CHRIS BROOKMYRE

FALLEN ANGEL

Little, Brown

LITTLE, BROWN

First published in Great Britain in 2019 by Little, Brown

1 3 5 7 9 10 8 6 4 2

A CIP catalogue record for this book is available from the British Library.

Hardback ISBN 978-1-4087-1083-8
Trade Paperback ISBN 978-1-4087-1082-1

Typeset in Caslon by Palimpsest Book Production Ltd, Falkirk, Stirlingshire
Printed and bound in Great Britain by Clays Ltd, Elcograf S.p.A.

Papers used by Little, Brown are from well-managed forests
and other responsible sources.

Little, Brown
An imprint of
Little, Brown Book Group
Carmelite House
50 Victoria Embankment
London
EC4Y 0DZ

An Hachette UK Company
www.hachette.co.uk

www.littlebrown.co.uk

For Marisa

Temple Family Tree

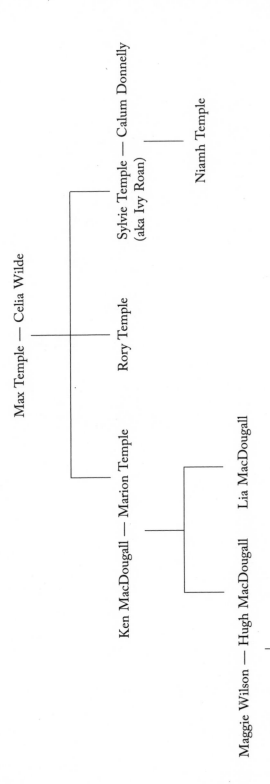

Max Temple — Celia Wilde

Ken MacDougall — Marion Temple

Maggie Wilson — Hugh MacDougall

Lia MacDougall

Emily MacDougall

Rory Temple

Sylvie Temple — Calum Donnelly
(aka Ivy Roan)

Niamh Temple

Prologue

Human beings find it impossible to make sense of death. The sum of our civilisation and learning has left us uncomprehending of its finality, stalked by its inevitability and yet stunned by its caprice. It is surprising then that we do not take greater solace in the knowledge that some people truly deserve to die.

In such circumstances, death can seem magical, killing a liberation. A figure who loomed so large as to sometimes dominate all my thoughts, instantly rendered null. A once terrifying threat extinguished, an unforgivable wrong avenged. And the greatest transformation of all is that there is no reason for me to be afraid of him any more.

Undoubtedly, his memory will echo, but that is all he can now do.

He is slumped over his desk, his right hand extended as though reaching for one of the documents piled next to his monitor. This was his sanctuary, a place he must have imagined he was untouchable. But such was the hubris of one who so clearly disdained other people for being as stupid as they were powerless.

There are books and papers all around, as befitting a learned individual with a busy mind. Framed certificates on the walls, conspicuous badges of achievement. They are trappings of respectability, part of the façade that disguised the man he truly was, what he was capable of and how low he was prepared to sink.

If someone walked in they might think he had fallen asleep on the job, or perhaps read a particularly depressing email. You would have to come close and look in his eyes to see that he is dead.

It will look like a heart attack. They will not find the tiny needle mark. They will not know to test for insulin. For what he had done, for what he had taken away, he did not deserve that it should have been so quick or merciful.

1

There is no noise from outside, a sense of respectful stillness surrounding the building, like the world itself is acquiescent of the deed. It feels strange that killing should be so quiet, particularly when that killing is both an act of vengeance and in defence of what is right and true. In real life it is not accompanied by a swell of strings or, in this case, even a cry for help. There had merely been that gasp of horrified astonishment, followed by a look of resignation. It was as though only in this moment did he understand the inevitability of it ending like this, the crushing knowledge that he had brought such a fate upon himself.

What were his last thoughts as he slumped forward onto the mahogany, before the light faded in his eyes and darkness descended for ever? Were they of those he had loved, those he had betrayed? Were they of his life, his career, his achievements, his regrets? Or did his fading mind allow him one last picture of blue skies and a sparkling sea: a place he once believed he was king, but where he had sown the seeds of his destruction?

PART ONE

The most effective conspiracy has the smallest number of participants. By definition the minimum is two. That is also the ideal maximum.

Max Temple

2018

Ivy

Rain is lashing down as she emerges from the Tube station, gusts of wind angling the deluge almost to the horizontal. A tenaciously brutal winter had relinquished its grip only with grudging reluctance, giving way to some unseasonably hot and sunny late spring days, but this meant that it caught everyone off-guard when the heavens opened this morning.

Ivy had overheard a woman in the carriage talking about the recent warm spell's contrast to the Beast from the East, saying she had almost forgotten what it was like to feel the sun on her shoulders. Ivy realises this is true of her too, but that doesn't mean she has missed it. Living in London, she seldom spends much time out of doors. Her office and her apartment are climate controlled to within a decimal point of perfection. What does she need sunshine for?

Sunshine is a disinfectant, people say, as though bringing simply anything into the light is an unambiguously wise and healthy thing to do. As far as Ivy is concerned, the only value of sunshine is that it casts shadows, and that is where she operates.

The problem with sunshine is that it makes people believe everything is going to be all right, and in her area of PR, that isn't good for the bottom line. It isn't good for clients' welfare either, to be honest. Clients need to be able to envisage an approaching worst-case scenario, so that they can take appropriate steps to avoid it, and the most appropriate step, always, is to retain her services.

She reaches Lincoln House on Remnant Street, where the Cairncross Partnership occupies two floors, hurrying through the revolving doors out of the downpour. There is a trail of water on the floor ahead of her, leading to where a woman has stopped to

7

shake off a dripping umbrella, this action complicated by one of its spokes having bent. Ivy estimates her to be in her forties, probably a mother of teens from the look of her; lower-to-middle-tier management, if that. Her body language is cowed as though apologising for her very existence: someone who has reached that point in life at which she realises all the things she once thought she might achieve or experience are never going to happen. Probably been kidding herself for the past decade and a half that the kids would make up for it, telling herself that raising them was a worthy achievement in itself before coming to realise – too late – just what a wretched con that was.

Somewhere between the revolving doors and where she now stands, it must have struck the poor cow that the price of a replacement was worth more to her than her dignity in trying to salvage a conspicuously buggered brolly in front of other human beings.

Glancing down, Ivy notices that her own umbrella has a kink in one spoke too, from being caught by a billowing gust only yards from the entrance. It is an Aspinal that she had bought yesterday on the way home, having checked the forecast. In a business entirely about appearances, it doesn't look good to turn up drenched, not least because it betrays that you didn't anticipate a coming storm.

The woman glances her way and offers a smile of solidarity as she clocks the damage. Ivy feels a familiar surge of revulsion. No, bitch, she thinks. In her world, there is no such thing as 'me too', whether that is a bent brolly or anything else you might delude yourself into thinking you have in common.

Ivy holds her gaze for a moment, unsmiling, before jamming the two-hundred-quid Aspinal into a nearby bin.

She proceeds towards the lifts, pulling out her swipe card and fixing her gaze on the barriers as she passes reception. Her singularity of purpose proves insufficient to prevent an unsolicited greeting from behind the desk.

'Morning, Ms Roan.'

Ivy responds with the tiniest, most cursory micro-smile: one so fleeting and perfunctory as to convey the extent to which she begrudges the burden of such a courtesy.

She takes the lift to the twelfth floor and strides towards her office on swift feet, rounding a corner in time to see one of the junior account managers notice her approach and warn his colleagues. At that distance she can't hear what he says but she doesn't have to be much of a lip reader to discern his two-word heads-up: 'Poison Ivy.'

In a supposedly creative business, it's hardly the most imaginative of derogatory nicknames for them to have come up with, but she is nonetheless rather proud that it has stuck. She doesn't need any of them to like her. Her job is to make you like other people, and their job is to help her do that.

Her phone buzzes in her hand as she strides between rows of desks. The contact ID flashes up, the caller listed simply as L. She knows he is about to get on a plane, and it won't be anything important. 'Just phoning to hear your voice,' something like that. She sighs and declines the call. Again. A few moments later there is a text, telling her his flight is on time. Good to know.

She gives a beckoning nod to Jamie, her assistant. He terminates the call he is on and follows her into her office.

Jamie is as loyal as he is dependable. He doesn't call her Poison Ivy, even among his junior peers. She knows this because she has eavesdropped on occasion and has only ever heard him refer to her as Ms Roan.

She is not sure whether she respects him more or less for this.

Jamie gives her a breakdown of where they are with various accounts. He tells her nothing she doesn't already know, but it functions as an opportunity to review matters in the light of any new developments, and to prioritise accordingly. Theoretically, it also allows her to delegate, but that's not going to happen. That's when things go wrong.

Her eyes stray towards her mobile as Jamie speaks. There's been a dozen alerts since, but she is thinking about the text from L stating when his flight is due in. She can picture his face as he urges her to let someone else shoulder some of the burden, or at least the scut work, so that they can spend a few more waking hours together. There's a part of her that wants that, but that's the part of her she's afraid of. She can't afford any oversights. In this job, control is everything.

L scores points for never actually using the word 'workaholic' but she knows she's one of the few people this cliché could be accurately applied to. It's an addiction for sure. Ivy knows, because she's been back and forth on most of the other ones: drinking, drugs, eating, not eating, stealing, and of course, sex. Someone once said of alcohol that the crucial thing is to be getting more from it than it takes from you. Work is the one thing that distinction has proven true of. It is the one addiction that has served her.

Jamie has bought her 'lunch' first thing, as per: a bottle of still water and an apple. He puts this meagre offering down on the desk and stares at it a moment, plucking up the courage to state his concern. He makes it sound breezy to disguise the fact that he knows it's none of his business but he's wading in nonetheless.

'I don't know how you can function on so few calories.'

If it was anyone else in here, she'd add a few more calories by biting their heads off, but she likes Jamie. She knows that's probably not a good thing – for him, anyway. He deserves better. He is genuine and solicitous, with an eagerness that is not purely career-driven. All of which will get him abused.

'I burn fuel very efficiently,' she replies.

This is a paraphrase of something L said to her: his typically elliptical and sensitive way of suggesting she might be unhealthily thin.

'You wouldn't like me if I was fat,' she'd told him, a banality intended to shut the issue down.

'Who says I like you?' he had hit back.

But she knows he does. That's the problem.

To think that she slept with him that first time because she thought he was a safe bet: and by safe bet she doesn't mean someone she was guaranteed to tempt back to her place within hours of meeting. She means someone she was sure would get lost sharpish after. A safe bet that he detested her as much as she detested him; that it was a mutually understood grudge-fuck.

Her judgement has proved way off on this one, which worries

her, but L will soon go the way of all the rest. It's been almost two months, and that's roughly how long it takes for them to see who she is. Or rather, the point at which she ditches them before they begin to see who she is.

Jamie is hovering, his hesitation telling her not only what he is about to mention but inadvertently how he feels about it. When he speaks he does an impressive job of sounding neutral, but it's already too late. Even without the momentary reluctance, she'd have picked up on details in his intonation, and the briefest involuntary pause before he mentions the name of the prospective client.

'Sir Jock would like a meeting to discuss whether you've had any further thoughts on the DKG thing ahead of the client dinner.'

Any further thoughts. Deftly self-insulating as ever on the part of the boss, Sir Jock Davidson. He's known in the game as Raffles, as in the gentleman thief, in reference to his rapacious billing practices. Like her, he is aware of the nickname and has embraced it, but there are other aspects of his reputation he is more protective of. That's why he wants her to make his mind up for him, and by that she further understands that he wants her to take the blame if she gets it wrong.

This is a firm where they are necessarily flexible with regard to the ethics of who they represent and what means they deploy in the service of that representation. But even here there is some division over whether they should go down the road DKG wants them to. For some – such as Jamie – it comes down to moral squeamishness; but for the likes of Sir Jock and the other partners, their reservations relate to potential blowback for the shop.

Any further thoughts. Ivy's had plenty, yes. And one of them is that you're not much of a PR outfit if you don't believe that come the worst, you can always launder your own reputation.

'I've still to make a final decision,' she tells Jamie. He tries to hide it, but she can see a hint of sadness in his expression. He believes she has already made up her mind. He's probably right.

She wakens to see L standing in the doorway. She was sleeping light despite the alcohol, aware that he was due here sometime in the

11

night. She feels woozy as she sits up, not quite sure whether she's already hung-over or still drunk. She sharpens at the sight of him, though. It's game time. She sits up so that he can see she's naked, and her movement causes the figure alongside her to stir. Peter, she thinks his name is. He works for DKG, and they met at the client dinner earlier in the evening.

She had detected something irresistibly calculating and self-assured about him: coldly analytical, reading his environment for possibilities the second the business part of the meal was concluded. It had given rise to just this flash of a moment, their eyes meeting and recognising the same thing in each other. She had leaned over deliberately, pretending to retrieve something from her bag but making sure her blouse fell open just enough. She caught him looking. It was something she could have used any way she wished: made him uncomfortable, pretended to take offence. Tonight though, she had thought of L and simply decided: it's time, and you'll do.

But not before a few more martinis and a couple of lines.

There is a thumping in her head, behind one eye especially. She tells herself it's a hangover symptom, but it usually means something else: stress.

Peter sees the figure in the doorway and sits bolt upright.

'Oh, fuck.'

He gets the picture pretty quickly. Fright and panic give way to feeling embarrassed and apologetic. He's looking from L to her and back again. Give him this much, he knows which one to feel sorry for.

L by contrast looks shell-shocked. He just doesn't get it, didn't see it coming at all, and why would he? She gave him the entry code only a week ago, before his trip, and this is the first time he's used it. It was ostensibly a gesture of opening up, taking the next step. Maybe a tiny part of her even believed that at the time. But a larger part knew that she was giving it to him so he could come in and find something like this. It wasn't the first time she'd ended one this way.

He still hasn't said anything. They've usually made it to the wounded male pride stage by this point. Sometimes they even cry, which she has enjoyed in some instances. She doesn't think she could take that tonight, though.

'You should just go,' she states.

Peter responds by getting to his feet and reaching for his clothes. She's actually talking to L, but Peter can get lost too.

She fears that she's going to be sick. It's not pleasant, but nonetheless, there's something reassuring about the familiarity of the sensation, and of the moment: getting rid of a problem. Getting rid of a threat.

Finally, L finds his voice.

'There's something wrong with you.'

'Hardly a scoop. You know, they say that when someone tells you who they really are, you should listen.'

L steps aside momentarily as Peter ambles awkwardly past, clutching his clothes. He's so spooked he walks right out the front door, presumably intending to get dressed in the lobby.

L waits for the door to close before he speaks again.

'You wanted me to see this.'

'Brilliant deduction. I guess all the things I've heard about your powers of observation are correct.'

There is an easeful coldness to her delivery. It comes readily enough but on this occasion it feels like an act. It puts her at one remove, saves her from truly feeling anything. This is particularly valuable tonight, because what she is feeling frightens her.

'Look, this is a mess, but this doesn't have to be *it*,' he says. 'We can talk. *You* can talk. I can listen. Believe me, I can listen.'

Ivy swallows.

'You can fuck off . . .'

She pauses at the end, aware the sentence is incomplete. She stopped herself saying his name, because the only one she's ever regularly called him by is a term of affection. Right from the off, it was a pet name: an inside joke, his middle initial. L. Lately when she sees it flash up on her phone, she's become afraid it might stand for something else. That's why she had to do this.

He doesn't slam the door. It would be easier if he did. He closes it softly, considerately, like everything else he does.

13

She tells herself this is in his best interest, that he deserves better. This part is true. She tells herself that she doesn't deserve him. This part is true also.

She tells herself it is what she wants. This part is not.

She looks at her mobile to check the time. It's half past three, which means she'll have to decide whether her next move is to have a coffee and get up or to down some Glenmorangie and hopefully manage a couple more hours' sleep. Either way she needs a shower after what she just did. And she doesn't mean the sex.

As she stands under the jets and the wetroom fills with steam, she hears a buzzing from one wall, where her phone and iPad are lodged in waterproof pouches. Instinctively she calculates what the time is in various cities as she wonders who it could be. She is already moving her mind into the workspace, away from the shit she just went through. Business always serves her.

She wipes condensation from the plastic and sees the name of the caller. It's her sister, Marion. Ivy hasn't responded to her in three years, instantly deleting the voicemail messages she has occasionally left. She declines as a matter of reflex but then asks herself why Marion of all people would be calling at this hour.

It's a question to which she immediately realises there can be only one answer.

She turns off the water and fishes the mobile from the pouch, preparing to return the call. Before she can do so, it buzzes again. Ivy presses to accept and holds the handset to her face.

Marion communicates everything in just two words.

'It's Dad.'

2018

Amanda

'Amanda, you almost done, babe? The taxi's gonna be here any minute.'

Kirsten's words bounce their way along the corridor and reverberate around the room, causing me to glance anxiously to where Arron is asleep in his car seat. I can't afford to have him wake up right now, and he tends to respond to his mother's voice like siren song. To my ears it's less song and more siren, but I guess I'm not as used to her accent.

I'm having what feels like my fourteenth attempt to reconfigure the contents of a suitcase so that I can close the goddamn thing. It's like some kind of extreme 3D version of *Candy Crush*, with all my efforts undermined by the suspicion that the task might actually be impossible. Kobayashi Maru. We're only going away for a week and yet there's more stuff needing fitted into this case than I've brought from Canada for a stay of three months. Who knew babies could need so much equipment? You'd think we were planning on occupying Portugal, not vacationing there.

I take a breath and bite back a response to Kirsten hassling me. It's not like the lady of the house has been a lot of help. She seemed more concerned with making sure she's got her gym gear and her beach wardrobe looked out, and consequently left packing the baby's stuff to me. As a result, despite the amount of shit I'm trying to jam into the case, I am dogged by the anxiety that I may have forgotten something.

I think Kirsten must be wrong anyways: the taxi isn't due until eight.

I look at my watch and with a jolt it registers that it's ten to.

Where the hell has the time gone? Last time I checked, it was just gone seven. I haven't even organised my own shit yet. Truth is, I've barely unpacked it. I arrived here in Stirling from Toronto less than forty-eight hours ago, with no idea I was going to be back on a plane so soon.

Vince and Kirsten are friends of my parents, or Vince is at least. They never met Kirsten. I think maybe he was their lawyer at some point, back in the day, but the details are fuzzy, mainly because I wasn't paying attention when they talked about it. I was too fixed upon the fact that Vince had offered the opportunity to come and stay in Scotland over the summer, before I start college in the autumn. I stopped listening after that because my head was already filling with the possibilities.

It was a chance to base myself in the UK for three months, see some sights, maybe do a bit of travelling. The deal was that I would get to stay for free, and even get some spending money, in return for helping out with their kid. I didn't need to be asked twice. Who doesn't love babies?

Yeah, it all sounded pretty good when I got on the plane at YYZ. Not so much now that I'm in the middle of it. On the basis of what's happened so far, my side of the deal appears to be not so much helping out as doing all of Kirsten's job as a mother for her.

I yawn, my fatigue not doing much for my judgement in trying to solve this puzzle against a ticking clock. The kid kept me awake most of the night. Or rather, it would be more accurate to say that I couldn't get to sleep until the small hours because of the time difference, and then the point at which I finally nodded off seemed to coincide with the point at which Arron woke up and decided it was morning. It gets bright here real early, I have discovered, after failing to deduce the significance of a blackout shade when I drew the curtains the night before. Like an idiot I had thought: what the hell is that doing in here? Wouldn't total darkness freak out a little baby? Now I understand, but it's not like you can pull down the shade at 4:15 a.m. and tell a baby it ain't time to get up yet.

I haul two bags of toiletries back out on to the bed and buy myself more room by squishing a load of Babygros between the ridges at the bottom of the case. With the toiletries pressed back in, I am still prevented from getting the case closed by the awkward bulk of a semi-transparent object identified by a sticker as being a 'microwave bottle steriliser'. The kid drinks formula milk, for God's sake. It's not like they don't sterilise that stuff before they seal it in the cartons. (And why isn't Kirsten breastfeeding anyways? Dumb question: I've already heard her talk about getting her abs back after pregnancy, so I'm guessing stretched titties were never going to be acceptable.)

I twist the steriliser through ninety degrees, which finally allows me to close the lid. I lock the hasps and haul the case towards the stairs. It's not so heavy, but it is awkward, especially as the staircase is so narrow. I kinda thought the house would be bigger, to be honest. My parents made out Vince had money, or maybe I just got that impression because they said he's a lawyer.

As I begin to descend I can hear Vince on the phone.

'I'm glad you're seeing sense on the matter,' he says.

He's sounding firm but trying to keep his voice low. Kirsten is still up in their bedroom, applying more make-up probably. I've heard her complain that Vince is unable to disengage from work and make it clear she doesn't want it to be an issue on their vacation. That's why he's staying out of her earshot to make a call.

'If you're saying you need me to move on this as quickly as you're suggesting, I have to be absolutely sure you're putting your money where your mouth is.'

It has become rapidly apparent to me that one of the reasons I've been offered this gig is that Vince is not exactly a hands-on kind of dad. He works long hours at the office and seems to spend a lot of time on the phone or on his laptop when he *is* in the house. I can't say I'm surprised, given he's kind of ancient. Guy's in his fifties. As I asked my parents, who would want to be taking on fatherhood at his stage in life? Now I know the answer: somebody who married a woman half his age. A woman less than half his age even, who doesn't appear to harbour any ambitions for herself other than as a home-maker, and it appears she intends to outsource much of the home-making to cheap Canadian labour.

17

'The nature of the proof isn't something I'm prepared to disclose,' he says. 'No client would expect me to show my hand at this stage of the negotiation. But I can tell you this much, the evidence speaks for itself.'

He is standing in the living room as I place the suitcase next to the front door. He's looking relaxed and pretty pleased with himself. He seemed kinda jumpy last night and first thing this morning. I thought it was anxiety about getting ready for a first trip with his baby, but clearly there's been some deal he's negotiating that's got him all excited.

'It's not going to come down to nuanced interpretation or complex argument over detailed points of law. It's a slam-dunk, and I think you know that, otherwise you wouldn't be on this call.'

Looking at my watch, I realise I won't have time to select what I need myself for this trip. As I haven't actually had the chance to properly unpack since getting here, it will just be a case of grabbing my rucksack as is. At best I might have time to remove a few unnecessary items to lighten the load, but even as I think this, I hear the already too-familiar sound of Arron crying.

He was asleep last time I looked, and no wonder, as he'd been awake for about five solid hours, reacting to all the activity and excitement around him, no doubt. He had nodded off just when I thought: At least this might mean he'll sleep on the flight.

I run upstairs and back to his room, where I pick him up to comfort him and immediately catch a strong whiff of why he's not happy. God damn it.

I put him down on the changing mat, pop the fasteners on his Babygro and observe that he's managed to spray brown liquid all the way up his back. I'm looking at more than a few quick strokes with a wipe and a new disposable diaper.

Having cleaned him up, I go to the drawer for a fresh outfit, which is when I recall that they've all been packed at Kirsten's insistence. ('He once puked and crapped his way through twelve in a single day,' she explained.)

I allow myself a sigh. I would count to ten but there isn't the time to spare. I run down the stairs and flip open the suitcase, where I have to fish out a new one-piece from where I so cleverly stuffed it between the ridges at the bottom.

Vince glances across as I root through the clothes, a look of curiosity on his face but clearly no intention of lending a hand. He's still on his call.

'Well, this is very much the eleventh hour. I'm just leaving for the airport. You're telling me it's not brinkmanship but for me to believe that, you're going to have to deliver cash on the barrelhead.'

I can hear Arron start to howl again. *God damn it, I'll be right there*, I think.

I manage to pull the outfit free without disturbing too many other items and I hurry back, but as I crest the stairs I see that Kirsten has reached the doorway before me.

'You've left him lying there on the mat, naked and unattended?' she asks, making it sound like I've lain him out in the snow for wolves to feast on. Kirsten's from a place in England called Essex, and her accent makes me wonder if everyone there speaks with a constant edge of aggression.

'I needed a fresh Babygro and they were all in the case. This one's covered in poop.'

'You should have shouted me in. He'll catch a chill. It's freezing in here.'

It really isn't, but I'm not about to argue. I kneel down and get busy putting on the new diaper, Arron howling in response. Flustered, I put it on back to front. Kirsten sighs as if I am hopeless and nudges me out the way.

The effect is remarkable. The kid just stops crying, then stares at his mom like he's entranced. Kirsten has also undergone a rapid transformation, her scowl and sharpness replaced by soft cooing noises as she does up the buttons.

She hands him to me with the instruction to put him back in his car seat ready for the trip, which is when Vince appears in the doorway.

'Is that the taxi?'

He has a sheepish expression.

'No, but it's due any moment.'

19

'What is it?' Kirsten asks, interpreting that an announcement is coming.

'Look, I'm really sorry, honey. I'm going to have to catch up to you all at the airport.'

'Oh, you have got to be joking me,' his wife replies, in a tone that says the explanation had better be tip-top.

'Just got to run . . .' he sighs mid-sentence, 'past the office, sort one thing.'

'Vince, you said—'

'One thing. And believe me, you'll be happy I did it. This is worth a lot of money, but I have to tie it up now.'

This seems to change her tune. She checks her watch.

'Have you got time?'

'Honestly, I'll be a couple of minutes at the office. You get the bags checked and I'll catch up to you in Departures. We'll be toasting this with Champagne, I promise you.'

2018

Celia

Celia is thinking of Max as she lifts her shoes from a grey plastic tray in the Glasgow Airport security area. She can hear his voice, the things he used to say when he was standing here beside her doing this.

'It's a pretty poor return on effort for those Islamists who aspired towards a worldwide caliphate. Though I suppose that subjecting millions of people to a tedious inconvenience only necessitated by their threats of violence is a fitting achievement. Religion's principal impact throughout human history has largely been one of pointlessly making things harder than they need to be.'

Her reflection is interrupted by a voice that hauls her back to the here and now.

'I was so sorry to hear about your husband.'

The woman is standing next to her as she unpacks her toiletries from a see-through plastic bag and transfers them to her hand luggage. Celia strives to place her for a moment, then understands why she cannot. The woman wears a look of warmth and pity; the kindness of strangers indeed. Yet at that moment she had been lost in idle thoughts that were a rare respite from contemplating her bereavement. People mean well but they don't think about what it takes out of you to acknowledge a loved one's death over and over again.

Celia draws upon her depleted reserves of inner strength to offer a sincere smile and say simply: 'Thank you.'

She feels like she's been crying for days. She hasn't, but each onset takes her back to the same feelings, seemingly erasing the periods in between.

The woman's expression changes suddenly and she appears acutely uncomfortable. Celia identifies the moment it occurs to her that she has just intruded upon the grief of a complete stranger, someone she has never met, albeit to offer condolences. It happens. Her face was all over the media in the days after Max's death. People recognise her and react to the familiarity. It is an extra burden upon her grief, during what ought to be a most private time.

It has been hard enough dealing with friends and acquaintances. On the surface it appears they are offering her something, an act of solicitousness, but inside it feels like she is the one doing them a courtesy: allowing them to discharge an obligation. Everybody feels the need to say something, as though afraid they will be judged for the sin of omission, so she is granting them status, stamping their card. They don't realise they are asking her to revisit – however briefly – her pain and loss when her mind might have been somewhere else.

Nonetheless, the only way out is through, and this encounter with a stranger is an important reminder that a little bit of Max belonged to everybody.

'I'm so sorry if that was inappropriate,' the woman says. 'It's just, I forgot that I only know you from my husband's DVDs.'

'Don't mention it.'

Celia finds it that bit easier to forgive the intrusion now; indeed, she can't help feeling a little glow as she recalls the days when she would be recognised for who she was rather than who she was married to. In fact, there was a time when Max would have been primarily referred to as Celia Wilde's husband, but she had long since made her peace with the inversion. Life is all about finding new roles, welcoming different phases. Wife, mother, grandmother; love, family, birth and, unfortunately, death.

It's the constant remembering that's hardest: briefly forgetting and then being reminded that he's gone. Waking up in the morning, coming to slowly and expecting to find him there, seeing that he's not and being hit once again with the knowledge that he never will be again. She wasn't ready for how it could catch her dozens of times a day. The many micro-plans that factor him in, out of habit and reflex. What to have for dinner. What they need from the supermarket. Pondering whether to go out for a walk now or wait until Max is finished whatever he is working on and comes downstairs from his office, his sanctuary as he called it. Hearing the phone ring and briefly wondering whether to leave it for him to answer.

It's like being repeatedly slapped in the face. She wishes she could get her brain to accept it, to stop anticipating his presence every moment, but that's what you condemn yourself to when you've been married to someone for close to fifty years.

One of the things she's been reading about bereavement is that she will need to work on recovering her identity as an individual rather than half of a couple. Memories of those earlier times will help, but they feel woefully ill-matched to the weight they are up against. Right now, the greatest comfort is that she has always been part of something else: her family.

This thought prompts her to reply to the text Marion sent her a while ago, asking where she's gotten to. Celia lets her know that she is just coming out of Security and about to go through the duty free. She dallies awhile amidst the perfumes, accepting the attentions of the women offering scent samples. A strapping young man in a stylishly informal kilt offers her a whisky liqueur from a tray, a dozen thimble-sized drams laid upon a silver salver. Ordinarily she wouldn't even think about it at this time of the morning, but she is on holiday, and God knows she deserves some indulgence right now.

'Can I interest you in a wee snifter, ma'am?'

'Any excuse to tarry next to you in that fine garment, young man.'

There's a sparkle in his eye as he smiles in response. He knows how to take a compliment. She likes that.

She knocks back the liqueur, sweet on the tongue with a hint of a burn going down. She only realises how much she needed it as it hits her system.

As she emerges from the duty-free area, she can see Marion waiting for her at Starbucks, holding two coffees. Her daughter looks her age and more: mid-forties and weary with it. Celia doesn't know why that should seem surprising. Maybe it's just that she has all

23

these images of her at different stages in her life and she is always expecting to see a younger version. It's silly. Marion is a grandmother herself now, after all.

Celia accepts one of the coffees and leans into her daughter for a brief hug.

'How are you doing?' Marion asks.

'Oh, you know. As well as can be expected. I've only cried twice today, though it's early yet.'

Marion nods.

Celia takes a sip of the coffee, which tastes bitter after the sweetness of the liqueur.

'Is there vanilla in this?'

Marion looks defensive.

'No. You take it without sugar, I know that.'

'Actually, sometimes I like a little bit of syrup. When it's a latte.'

'I didn't know.'

Celia sighs.

'It doesn't matter. How are you doing?'

'OK, considering.'

'You look a little tired.'

'I didn't sleep great.'

'Maybe it's just that jacket. I'm not sure the colour is the ideal complement for your skin tone.'

Poor Marion. She never did know quite how to dress herself. 'She gets that from me,' Max used to say. No point in chiding her for it though. She wasn't going to change.

'Perhaps we all just need some sun,' Celia says. 'I'm certainly looking forward to wearing something a little more flamboyant. I've had to move from the winter wardrobe right into mourning dress. The hardest thing is being aware that people might be judging you for, I don't know, some kind of sartorial impropriety if you're not going around in black.'

'You know, Victorian widows had to wear mourning garb for two years and a month,' Marion says.

Celia doesn't see how this is supposed to be helpful.

'Max would want me in bright colours. I know that much.'

They proceed towards the main body of the departure lounge, which is like an over-lit shopping mall these days.

'Ken ran into a friend,' Marion says. 'He was blethering away outside Dixons. He'll catch up.'

Ken is Marion's husband. Boring Ken, the plumber. He's nice enough, and their marriage certainly went the distance, but Celia has never been able to get past the thought that Marion could have done better. Perhaps every mother feels that way about her daughter.

Celia leads Marion into WH Smith. She already has her Kindle but she likes to browse the books and magazines, part of a pre-flight ritual. They are standing next to the airport exclusives when she turns her gaze across the concourse towards the permanently bustling Starbucks. Marion notices that something has caught her eye.

'What?' Marion asks.

'Think I just saw Vince.'

'From the villa next door? He must be on the same flight. Where is he?'

'Don't look.'

'Over in Starbucks?'

'I said don't look. He hasn't seen us, so we've got away with it. We'll be seeing plenty of him soon enough.'

'Didn't you say his wife was pregnant the last time you were over? October, wasn't it?'

'That's right. She'd have been due sometime in the new year. Though to be honest, when I found out she was pregnant I was astonished. I wasn't sure she was old enough to be menstruating. Best watch out: she might be in here too, buying herself a comic and some sweeties.'

'*Mother*,' Marion scolds, but she's laughing with it.

'Now, what about Hugh and Maggie and the wee one?' Celia asks. 'Are they here in the departure lounge or are they due in soon?'

Marion looks confused.

'They're meeting us at the villa.'

'But I thought we were all meeting up here and getting the same flight?'

'Why would they do that? They're flying from Manchester.'

'And Rory?'

'He's changing in London off a flight from San Francisco.'

'Didn't we agree we should all meet up at Glasgow and fly on to Faro together?'

'You mentioned it, Mum, but it was way too complicated.'

Celia can't suppress a sigh.

'I just miss the days when we all went on the same plane.'

'We weren't all coming from five different places back then. The main thing is that we're all going to be there at the villa.'

'All of us?' Celia asks pointedly.

Marion doesn't say anything at first.

Celia is not sure what answer she even wants to hear, though she knows what Max would have wanted, so she lets that be her guide.

'That remains to be seen,' Marion eventually replies.

'All I ever wanted was for us all to be together at the villas one more time, like it used to be. That's what Max wanted too. It's just such a shame it's taken his death for it to happen.'

'I invited her as you requested, but that's as much as we can do. It's not like she doesn't know where to find us, or that she's not welcome.'

'She knew all that about the funeral, but she didn't come to that,' Celia notes.

'She's still very paranoid about her privacy, concerned it wouldn't be too difficult for someone to join the dots.'

'It was a small private service. Not some huge public affair.'

'Yes, and that would have made it even easier to single her out. It was private inside the building, but there were cameras and a couple of reporters in the grounds of the crematorium.'

'I suppose. She's not the only one it affected, though. She seems to forget that.'

Marion says nothing, which means she disagrees but isn't prepared to get into why.

The service was difficult: moments of feeling nothing interspersed with the fear of totally losing it in front of everyone. She had numbed herself. She was supposed to be thinking about him, and everybody was talking about him, but the whole time she was banishing him from her mind. It was the only way to get through it.

26

The holiday is going to be painful in its own way, but she knows it will help her heal. It will help the whole family to heal. The funeral was merely a ceremony. This will be his memorial: everyone who loved him gathered in a place where they shared so much happiness down the years. They returned time and again to the villas, each visit building new memories on the strong foundations of the last.

Until.

So much was taken away from her in that one night. Even in the early shock and grief, what none of them realised was that the tragedy was merely the beginning of their ordeal.

People talk about adding insult to injury. They have no idea.

2018

Amanda

An alert on my phone tells me that K-Xander29 has posted a response video to my latest effort. Previously I'd have been able to just drop everything and watch it, then start composing a counter-argument, but Arron is wriggling in his buggy, a frustrated look on his little face which I have already learned to recognise as a pre-cry expression. Kid seems to have like zero attention span.

I've been told the flight from Glasgow to Portugal will be around three hours. This sounded like nothing at the time, coming soon after my seven-hour flight from Toronto. However, trying to keep this little guy from kicking off here in the departure area suggests being confined inside a narrow tube with him might be the longest three hours of my life.

I pick Arron up and start bouncing him on my knee as a distraction, my phone open on the seat next to me. I am scanning the comments posted below the new video for clues as to its content, but there are only four and they aren't saying much beyond congratulating K-Xander29 for making points they agree with.

I close it again as I spot Kirsten approaching. Arron's mom doesn't appear to have much of an attention span either. She hasn't sat down for more than a couple of minutes. First she went to the bathroom, then to buy sunglasses, then off to the duty-free store, from which she is returning now with – impossibly – more make-up on. She sits down amid a cloud of scent, having dabbed so many perfume samples you'd think she was a drug smuggler trying to outwit sniffer dogs.

Kirsten takes out a magazine, which she places on her lap but doesn't read, choosing instead to watch people file towards their departure gates. Suddenly she lifts her head and puts on a smile as I become aware of two women stopping in front of our seats.

'Oh, hello. It's Kirsten, isn't it?'

It's the older of the two who speaks, an elegant woman I estimate to be in her early seventies. The word glamorous leaps to mind, but that has connotations of being showy, whereas this woman is simply well-presented in an effortless kind of way: someone not trying to look younger than her age, but who simply looks good and never mind how old she is. I immediately like her for that.

'Yes,' Kirsten replies. 'Hi there, Celia. You off to Faro again too?'

'Indeed. This is my daughter Marion. We're having quite the family reunion over there.'

Kirsten smiles at Marion, who looks to be in her forties. It strikes me that this is still maybe a decade less than Vince, which brings it home all the more just how young Kirsten is to be married to him. I've been hoping to get a look at her passport to confirm just exactly what age she is, but it can't be much more than twenty-five. Twenty-seven at the absolute most.

Marion looks like a schoolteacher. She seems kind of dowdy, but maybe that's just by comparison to who she's standing beside.

'We're off on our first family holiday,' Kirsten replies, indicating the baby. 'This is Amanda, who's helping out.'

We all trade smiles.

'We just saw Vince in Starbucks,' says Marion.

'Oh, so he's made it,' Kirsten remarks. 'He had to get here via the office. Some work thing came up at the last minute.'

'Same old Vince, then,' Marion observes.

Kirsten doesn't respond and I wonder whether this is delicate. These people have clearly known Vince longer than she has. I remember hearing he had a previous wife, and they probably knew her too.

'And is this the little one?' Celia asks, sensing the awkwardness. 'I remember you were pregnant last time. What's his name?'

'Arron.'

'Look at you,' she says bending over, her voice suddenly sing-song in a way the kid responds to with a fascinated gape.

29

She straightens up again.

'I've a few things to pick up, so we'll leave you to it,' Celia says. She is about to walk away when something occurs to Kirsten.

'I was so sorry to hear about your husband,' she says.

Celia gives her a glum smile and briefly clasps Kirsten's hand. 'That's very sweet of you, dear.'

Kirsten has a concerned look as the pair walk away.

'I hope I didn't say the wrong thing,' she confesses. 'You've got to say something though, haven't you?'

'Who was that?' I ask.

'They've got the villa next door. Think Vince's known them for ever. Celia's husband just died a couple of weeks ago. I met them both last time I was over. I didn't realise he was kind of famous until I saw something about his death on the telly. Think he was a scientist or something.'

'What was his name?'

'Max.'

I can't believe it. Surely not.

'Max Temple?'

'Yeah, I think that was it. I'd never heard of him though.'

'As in Temple's Law?'

'I wouldn't know. What's that?'

I am about to reply when Arron lobs his teething ring on to the floor. As I bend to retrieve it, Kirsten has got to her feet again.

'I'm gonna go get us a drink,' she announces.

'I can do it,' I offer, hoping for a change of scene.

'No, you're all right,' she replies. 'Just stay put in case Vince is looking for us.'

And she's off again, this time for longer than before. Long enough, in fact, for me to think that she has hooked up with Vince and they're kicking back in a bar while some other sucker is holding the baby. I might have to get used to that. To be fair, if they haven't had any help until now, I wouldn't blame them for wanting to make the most of some me-time. I've been looking after the kid for less than two days and I already want an extended break from him.

30

I think about taking him for a wander in his buggy, but Kirsten told me to stay put. She'd have a fit if she came back and found her baby missing.

I grab a look at WhatsApp, which only serves to make me feel all the further from home. The time difference means my friends are in bed right now, and I missed all their chat while I was failing to get some sleep. Weird how it all looks so dumb and inconsequential when you're not part of it. On the upside, Megan said Chvrches are gonna be playing Toronto. I'll need to look into that.

Our gate is showing on the display when Kirsten comes ambling back. She hands me a bottle of water while she sips from a plastic tumbler containing something clear and fizzy. I can't identify it, but it smells strongly of alcohol. I note that it's only just gone ten.

'Is Vince not here? They've given the gate.'

Kirsten glances at the screen and places her drink down on the floor as she produces her phone. She shakes her head after a few seconds, then begins thumbing a text.

We proceed to the appointed gate, where they are making a pre-boarding call for passengers with small children or needing special assistance.

'It's just like him to wait for the last minute to turn up, so I'm left looking after Arron the whole time.'

'Did you get a reply to your text?'

'Yeah. "Just grabbing some last-minute shopping." I bet he's in the fucking bar. Should probably be grateful he even booked himself on the same flight.'

A new possibility causes Kirsten's face to darken.

'Come on,' she commands, marching purposefully to the desk where the check-in agents are gearing up for boarding.

'Excuse me, can you just confirm that my husband is booked on this flight? His name is Vincent Reid.'

The agent looks at her computer.

'Yes, he's checked in and according to the system, he passed through security at 09:07.'

That was almost an hour ago.

'What the hell is he playing at?' Kirsten asks.

31

'I can put out a call,' the agent offers.

'Please.'

Kirsten turns to me.

'You go ahead and board, get sorted out with Arron. I'll wait this side for Laughing Boy.'

I have to collapse the buggy and hand it over to an agent at the gate. I hear the call over the PA as I carry Arron towards the gantry, loaded down by the weight of the baby-bag on one shoulder and the kid in my other arm.

I can't help but wonder where Vince has gotten to, and about the implications for the atmosphere between him and Kirsten throughout the coming flight when he does finally show up.

I squeeze myself into the seat and a flight attendant comes along to give me an attachment for my seatbelt so that I can secure the baby in my lap. I have barely got it fastened when Arron starts to grizzle. I hope he hasn't pooped again. It's been a while since he had a bottle, though. There's one in the baby bag, but it's down on the floor, so I need to unfasten Arron and lie him on the seat next to me as I reach to retrieve it. I'm wary of him rolling himself off, though I'm not sure if he's that mobile yet.

A few seconds later he's wolfing the bottle with an eagerness bordering on desperation. His face gets kind of red, like he's ready to burst. I figure he needs burping. I've only been shown how to do this once and I'm not sure I've quite got the hang of it.

Arron's not happy about the bottle getting taken away yet, so I let him have some more. Eventually he lets go, physically pushing the teat away with his little hand. Kid looks inflated. I turn him to face me and rest him with his head looking over my shoulder like Kirsten taught me. I pat his back gently then hear a gurgle and a splash. There is a warm sensation down my back. Great. He has barfed all down my shirt and I'm going to smell like Parmesan the whole way.

I feel a surge of relief as I glimpse Vince emerging through the door of the plane, but it fades when I see it's not him after all: just another bald middle-aged dude in a jacket similar to the one he had on when he left. To be honest, I'd struggle to pick Vince out in a line-up, as I've only known him a day and a half and he's barely been present for a few hours of that.

The stream of boarding passengers reduces to a trickle, then to nothing. I see flight attendants checking manifests. I start to wonder what I should do. They're not going to take off without Kirsten, are they? No, they'd need to get her cases out of the hold. But what if they do that? Nobody has come to ask me about the empty seats beside me. Is that because they're cool to wait or is it because they're no longer expecting them to be filled?

Calm TF down, I coach myself. Kirsten isn't going to abandon her baby.

Sure enough, Kirsten hastens through the entrance a moment later, looking flustered and pissed off. There is still no Vince. She sits down with a thunderous expression. I am scared to say anything dumb, but I gotta ask.

'Did you hear anything from him?'

'He's not answering his calls or texts. It's going straight to voice-mail. Arsehole. I'll keep trying.'

She doesn't get the chance, though. A flight attendant comes over and tells Kirsten she needs to turn her phone to flight-safe mode.

'My husband hasn't shown up,' she says. 'He's the passenger supposed to be sitting here.'

'Yes, we've put out several calls. The manifest shows he doesn't have checked luggage. We're going to have to close the doors.'

'Can you give it a few more minutes?'

'The ATC schedule is very busy today. If we miss our slot, we're going to be pushed back half an hour, and that will have a knock-on effect for several other flights.'

Kirsten looks at her phone, her finger paused above the flight-safe icon, as though one more second might see Vince respond. It doesn't.

She and I look at each other. It's clear neither of us knows how to deal with the situation.

'I can't bleedin' believe this,' Kirsten says. 'I've been rained on and freezing for six months when I've not been stuck in the house with Arron. I've never felt so in need of a holiday and this shit happens.'

33

'Should we get off?' I ask.

Kirsten looks down the aisle to where an attendant is getting ready to close the door.

'Nah. Fuck him,' she says.

She stabs at the flight-safe button and fastens her seat belt.

2018

Ivy

With the aircraft at cruising altitude and a large gin on the tray in front of her, Ivy plugs in her headphones and launches the video. The drink is an indulgence so early in the day, but she's going to need it. She downloaded the file last night and toyed with watching it then, before changing her mind and deciding it was safer to wait for the flight. The fear was that she might get so emotional that she'd change her mind about coming. This way, she's already committed.

She is flying out of Edinburgh, as she had something she had to take care of locally before she could head off to Portugal. She will be flying back directly to London, though. The only question is how soon.

She feels a tingle in her gut, an anxiety over what she's about to go through. She is making herself watch it, despite the pain she knows she will feel, because this is the way the world will remember him.

The clip dates from 2002. It is a segment of a now discontinued teatime chat show on Channel Four, featuring guests from all fields – politics, sport, showbiz, science – engaged in breezy discussions with a cheery presenter. The kind of thing you could tune in and out of while you chopped veg for the dinner. It was the perfect fit for the pop-psychology book Dad was plugging.

The presenter is Abby Cook. She is bubbly and attractive in a non-threatening way, someone who cut her teeth presenting zoo-TV shows for older kids. By 2002 she had moved a few hours later in the schedule, after boosting her profile with a half-naked cover shoot for *FHM*. She has subsequently shifted hours again, these days earning a shitload on ITV's flagship mid-morning show, but whether late vintage or early noughties Abby, the secret of her success is the same. She has a folksy girl-next-door charm, the type of presenter whose manner comforts the target audience by giving the impression she doesn't understand the big words either.

That was very much why it happened. Abby was out of her depth.

'And next on the couch, someone I'm super excited to be talking to. I'm sure you all recognise none other than Jason Cale, best known these days for presenting *Paradigm Shift* on the BBC. But, of course, the reason I'm excited is that many of us remember Jason as Danthos, from the classic British science fiction series *The Liberators*.'

Ivy's laptop screen is briefly filled by a grainy clip showing a younger Jason, stripped to the waist as he fires a laser blaster against what is supposed to be an alien landscape but was probably a quarry in Wales. It cuts back to show him on the couch for a reaction shot, a perfectly pitched combination of bashful pride and 'surprised' cringing.

'Now I'm sorry to spring that on you, Jason, but the reason we showed it is of course that you are accompanied this evening by Max Temple, and Max's wife – a little bit of trivia for you all – is Celia Wilde, who played the very sexy Kurlia alongside Jason in that show.'

There is mercifully not a clip, but merely a still showing Mum in her iconic costume, before the director displays even greater humanity in not cutting back to Dad's face right then. Instead the camera is back on Abby.

'Max is an esteemed psychology professor from the University of St Andrews, and he and Jason are here tonight because they have teamed up to write a book. It's called *Behind the Mask: How To Tell What People Are Really Thinking*, and I'm fascinated to hear how this collaboration came about. Jason, can you tell us . . .'

Jason does most of the talking, which is for the best. He knows how to keep it light and accessible, sometimes talking over Dad when he threatens to get too technical. Dad looks like he's merely tolerating the ordeal, waiting for it to end. He's not actually awkward in front of the cameras, but even if you didn't know him you'd deduce he is unused to this atmosphere of enforced joviality. Even now Ivy feels a tension every time Abby asks a question: despite knowing it never happened, she is still on edge in case Dad gets all brusque with her for being so anodyne.

However, that was very much Jason's intention in making him part of this double act. Coming across as kind of aloof actually worked for Dad in this context, emphasising his academic gravitas in contrast to his co-author's chatty, populist style.

Abby wraps up the discussion of *Behind the Mask* and they shuffle along the settee to make room for the next guest. She introduces him as Toby Cutler-Wood and informs the viewers that he is a former police detective. He is a slim, white-haired man in a three-piece suit whom Ivy suspects is affecting to look like an academic. As an ex-cop, he should have read the evidence in front of him and deduced that the presence of a genuine academic meant it was a bad night for pretending to be something that you're not.

'Since retiring from the police six years ago, Toby has turned his detective skills to uncovering a different kind of fraud, on a quite startling scale. Honestly, this will really blow your minds. Toby is here to tell us about *The Apollo Conspiracy*, his bestselling book claiming that the moon landings never happened but were actually *faked* by NASA.'

Toby doesn't have Jason's facility for banter and small talk, ploughing headlong into his pitch. The screen is briefly filled with a photograph of the surface of the moon, a lunar lander in the right of the foreground, an American flag erected to the left. Another image takes its place, of two astronauts in front of the same lander. In both images, beyond the horizon all is black, and that is what he is focused on.

'What's wrong with this picture?' he asks Abby, though he doesn't wait for an answer.

'There are no stars! There should be thousands of stars visible. The very reason the Hubble telescope was put into orbit is that the view of the cosmos is so much clearer beyond the atmosphere, and yet in this image, supposedly taken from the surface of the moon, there is not a single, solitary star.'

He talks excitedly about how the solar wind trapped in the Earth's magnetic field has created a series of high-radiation zones, known as the Van Allen Belts, beginning four hundred miles above the planet and extending for as much as forty thousand miles. Not only would this radiation damage the scientific instruments that would have been crucial to a moon mission, he informs Abby, but it would prove lethal to the personnel. Then he moves on to the temperature of the lunar surface, how it reaches one hundred and twenty degrees and thus would have killed the astronauts if they were exposed to it.

Ivy can't help but smile as the camera picks up the first indicators that Dad is getting exasperated. He is squirming in his seat and rolling his eyes. As this escalates into audible tuts and sighing, Jason begins to look uncomfortable, clearly concerned that his sidekick is about to blow their media profile by demonstrating that he can't play the game.

Abby seems genuinely gobsmacked as Toby piles on the evidence and the shocking implications begin to sink in.

Ivy recognises the response, stuff her dad would later write about: how intoxicated Abby is by hearing seemingly compelling evidence that alters something she had previously regarded as unquestionable.

'And speaking of the surface, do you notice the dust, and the footprints in the dust? The *Apollo* landing module had a rocket to slow its descent, delivering ten thousand pounds of thrust, which should not only have left a scorched crater, but blown all of the dust away too. NASA faked up what they thought we imagined the surface of the moon to look like, but forgot about the impact their own vehicle would have had. They were sloppy, but the insulting thing is that they clearly think *we're* all stupid.'

The focus is still on Toby, but Dad's voice cuts across from off-camera, in a tone so familiar that sitting on a plane sixteen years later, Ivy can't help but let out a chuckle.

'I'm sorry, but this is just the most preposterous garbage.'

Ivy pauses the video to hand her empty gin miniature to the flight attendant. As she does so, the man in the seat next to her indicates the screen.

'I remember that interview,' he says warmly. 'Guy was a legend. Shame he's gone.'

Ivy flashes him a micro smile, a gesture of basic courtesy the brevity of which ought to convey that she doesn't wish to discuss it further. It gives her a glimpse of how much more unbearable things would be right now if anyone knew who she was. But then, that is precisely why she went to such great lengths to alter her identity.

If anyone were to discover she is Max Temple's daughter, they might find it incredible that she's never seen this legendary clip all the way through. It would be like a rock star's offspring never having heard his greatest hit.

It's different when it's family though. You're not defined in each other's eyes by the things that shape your public perception.

The evening it aired, she didn't hear a word of it because Niamh was screaming for a solid hour, by the end of which she was crying too. There was never a good time to watch it back then: never *any* time. And in the years since, there have been too many conflicting emotions, too many reminders of how things were.

It's different now that he's gone. There are still the same conflicting emotions, but what changes it for Ivy is that *nothing* can change now. Max Temple can't become anything more, anyone new. He can only be what people remember, so she can choose whichever version of him serves her best.

Back on the screen, Abby's instincts prompt her to assert control and calmly defuse the situation. Unfortunately, these instincts were honed by years on kids' telly and work better on pop singers and *Hollyoaks* actors than on academics accustomed to a certain degree of deference.

'Now, Max,' she says, like she's humorously telling him off. 'You've had your time, so let's all be polite.'

'A lot of people get defensive when you show them this stuff,' Toby says, eyeing Dad. 'Because it shakes their world view.'

Abby nods.

'It may seem shocking,' she agrees, 'but you can't argue with the evidence.'

That's when Dad weighs in more forcefully, addressing Abby directly.

'No, the problem is that *you* can't argue with the evidence. You don't know which questions to ask, which is not your fault, because you haven't been briefed properly, but that is what this gentleman is relying upon in order to con you and your viewers.'

At this point, Abby must have got a message in her ear from her producer to let this play, because she suddenly goes from trying to break up the fight to holding the jackets. She looks to Dad with an inviting expression.

'What questions would you like to ask?'

It is the moment that changed Max Temple's entire career.

Ivy remembers how the phrase became something of a meme, a line people quoted when someone has been getting away with their bullshit for too long, but their easy ride is about to end.

What questions would you like to ask?

Because there are ten minutes of the show left to run, and until the credits roll, this poor bastard is trapped in Max's house.

'Just to be clear, you're saying the brightest scientific minds at NASA concocted the greatest hoax in human history, faked the lunar surface on a soundstage somewhere in order to produce their photos and TV broadcasts, but forgot to put stars in the pictures?'

'I said they were sloppy,' Toby replies. 'I worked twenty years as a detective, and if there was one thing I learned it was that when you're making up a lie, you will inevitably get tripped up on the detail. That's what happened here. Hence no stars.'

'Well, there's your ans—' Abby starts to say, but Dad doesn't let her end it there.

'There are no stars in the photo because here on Earth nitrogen molecules in the air scatter the sunlight, so that by the time it reaches us down here, it looks like it's coming from every direction at once, rather than a straight line from the sun. On the moon, there is no air, meaning the sky is black even in daytime. If you are trying to take a photograph of your fellow astronaut who is brightly lit by the sun, you need a short exposure time. Photographing stars requires long exposures. If you were to go outside tonight and take a picture of the sky using the same settings the astronauts used, there would be no stars in that picture either. This isn't rocket science, it's basic photography.'

Toby looks suddenly pleased, animated in a way that suggests he's about to spring a gotcha.

'In that case, in the absence of scattered light, how come the areas in shadow are not totally black? In the single most famous photograph of the Apollo missions, we see Buzz Aldrin standing on the surface, lit by the sun behind and to the right, which we can tell by the shadows.'

The director is on the ball. The photo appears on screen even as Toby is still speaking.

'So, if the sun is behind him, how come we can see Neil Armstrong and the lunar lander reflected in his visor? There is clearly a second light source nearby. Are you saying they brought a spotlight to the moon for taking photos?'

Abby looks impressed by this counterpunch. She doesn't know Dad.

'There *is* a second light source: the surface of the moon is highly reflective. Sunlight bounces off it – that's why you can *see* the bloody moon. Any astronomer could tell you that a full moon is not merely twice as bright as a half moon, as you might think, but ten times brighter. This is because of a phenomenon known as backscatter, which is particularly pronounced on the moon due to the lunar soil, though you can see the same effect on a dusty piece of ground, or on the grass of a dewy morning. Stand with your back to the sun and you will see a hazy halo around the shadow of your head.'

'Well, these properties all sound suspiciously convenient,' Toby counters. 'But you can't argue with the harsh fact that the Van Allen Belts—'

Dad cuts him off, the camera panning straight to him. It's like he's hosting the show at this point, and Abby is one of his guests. Clearly the director is loving him.

'What do you know about the trajectories of the Apollo missions, Mr Cutler-Wood?'

Toby looks rattled by having been given such a direct question.

'What would be the point in me studying theoretical trajectories for a mission that never took place?'

'The point would be that the trajectories were plotted so that the spacecraft only glanced the very inside edge of the inner belt, minimising the astronauts' exposure to the radiation. They spent most of the mission in the outer belts, where the levels are not so high, and the metal walls of the spacecraft protected them from the worst of it.'

Toby tees up for another gotcha, but he seems half-hearted. Ivy can tell he already suspects it will fail.

'You're saying they sent them in a spacecraft lined with lead?' Toby asks. 'How would they have ever shot something so heavy into orbit?'

'You don't need lead shielding to protect yourself from radiation, of which there are many different types: alpha particles, for example, are helium nuclei that can be stopped by window glass.'

Dad shakes his head then fires off another volley.

'I mean, honestly, did you do any research that might contradict your theory? Have you ever heard of the null hypothesis? Does the name Karl Popper mean anything to you? It seems clear to me that you started with your conclusion and then merely conducted a search for evidence in support of it, which would suggest that every criminal conviction your investigative abilities were instrumental in securing should now be ripe for appeal.'

We have reached the stage where Abby feels she needs to rescue the guy, as he is starting to look punch-drunk.

'There's no need to make it personal,' she warns Dad, still trying to keep her tone jovial. 'I think we can all agree that Toby has raised some controversial points with his book, and it just proves there's two sides to every story.'

'Yes, but sometimes one side is objectively wrong,' Dad replies. 'These points Toby presented might seem arresting – if you'll forgive the pun – but only to people who haven't studied the facts. It's like the Kennedy assassination. It sounds very shocking to hear how several witnesses claim to have heard four or more shots when the official version claims there were only three. However, the reason the official version concludes that there were three shots is that *eighty-one per cent* of witnesses reported hearing three shots, as opposed to *five per cent* who claim it was more.'

Abby looks like she just had her mind blown. It is the effect she experienced earlier, but in reverse. She had probably accepted the conspiracy version of the JFK assassination like she had accepted the truth of the Apollo missions, and is excited to hear it challenged with new information. Consequently, she is now happy to sit back and let Dad off his leash.

'There are two sides indeed, Abby, but it only sounds shocking when you don't hear both. Toby is right that the temperature of the lunar surface does indeed reach one hundred and twenty degrees at a maximum. It also gets down to minus a hundred and twenty at its coldest. However, the lunar day is four weeks long: the moon spins on its axis every twenty-seven days. The surface heats up gradually over several days, which is why NASA planned the missions to take place when the sun was low in the sky. Which is to say nothing of the fact that powdery materials are a terrible conductor of heat, and speaking of the lunar dust—'

Finally, it is Dad who gets interrupted, Abby placing a hand upon his arm as she is forced to cut him off.

'I'm afraid we're almost out of time, Max, but it's been a fascinating discussion. So, a special thank you to our guests tonight, Max Temple, Jason Cale and Toby Cutler-Wood. Join us again tomorrow evening when we'll be joined by . . .'

Though the camera pulls out to show all three guests on the sofa, Toby is the one to which the viewer is drawn, looking hollowed-out and blank-eyed. It is an image which has reappeared on social media since Dad died, rediscovered by a new generation and spreading. Ivy has seen it on web forums down the years: like the Captain Picard face-palm for expressing exasperation, this became the image synonymous with abject defeat. The irony of course being that sixteen years on, more people than ever believe the landings were faked, and it didn't take long for Toby Cutler-Wood to bounce back either. He is making a fortune on the lecture circuit these days, mostly in the US, having expanded from the moon landing onto 9/11, that whole Truther axis of stupidity.

43

Ivy closes the laptop and downs the rest of her gin in one go. She feels about as uncomfortable as she anticipated, but it was worth doing, preparing her for everything she is going to have to process in the coming days. The clip presented as good a version as any by which to remember him: brilliant, funny, formidable; hectoring, authoritarian, manipulative; aloof, entitled and arrogant – though in a way that you couldn't help but adore. It accentuates her regret at the way the family fell apart: the time she didn't spend with him, and the knowledge that now she won't spend any more.

Most importantly, watching the clip serves as a reminder of the myriad ways in which everyone else perceived her father, the moment at which he became public property.

As she reflects on all he said on the show, what sticks with her most are his words to Abby about how seductive conspiracy theories could be. He went on to build a career talking and writing about this because it fascinated him far more than merely debunking the theories themselves. As a psychologist, he understood how much easier it is to fool people than to convince them they've been fooled: that it is possible to sell an enduring lie because once people invest enough of themselves in it, they will continue to believe, in the face of overwhelming contradictory evidence.

Right down the years, Ivy has been paying attention and taking notes. You can't pull off what she had unless you've learned from the best.

2018

Marion

The sun is a golden blessing as Marion walks through the doors at Faro airport, reminding herself what it is to feel warm after a relentless, bitter winter that served as a prelude to a different kind of cold. She stops a moment to let it play upon her face, her mum proceeding ahead of her alongside Ken as he pushes their luggage trolley. The colours are bright and vivid, the way she always remembers them in this part of the world. She's never been here in the winter months, so it's hard to imagine the place ever looking any other way. She puts on her shades against the glare but continues to gratefully soak up the heat. It makes her feel transported, not merely to another place but another time.

Marion is still all churned up inside after all that has happened, and in a state of trepidation at the prospect of everything she may have to face in the coming days, but the sunshine reminds her of simpler times, simple pleasures. That's when it strikes her that she has not merely been afraid of the bad memories, but the good ones too. They're the ones that hurt more, the packets of emotion she's most afraid of opening. As she takes in the blueness and clarity of the sky, she understands that if the alternative is to go on feeling nothing, at least this way there is a leavening of warmth to the hurt.

They reach the top of the ramp leading to the on-site car-hire offices, where they encounter Vince Reid's new wife again, stopped between a trolley and her son's buggy. She is fanning herself with a magazine, her phone held to her ear while Amanda, the nanny or au pair or whatever, offers the little one a bottle. Marion can't help but think that something seems to be wrong, not least the fact that

45

Vince isn't with them. She remembers hearing his name in an announcement over the PA back at Glasgow.

Mum puts a hand to Ken's shoulder, signalling him to hold.

'Is everything all right?' she asks.

Kirsten looks irritated by the enquiry. Marion can see that she would rather be left alone, but Mum isn't always the best at reading those kinds of signals.

'Not exactly. Vince missed the fucking plane.'

Mum blinks at the language but isn't deterred.

'Oh dear. What happened?'

'Don't know. Bastard's not answering his phone or replying to my texts. I haven't a clue what he's up to. But when I get my hands on him . . .'

'Are you all right for getting to the villa?' Marion asks, making a quick calculation. They're not going to fit five adults and a baby plus luggage into the car they've booked, but Hugh's flight is due in a couple of hours. Marion could let Kirsten and her group travel ahead with Ken and Mum, then hitch a ride with her son and his family.

'We're fine,' Kirsten says. 'I organised the car hire. I don't leave that kind of thing to him. I was his secretary long enough to know what he can and can't be trusted with. I just thought that getting to a departure gate on time came into that category.'

'Is there anything we can help you with?' Mum asks.

'No. Just getting Arron fed and changed then we'll hit the road.'

Mum gives Ken another tap on the shoulder by way of signalling him to resume their progress towards the car-hire place. It's the one at the end, but at least it's an office, and not the angry scramble in the car park that attends those who've gone for the cheaper meet-and-greet outfits.

'I wonder what the story is there,' Mum muses, looking quite delighted. She has always enjoyed other people's bad behaviour.

There's no queue at the rental office, so it takes Ken only a few minutes to deal with the admin before leading them across the tarmac to the hire car, a white Kia. It looks new, the rubber on the tyres giving off a sheen that suggests barely any mileage.

46

Marion grips the passenger side door but feels her mum's hand on her arm.

'Let's sit in the back together, and Ken can be our handsome young chauffeur.'

'He's forty-five,' Marion says.

'Forty-five's as young as you want it to be,' Mum replies. 'I know that from experience,' she adds with an unmistakable innuendo. Marion can see Ken blush as he adjusts the position of the driver's seat, no doubt grateful he has his back to them.

Marion has no such protection, and her own discomfort does not go unnoticed, or unrelished.

'Oh, Marion, you'd best get over your prudishness before we get to the villa, as I am very much looking forward to gadding about in my bathing costume. I'm sure your husband won't mind, will you, Ken?'

Ken says nothing, wisely keeping out of it. He is normally quite adept at flirty banter, but understandably not when it's with his mother-in-law.

'I'm certainly looking forward to seeing *you* with a few less layers,' Mum adds, not letting Ken off the hook.

'Oh, for God's sake,' Marion mutters. She can't help herself. 'It's hardly appropriate, Mum.'

'What, because Ken's a grandfather now? Because of my age? It's just a bit of fun.'

'No, because . . .'

She lets it hang. She can't say it. But Mum can.

'Because of Dad? Am I supposed to be all in black in accordance with your Victorian prescribed mourning? Your father wouldn't be having any of that. He was always very proud of how I looked. He liked it when I drew attention.'

Marion opts not to respond further. There can't be a woman born who is comfortable discussing her mother's sexuality, and she suspects Celia knows this only too well. On the plus side, she does seem quite chipper, which is a big relief, though with Mum there is always the possibility that she is putting on a performance to hide the truth. The woman was once an actress, after all.

For now, however, Marion is prepared to take her morale at face value, as she could do with the reassurance. Mum had been running late at the airport, which got her disproportionately worried. It was daft now, she could see, but as she stood in the departure lounge with ten minutes becoming twenty and her texts going unanswered, all manner of dreadful things had begun to go through her head. She recalled stories about bereavement in elderly couples who had been together for decades, how occasionally the survivor would suddenly die within weeks of losing their spouse, as though some part of them could not, would not live on without their partner. She also had visions of Mum sitting at home weeping, unable to face the trip now that the reality of it was upon her.

Then she finally got a text and shortly after that, Mum had walked out of duty free seeming more like her usual self than any time since it happened. She looked radiant and summery, a liveliness about her appearance that made Marion feel even more of a shambles. She had barely slept last night, thinking about what lay ahead of her today, and she knows she doesn't look that great at the best of times. Difficult to work on getting beach-ready when you're being double-teamed by bereavement and the early stages of the menopause.

She glances at Ken, looking carefree in the driver's seat with his shades on and the air con ruffling his silver hair. He looks like he's already been on holiday a week, relaxed and calm, which is what she loves about him.

He accelerates the Kia towards the A22. The motorway wasn't open back in the days when they first used to come here. The journey would take the best part of two hours, through a dozen coastal villages. These days it should take half that, though they will have a stop at Lagos to hit the supermarket.

Marion pulls out a magazine from her bag. She is almost surprised to see it there, as she has little recollection of buying it. She must have done so on autopilot. It is a copy of *New Scientist*, not something she would ordinarily pick up, but there is a little inset picture of her father on the cover, and the promise of an article inside: 'Remembering Max Temple'.

She flicks through it until she finds the double-page spread and remembers glancing at it in WH Smith at the airport, thinking it might help her reconnect with its subject. Her father has become something of an abstract to her in the past couple of weeks, her mind rendering him thus as a means of dealing with the pain. It was a necessary defence, but she fears she is losing touch with her sense of his presence. She needs to feel the pain in order to still feel him.

She scans a familiar summary of biography and achievements, pretty much the greatest hits in terms of his career and media profile. There are pictures from various periods of his life, and inevitably a screencap of that viral TV clip, the one with the moon-landing conspiracy guy wearing an expression like he wanted to die right then and there. She was never going to learn anything new from a glorified obit, but in a way, this kind of thing helps frame the context she is living with now: one in which he is dead. The only thing to arrest her gaze for any duration is, inversely, one of the shortest paragraphs. It states: 'Temple's detractors liked to depict him as emotionally aloof, but those close to him describe a warm family man, one whose life was not untouched by sorrow. In 2002, he suffered the death of his 18-month-old granddaughter, who drowned in a tragic accident at the family's villa in the Algarve.'

It feels jarring to see it reduced to a seemingly incidental detail in someone else's biography, described in terms that make it seem a small and quiet thing: a brief time of solemnity and sadness in a life otherwise full of achievement and celebration. The perspective is instructive. The journalist could not possibly know – nobody could know, who was not part of it – just how brutal it was for so many people, and how it wasn't quiet, wasn't brief and wasn't solemn. Mercifully, this same brevity ensures that the article does not allude to the innuendo, the smears and the conspiracy theories that added to their collective pain.

She becomes aware that Mum is glancing at the magazine, and feels oddly vulnerable and self-conscious, instinctively protective of her own grief.

'I've never been able to read in a moving car,' Mum says, with the unmissable subtext that Marion will not be permitted to do so on this journey. 'It was weird looking at the magazines at the airport, though,' she goes on.

'Seeing Dad?' Marion asks, wondering which others she missed.

'No, just remembering which ones I used to write for. It doesn't just seem a long time ago, it feels like it all happened to another person. I gave up my acting career to have my children, and I regarded raising a family as my second career, but then my columns became a part of that. I shared all that it meant to be a mother, a wife, a grandmother. Suddenly I was a journalist. Then that ended too. I'm wittering, but I think I'm just trying to remind myself that every ending is also a beginning, though you seldom see it that way at the time. That's why us all coming together again at the villas is so important. We think we've endured the end of something, but this can be a new beginning for our family.'

Marion finds it difficult to respond. Perhaps Mum is right, and this holiday will be the catharsis they all need, but her instincts are telling her otherwise. She doesn't see how it could possibly be a good idea for the whole family to gather again in that place where they will inevitably be reminded of the worst time in all their lives. That's why nobody ever entertained the notion throughout all the years that Mum's been suggesting it – until the present circumstances made it impossible to say no.

With every mile Ken drives her closer, she's getting more anxious thinking about what memories will be dredged up, what tensions.

What regret.

What guilt.

And she is afraid of what it might expose Hugh and Lia to. She was able to shield them back then, and fortunately they were too young to absorb the fallout. They're all grown up now, but her instincts have not changed. Marion knows how far a mother would go to protect her children. How far a mother *should* go. But not everybody sees it the same way.

Marion reminds herself she has been back to the villa plenty of times with her own family, but that was different. The dynamic was different, the memories different. It's not the place or the people she's afraid of, but the combination of the two. She has even been there with her parents, but never with everybody at the same time: and never with one person in particular.

She has never been back.

With that thought, she realises it would be wise to manage Mum's expectations: not merely regarding whether her youngest daughter will show up, but about what is likely to happen if she does.

'Mum, I don't think you should get your hopes up regarding Ivy.'

Mum scoffs at the name.

'See, that's what I mean. If you can't even accept what she has chosen to call herself, then it doesn't augur well for fostering a spirit of *détante*.'

'It's just typically pig-headed and self-obsessed, that's all.'

'Which is why, if she was to be there, you'd best prepare yourself for how she is rather than how you'd like her to be. She's not going to be the prodigal daughter, and she's not going to act penitent just because . . . you know . . .'

Once again, Marion can't bring herself to say it.

'Well, if she can't be contrite now, of all times, whenever would she?' Mum asks, proving that she has precisely all of the deluded expectations Marion fears.

'Mum, she's proud and she's haughty and she's a nightmare: we know that. She's not going to change, but the thing to remember is that just because she doesn't *act* contrite, it doesn't mean she doesn't *feel* contrite.'

Mum doesn't look at all convinced. She doesn't respond but folds her arms and stares out of the window in silence for the next twenty or thirty miles. Replaying incidents no doubt, rehearsing old arguments.

Ken drives them through the village of Praia Mexilhões, winding along the clifftop road. They are approaching a place that was a building site for years, construction abandoned following the crash in 2008, after which it lay untouched and overgrown. Back then Marion would have found it hard to say whether it was ruins or foundations, but now it's a two-storey villa surrounded by lush lawns, sprinklers irrigating them in wide arcs.

They pass that, then a couple of older isolated villas, and finally the familiar compound comes into view. Mum and Dad own two of three properties situated around a shared pool, Vince Reid owning the other. The development is officially named Baia Serena but the Temples have always just called it 'the villas'.

Marion feels that weird tightness inside, as she has done upon every return. Part of her wants to ask Ken to turn around and drive back to the airport, but she can't do that with Mum here, and besides, she can already see a hire car in the driveway. Rory must have got here first.

'She never, ever said sorry,' Mum eventually says. 'That's the thing I can't accept.'

'She admitted she made it up.'

'Yes, but she never apologised.'

'I'm sure she did at some point. Implicitly, at least.'

'Not to him. Not to Max, the one she hurt the most.'

'And yet he forgave her,' Marion reminds her.

'It would have meant more had she *asked* for his forgiveness.'

'She was too ashamed. Dad understood that. That's just what he was like.'

'Yes, but that's what made it so much more painful,' Mum protests, turning to face her. The mask of equanimity has slipped. There are tears in the corners of her eyes. 'Nobody loved her more than him. And yet she made that hateful accusation.'

'Mum, that's just it: she lashed out at him because that was the best way to hurt all of us. She lashed out at the one person she knew wouldn't hold a grudge.'

'Yes, but that doesn't mean it didn't hurt him. That's what she never asked forgiveness for. And now it's too late.'

'She can ask for it from us,' Marion suggests, but she knows how feeble that sounds.

'She could, but she won't. She's too far gone. Fabricating lies to manipulate people has been the making of her, remember. She has elevated it to an art form and it has made her a wealthy woman.'

Ken stops the little Kia alongside a bright red Audi. Marion thinks that it's not really Rory's style or budget, then she remembers he's got a new girlfriend, some San Francisco tech-industry hot-shot.

Mum lets out a sigh, one Marion recognises as the overture to her final say on something, except it's never her final say.

'I thought she might be the missing piece in putting us all back together, but realistically she's more likely to be the element that drives us all apart. She's done it before. This is not about her, and when she's not the centre of attention, she makes a drama until she is. So now that we're here I can see that it's probably for the best if she doesn't come.'

'You might want to hold that thought,' Ken says, opening the rear door.

They both look over the dry-stone wall and across the lawn towards the swimming pool, where a stick-thin figure is sitting on a sun lounger wearing only bikini briefs and a pair of Ray Bans. She's got two phones and a bottle of Sagres beside her on a table, a laptop open on her thighs, and is giving off an unmistakable sense that she owns the place.

Until this point, Marion would have said she was ambivalent about whether Ivy showed up, but one look at her sitting there tells her this was never true. She just didn't want to admit to herself how much she hoped her sister would stay away.

Most powerfully, our fear of chaos leads us to crave narrative. We construct apparently coherent stories that tie things together, part of a greater scheme, an all-encompassing truth. These stories make sense according to the way we already understand the world, but that understanding is already a flawed attempt to impose a pattern upon chaos.

Max Temple

2002

Vince

Vince was in the kitchen at the rear of his villa when he heard the slamming of car doors and a clamour of excited voices. He was fixing himself a very late breakfast: a *pastel de nata* left over from yesterday afternoon, and a glass of orange juice. He fancied a coffee but the espresso stove-top pot was still sitting by the sink, waiting to be emptied and cleaned out. Bit of a catch-22: he couldn't face doing that until he'd had a coffee, but . . .

He looked at the clock. It was almost quarter to twelve. Maybe not so surprising considering he saw three o'clock last night, having stayed up much later than he intended. He told Laurie he was reading, but in truth he had been working and he didn't want her to know. Sometimes he stayed up late to work and other times he got up before she woke, both for the same reason. He had promised he was leaving all that behind for a couple of weeks, but then they had both made promises about what they were and weren't going to do on this holiday, and neither was demonstrating much fortitude about it.

It wasn't as though she had been tempting him with a reason to come to bed at the same time as her.

There was a cereal bowl and a coffee cup next to the sink also: Laurie's breakfast. He wondered just how long she had been up. She was always an early riser: one of their many emerging incompatibilities. Then his eye was drawn to something further along the work surface: the smaller chopping board was lying out with half a lime sitting on it, a knife alongside.

Vince told himself it might be from last night, but looking closer he could see the glint of fresh moisture on the blade. She was already drinking. She probably wanted him to notice, too. He didn't have the energy to deal with that right now.

The commotion at the other villa provided a welcome distraction in the form of an excuse to be elsewhere. He devoured the *pastel* in two bites and wandered out through the patio doors towards the gravel drive between the villas.

When Vince and Laurie flew in, the only people at the other villas were Marion's family and her younger brother Rory, along with his latest girlfriend (who was way above the usual standard, Vince would have to say). Now Max and Celia must have arrived, which was a pleasing development. It looked like there were people with them in the back seat, but Vince couldn't see properly because Rory was in the way.

He spoke briefly to Marion yesterday but didn't ask whether her parents were coming too because he didn't want to come across as needy or overeager. He also didn't want to admit to himself that he was both of those things, or how disappointed he'd have been if Marion said no.

It's an odd thing: he would miss them if they weren't here, but it's not like he would go out of his way to see them otherwise. Their holidays overlapped frequently, especially given that they each visited several times a year, so they socialised when they were in Portugal, but they'd never discussed getting together back home, even though they didn't live so far from each other. It was one of those unspoken things, mutually understood: holiday friends. Not the same as home friends. Real friends.

It was what it was, part of the deal when you buy a place like this with a shared pool. You had to bump along with whoever you ended up alongside, take the hand you're dealt, and Vince would have to admit the hand he got dealt was a pretty good one.

He watched Max stretch after the drive, looking relaxed in tailored shorts and a peach polo shirt, his silver hair kind of wispy but sitting in a way that didn't emphasise the extent to which it was thinning. Comfortable in his skin: that's what Vince would call him. Probably every woman's idea of the wise and slightly sexy ageing professor: tall and slim, handsome in a chiselled, old-fashioned way, like one of those aristo-type actors from the Gainsborough Pictures era.

He was good company. Remarkably erudite and well-informed, as you would expect, but witty with it, if tending towards the waspish. The downside was that Vince always felt like he had to be upping his game in his presence, and he couldn't help feeling that the harder he tried to impress Max, the worse he came across.

It was easier when there was a crowd, and Vince could dilute himself in it. He wouldn't like to be one-on-one with the guy for any length of time, as he had the impression Max merely tolerated him. To be honest, he had the impression Max merely tolerated just about everybody. He was kind of remote that way: you could tell he thought nobody else was anywhere near as clever as him. He was probably right about that too, which was why Vince was content to be tolerated. He wouldn't get to spend time in such rarefied company under any other circumstances. And of course, it wasn't just Max's company that was the attraction. The guy's wife was Celia Wilde, for God's sake.

She had popped over to introduce herself the first time Vince and Laurie arrived here after buying the place. Vince was drinking a beer and had almost choked when she appeared at the patio. Talk about spank bank. For guys of his age, she was the face that locked a million bathrooms, indelibly etched in a generation's consciousness as Kurlia, the alien princess turned rebel mercenary in the iconic seventies British SF series *The Liberators*. It was a show largely remembered for camp charm and wobbly scenery, but for many its most enduring legacy was down to a wardrobe department not shackled by enlightened sensibilities. If its costume designs were not intended to be fetishistic at the time, they had certainly become so since. And nobody had worn them like Kurlia.

Celia was bent to lean into the open rear door of the newly arrived vehicle. He wondered if it was someone elderly who was arriving. They hadn't got out of the car at the same time as Max and Celia and appeared to be in need of assistance. Celia's parents or Max's, presumably. Either way, not an addition to the eye candy quotient.

59

Vince had been wondering about Sylvie, the younger daughter. She hadn't been here last summer, so he was unsurprised (if a little disappointed) that she wasn't part of the package this year either. She must be seventeen or eighteen by now. She had presumably reached the stage where she was ditching the family holidays to go off to Magaluf or wherever with her mates, getting shitfaced and pumping strangers.

That's certainly what he would be doing if he could go back to his late teens. When Vince was that age, he was either too busy – mired in shit-work and studies – too skint or too both to be making the most of it. Everybody else seemed to be off on summertime shagathons while he was cramming for resits or literally minding the store for his dad. It was all going to be worth it in the long term, he had told himself. He would get plenty of what they were all having soon enough: after the next exam, or the summer after this one. But then, bang: he woke up one day and found that he was in his thirties. He was still busy with work, still mired in stuff he needed to study, and though not exactly skint, still a long way from where he thought he would be financially.

Sylvie was half his age but he always liked being around her, hearing what she talked about: her energy, enthusiasm, aspirations and not forgetting her snark. A big part of him still felt like a teenager, or maybe it was that he never felt he properly got to be one. That was why he felt more of an affinity with Sylvie than with her big sister, who was much closer to him in years. Marion was hovering in the doorway right then, a typical pose: staying back from the action, hiding from attention.

Marion always struck him as one of those prematurely middle-aged types: mumsy and kind of dowdy. She never looked young. She already had a husband and a baby by the time Vince bought the villa. She was married to Ken, who struck Vince as shy to the point of dull. He wondered if Ken was closeted and it was a marriage of convenience. He certainly couldn't imagine the two of them at it very much. Sure, they had kids, but that didn't always mean anything. Ken was relaxed and easy-going, and unlike Max, Vince never felt he was out of his league being around him (quite the opposite), but he was way too quiet for Vince's comfort. When you're not getting much back from someone, you can get anxious that you're not going over well.

He saw Celia straighten up, stepping back from the car with the reason for all the excitement. She was holding a baby wrapped in a purple blanket: a little poppet in a pink sunhat that she was trying to pull off her head, frustrated by an elasticated chinstrap holding it in place. The tot was writhing energetically as though to escape her grandmother's grip. Celia didn't look keen to put her on the ground, despite her apparent eagerness to be free after being cooped up in a car for the best part of two hours.

Out of the same door emerged presumably the kid's mother, a chubby female climbing awkwardly out of the narrow gap. He wondered who she was: friend of the family, a cousin of Marion and Rory? Then with a wave of shock he realised this was Sylvie. She had rounded out a bit the last time he saw her a couple of years ago, but Jesus.

He remembered how she had developed through her early teens. He had watched her blossom and thought she was going to be a real heartbreaker. Too young for the spank bank at that time, obviously, but he wouldn't deny that his eye had strayed to the sight of her climbing in and out of the pool in a bikini. He couldn't help it. He had no designs on her, he wasn't a pervert, but you can't fool your body's instincts. It was a purely aesthetic appreciation of a young girl who was clearly the heir to her mother's looks.

Dear God. What had happened to her? She was a teenage mum and had blown up like a space hopper.

Celia must have noticed him hovering, and possibly also noticed the confused look on his face. She gave him a wave and beckoned him closer.

'Vince! Of course, you've not met the latest addition to the family. This is our granddaughter Niamh. She wasn't here last summer – she hadn't had her vaccines and was too young to fly.'

'She's gorgeous. Congratulations,' he added, addressing Sylvie. Part of him was instinctively unsure whether congratulations were appropriate, and Sylvie's ambivalent response indicated he was on the money. She gave him a cursory and joyless smile, then hurried inside. She looked knackered. More than that: defeated.

He wondered what the story was. She must have had the kid when she was sixteen – if that.

Vince heard the thump of someone closing the boot and saw an adolescent male standing behind the car, slinging a rucksack over his shoulder. He was pale and plooky, a mummy's-boy barely old enough to shave. Poor bastard must be the father. He looked knackered too. Vince calculated their travel schedule. The flight they got must have left Glasgow at six a.m. He'd been up all night. They both looked like they'd been up a lot of nights.

'This is Sylvie's boyfriend, Calum. Calum is studying law. He can pick your brains. Calum, Vince and his wife Laurie are both lawyers.'

Calum managed a shy hello and followed Sylvie into the villa.

'Vince, Marion has prepared an early lunch and we're going to get right to it. That's what I love about this place: no settling in – the second I'm here, I'm straight into holiday mode. You must come and join us.'

Celia was remarkable that way. She might have been up all night too, but she was instantly in charge, and so good at including everybody, putting you at ease. In contrast to Max, she was demonstrably friendly. Flirty even, in Vince's case, though he would need to have had a few drinks before he deluded himself that there was anything to it other than her naturally outgoing manner. He got the impression Celia liked him, with the caveat that she was once an actress. That said, someone merely acting as though she liked him was preferable to someone sincerely demonstrating that they didn't.

'I wouldn't want to impose,' he said, really hoping she would dismiss this. She did.

'Not at all. It's been a long time and I've been looking forward to just sitting outside and having a blether. You must go and get Laurie.'

'I'm not sure Laurie's feeling so great,' he said.

It was a lie that came easily, one that he worried they'd heard before. He wondered how much they could guess, to what extent feigned ignorance was a form of politeness. Or was such ignorance not entirely feigned, but a complicit blindness: because if even one of you acknowledged it, then you couldn't all pretend it wasn't there.

'Oh, go and ask. Maybe she'll perk up.'

'I'll give her ten minutes, then I'll see.'

He didn't know how many she might have had. If it had been an hour later, they could just about disguise it: no harm in a couple at lunchtime when you're on your holidays. If she was pissed before twelve, that was trickier.

Vince followed Rory and his girlfriend around to where the table had been laid on the villa's patio, overlooking the pool.

'This is Svetlana, by the way,' said Rory in his lugubrious register. He always sounded like either he could barely be arsed talking to you or was simply too stoned.

'Vince.'

'Pleased to meet you,' Svetlana said, in a strong accent Vince couldn't place.

The Lord giveth and he taketh away, and when it came to eye candy, what had been lost in Sylvie was more than made up for in Rory's new squeeze. Vince couldn't help noticing her out by the pool as soon as he had arrived. How could he not? She was stunning, like supermodel stunning. To be honest, he was disappointed she hadn't been topless yet, as she totally seemed the type. He assumed it was different when you were with your boyfriend's family. He'd have to keep his eyes peeled, as she was bound to choose her moment, when the rest of the family were off elsewhere and she had the poolside to herself.

Marion began bringing out the food, placing down a huge bowl of chopped salad. Ken was at her back, bearing two fistfuls of beers, the necks of three gripped between the fingers of each hand.

Vince had just put one to his mouth when he saw Laurie appear, making her way across the grass. He tensed up at the sight, then relaxed when he judged that she was okay. He could tell from the walk, and from the fact that she wasn't covering her eyes with shades. Perhaps the slice of lime was just to go with some fizzy water. Club Soda, the Yanks called it: made it sound so much more sophisticated.

'Laurie, pull up a chair,' Celia said, placing down a selection of those tuna and sardine pâtés that they ate here.

Sylvie and Calum appeared, the former cradling the tot. Vince anticipated another round of introductions, but they were not forthcoming. Then he remembered that Laurie had come out here for a few days around Easter. They must have all met then. He wondered why she never said anything about Sylvie and the baby. More evidence that it was a sensitive area, perhaps. Or maybe she'd been drunk most of the time and didn't remember. He had figured that was why she went: so she could drink away from his monitoring and disapproval.

Marion appeared again with a board of fresh bread from the bakery down in the village. The locals could clean that place out if you weren't sharp, so somebody must have been up early, and he could guess why. With that thought he realised something was missing, then he heard a scream and a whiny cry, and the usual picture was complete.

Marion's daughter Lia came wandering around the corner from the other villa, tear-streaked and bawling.

'Hughie hit me again,' she wailed, a familiar lament in Vince's experience.

Hughie turned up at her back, protesting his innocence, but the fact that he followed her out here in anticipation of what she was going to say didn't do much for the credibility of his defence. Nor did the fact that he had a massive charge sheet of previous.

'Why don't you go and play on your own,' Marion suggested to him.

'I was,' he protested. 'But she came and annoyed me.'

This set off more bawling.

'He was hitting my dollies.'

'No, I wasn't,' Hughie retorted, unconvincingly, before stomping off.

'Come, look,' Marion bade the howling Lia. 'Auntie Sylvie's here with baby Niamh.'

The apparently inconsolable Lia's tears seemed to dry miraculously as she suddenly noticed her cousin. It was amazing how distraction could be so effective at that age. The thing that mattered so much two seconds ago was immediately forgotten and a new imperative replaced it. When were Vince's woes and cares ever lifted so suddenly?

64

Lia ambled over to where Sylvie was sitting and gave the baby a hug, but this didn't seem to satisfy her.

'No, I want to hold her myself,' she complained.

'She's heavy,' Sylvie replied. 'She's not one of your dollies.'

It looked like she was going to kick off again, but Marion intervened.

'I'll hold her in my lap,' she said.

'Gan, Gan,' said Niamh excitedly, reaching her arms to her grandmother.

Sylvie willingly handed over the tot and Marion arranged herself so that Lia could sit on her lap and 'hold' Niamh.

Lia looked very pleased with herself. The baby seemed to tolerate it, a baffled expression on her little face.

'I'm going to give her a bath,' Lia announced.

'Yes, you can help Auntie Sylvie give her a bath later.'

'I'm going to give her a bath myself.'

Marion let this go, which was par for the course. In Vince's experience as an observer, the word 'no' was not one that either of those kids heard very often from their mother.

Their collective attention was raised by a clattering sound from over by the dry-stone wall that bordered the driveway. Hughie was whacking it with a plastic sword, alternating chopping strokes with thrusts that drove his blade into gaps like he was running some poor bastard through. He was going at it with some real passion.

Vince and Laurie had long ago nicknamed the kid Damien. Vince thought he might have mellowed now he must be eight or nine, but if anything he seemed more intense and slightly unnerving.

'He seems to have a thing about stabbing,' Calum suggested, a hint of concern in his tone. Vince wondered what else Calum might have witnessed at family occasions back home.

'He's just playing a game,' Marion said.

'He's obsessed with *The Fellowship of the Ring*,' Ken added. 'Watches the DVD over and over. That and *Robin Hood: Prince of Thieves*.'

'He chopped my dolly's hands off,' Lia said, pouting.

'That's healthy,' muttered Celia. A joke and yet not a joke.

65

Marion looked uncomfortable, defensive.

'There's a scene at the start,' she said. 'Someone gets their hand cut off for stealing. He likes re-enacting it.'

Vince didn't recall much about the film other than that bloody Bryan Adams song. Oh, and that guard leering over Mary Elizabeth Mastrantonio, saying, 'I've never seen the breasts of a noblewoman.' Need to watch *The January Man* for that, mate, he remembered thinking.

With Marion looking at her son, Lia chose this moment to reach for some bread, letting go of the baby as she did so. Niamh almost tumbled but Marion sensed the movement and retrieved the situation, just. She got a sour look from Sylvie, who made a slight drama of taking the baby back.

Having snagged a snack and exhausted her interest in the baby, Lia wandered off, just as Max emerged from the villa bearing two bottles of cava.

'I thought it would be appropriate to kick off our holiday with a little celebration.'

'What are we celebrating?' Vince asked.

'Dad got this huge book deal,' Marion explained. 'Just him this time, I mean, on his own.'

Of course. Vince hadn't seen Max since everything went crazy.

He was already the co-author of a pop-psychology book, along with Jason Cale, a popular TV presenter who used to be the male lead on *The Liberators*. Cale's was the name that sold the book, and Max had been brought in to lend academic cred. It was safe to say Prof. Temple had left him in his slipstream after what had happened in recent months.

'Yes, congratulations,' Vince said. 'How is Celia handling not being the most famous one in the house?'

Max laughed. Celia merely smiled, though maybe not with her eyes. Vince felt afraid he'd said the wrong thing. Or was he just imagining it? With Celia he'd never know. She was always able to throw a convincing veil of politeness over things. Maybe he was just over-cautious because he wanted her to like him.

He wasn't normally drawn to older women, but there was just something about her. It wasn't merely that she looked good for her age: the way she carried herself, she made it look a sexy age to be. Maybe she was just hard-wired into his libido. Like many guys of his vintage, a fascination with Kurlia had served merely as an overture to discovering the Hammer horror movie she had appeared in before *The Liberators*. He had recorded it off Channel Four in his teens, on a videotape that eventually went fuzzy at the good bit from being replayed and paused so many times.

She was still in great shape. More busty than that Hammer clip would suggest, though she would have been only eighteen or nineteen at that time. He'd love to get an eyeful of the real thing.

He had always thought Max Temple was one lucky bastard, and he'd just got luckier. The guy had been all over the media since that TV show. A go-to talking head on any number of subjects, and now a book deal. Beautiful wife, loving family, distinguished career, money rolling in and now a sprinkling of fame: he seemed to have the perfect life. However, Vince only had to look across the table to see that wasn't so. His teenage daughter getting up the duff at the age of sixteen fairly messed up the picture.

Sylvie seemed uncommonly quiet. In the past, she was never short of something to say for herself. Very spiky with it: cutting and cruel, the way teenage girls could be. She was indulged for it too. Celia would occasionally try to rein her in, but she'd just pout and tut. Max seldom intervened against her. It wasn't hard to spot the dynamic there. She was the apple of her father's eye, and God she knew it.

What had happened to her since must have been quite the humbling. She seemed diminished, in every way except the physical. Poor lassie was twice the size.

'Hammer of the Charlatans, someone called him recently,' said Celia of Max.

'Is that going to be the name of the book?' Vince suggested.

'No,' replied Celia, 'but we should get a Temple family coat of arms made, with that as the motto. What's Latin for hammer of the charlatans?'

'The origin of the word charlatan was about fifteen hundred years too late for Latin,' Max told her. He could be very literal in his interpretation of things, not always tuned in to when something was just meant to be fun.

'That poor bastard, the moon landing guy,' Vince said, shaking his head. 'Never seen anyone get so comprehensively emptied on live television. Max threw him around like a wet tracksuit.'

'We should be grateful to the man,' said Celia. 'He's made Max a star.'

'I actually feel a bit sorry for him,' said Marion. 'He's become the face of defeat and humiliation. That's kind of tragic.'

'Don't waste your sympathy,' warned Max. 'The truly tragic thing is that he will still be out there giving talks on this like it never happened. In fact, by this point, *I* will be part of the conspira—'

Max's words were cut off by a piercing scream.

Marion and Ken both got to their feet in a hurry, reacting to what sounded like genuine distress in their daughter's cry. The whole table responded automatically to the sense of urgency, getting up and following in the direction of the sound. They all must have had the same fearful thought. It came from the other side of the villa, where beyond the hedge only a wooden railing hemmed off the clifftop path from the drop. However, if Lia had fallen, she wouldn't be screaming, and to Vince's ears it sounded more like a response to something she had seen.

Vince ran around the corner in time to see Ken glance back towards him, bearing an expression combining embarrassment with weary humour: a parent's lot. Vince wasn't sure he found what he was looking at so funny.

Lia was being comforted in Marion's arms, while before them two of her dollies dangled from slipknots. Hughie had used a section of the railing as a gibbet and had staged a hanging.

'It's from *Robin Hood*,' Marion said feebly, as the whole gathering took in the sight.

Celia raised her eyebrows in a subtle gesture of vindication.

'Like I said. Healthy.'

2018

Amanda

The sun is going down as I watch Kirsten swim laps in the pool. Her stroke is practised and elegant, barely making a splash as her hands cut the surface. It was hot when we arrived but there is just a hint of a chill in the breeze as evening falls. Two hours ago I would have believed it was the height of summer, but the goosebumps on my arms are a reminder that it is early June.

Arron is at my feet on the patio, my left foot rocking his car seat. He is quiet right now, having just had a bottle. He is staring at the wall, where the sun's reflection off the pool is causing a dance of light that he seems to find fascinating.

Kirsten hauls herself up the ladder and stands on the flagstones for a few moments, letting the water run off her before picking up a towel from her nearby sun lounger. She is wiry and lithe, only the smallest bump around her middle beneath the swimsuit. The woman gave birth only a few months ago. She must be hitting the gym like a sonofabitch. She hardly seems to eat anything either, but she talks constantly about food or about being hungry.

'Is he all right?' Kirsten asks.

'Seems quite settled.'

'Think we'll hang on a bit before his bath then.'

'Sure.'

Kirsten takes a seat next to me, a towel wrapped around her shoulders, gazing out to sea. She's got a glass of wine on the table between her phone and a plate of chopped celery sticks. The sky is clear and the water a dark blue, flecked with white further away amid the roiling waves. I can see a windsurfer about a quarter of a mile out. He's really booking, indicating a surprising wind speed.

'It's lovely here, isn't it?' Kirsten says, lifting her glass by the stem with relish. 'When Vince first told me he had this place I thought it sounded boring, a bit too quiet, but I really like the calm now. This is my favourite time of day, when the sun's going down but it's still warm enough to sit out.'

'It's a chill vibe,' I agree. 'I've never been to Portugal before. Never been to Europe, in fact. Will there be much chance to get around?'

'Oh yeah, the village is only five minutes in the car. Twenty minutes, half an hour to walk.'

'I kinda meant elsewhere in Portugal. For instance, are we anywhere near Lisbon?'

Kirsten looks like I asked if we were anywhere near Uzbekistan, indicating that she has as little desire to go there either. I am very quickly discovering that me and Kirsten probably ain't gonna have a shitload to talk about other than the baby.

'Lisbon's bloody hours away. Plenty to do here, though. Down at the beach in Praia Mexilhões there's surfing and windsurfing, paragliding, all that stuff. There's also a quieter little beach at Saloma, which you can get to using the clifftop path. What kind of stuff are you into?'

'I'm not like super outdoorsy.'

'Vince said something about you being a blogger or something.'

'Vlogger.'

'Yeah. You make little videos. About what?'

I really don't want to get into this.

'I just sort of talk about stuff,' I say, hoping not to encourage further questions. I wouldn't want Kirsten poking about in my YouTube channel, a thought that reminds me I really ought to get around to deleting some of my early efforts. Plus it's not likely to initiate an in-depth discussion about the cross-over between men's rights activism and the rise of alt-right neo-Nazis. I'm guessing if I mentioned Jordan Peterson, Kirsten would think he was in the NBA.

'To camera?' she asks. 'Are they on YouTube?'

I think about lying but I feel cornered.

'Yeah.'

Kirsten beams.

'Have you seen that one where the guy's getting interviewed and his kids burst in? I almost peed myself watching that.'

I feel relief wash through me. Both of us sit there quietly a moment, our eyes drawn to one of our neighbours getting up from her lounger, gathering her things and making her way inside her villa. I don't know who she is. She had been sitting apart from everyone else, tapping at a laptop or talking quietly into her phone. She spoke to no one and she made no eye contact when I had taken the baby for a wander around the gardens.

I get that it can be awkward when you've got three villas sharing a pool: you may not want to get totally social with relative strangers, but what would a nod cost you, lady? It's possible she was dealing with something intense on her computer and it wasn't the right moment, but I suspect it more likely she was laying down a marker. There was a strong scent of 'fuck off' wafting from her direction.

Kirsten picks up her phone, scrolls with her thumb for a few seconds then puts it back down. Every time she does that, I want to ask if she's heard anything from Vince, but it's a damn stupid question and I don't want to be annoying. Of course she's not heard anything: she would have said. But at the same time, I don't want Kirsten thinking I don't care, or that it isn't a little uncomfortable to have come all the way over from Canada and potentially found myself in the middle of a marriage crisis.

Maybe it's that she's here in the sunshine and already hitting the dry white, but Kirsten doesn't seem half as concerned as I do. It's like she's through the anger and irritation stages, into something altogether more relaxed. She seems resolved and determined to enjoy herself.

Kirsten reaches for a celery stick and crunches it between noticeably whitened teeth.

'You know, you use more calories to eat raw celery than the celery contains. Can't get enough of it since I read that – literally.'

She seems pretty pleased with this nugget of information, because she must have told me like three times in the short period we have known each other.

Kirsten catches me looking towards her phone and reads my thoughts.

'Still haven't had so much as a text since the airport,' she says, a hint of amusement in her tone.

'Has he done anything like this before? You know, disappear and go incommunicado.'

'He's very good at finding mobile reception blind spots when it suits him. I've heard him tell people he's about to drive into a tunnel when he isn't, just so he can cut off the call.'

'But, like, isn't it weird that he was at the airport, in the departure area, and he bailed without coming up and telling us what's going on?'

'Not that weird considering he knew I would kick off and make a scene if he told me he had to skip the flight. He's been a bit furtive recently, because he was supposed to be easing off and I reckon he was doing the opposite. I bet his bloody phone went, and whatever he was dealing with turned out to not be as tied up as he thought.'

Kirsten holds up her glass as though toasting the view, savouring another mouthful of wine.

'I'm not going to try calling again. It's on him. I don't know what the idiot is up to, but the fact is, we're here in the sun and he's back there in the rain, and that's his choice.'

Arron is starting to get restless, wriggling in the car seat. I bend down to pick him up, but Kirsten taps me on the shoulder.

'I'll get him. You go and get yourself a glass of wine too.'

'I don't really drink it.'

'There's beer then, or a lemonade, whatever. You're on holiday. Or it's vacation you say, isn't it?'

'That's right.'

I go to the kitchen and grab a Coke. I wouldn't mind a beer buzz but I'm still feeling the time difference and with the baby I know I'm not guaranteed a night's sleep.

Kirsten is cradling Arron in her arms when I come back outside. He is staring up spellbound by his mom's face. It's incredible to think this serene little bundle is the same kid who was screaming until he puked when we first got him into the villa.

'Vince told me you're going to uni in the autumn,' Kirsten says. 'Does that mean you've just had one of those proms?'

'Yeah,' I say neutrally. I don't want to encourage Kirsten down this line. It's not that anything bad happened; just that nothing much happened at all, and that's not going to satisfy someone who's seen too many high school movies. 'I'm going to college at home in Toronto. I'll be studying English and Broadcast Media. I want to go into TV journalism.'

'I'd love to be a TV presenter,' Kirsten says with a smile. 'Like on one of those travel programmes. Never gonna happen, though. Are your mum and dad in that line?'

Here we go, I think. The moment when nobody fails to disappoint, either by being an asshole or by trying too hard to make out they're okay with it.

'Actually, it's my dad and dad.'

Kirsten's glass pauses momentarily on the way to her lips.

'Oh, right,' she says, curiosity in her tone. There's going to be questions. I had best saddle up.

'Rob is a set designer, mostly for theatre but some TV, and Sadiq works in IT for a bank in Toronto.'

From the look on Kirsten's face, I can tell what she's thinking. People usually tread lightly here, but Kirsten seems less tactful about these things so I'm ready for it.

'Sadiq? So I take it Rob is, like, your natural father.'

I suppress a sigh. Why does this shit matter? I know people would say they don't mean anything by it, but if it doesn't mean anything, why do they need to point it out?

'Yeah. But they've been together since before I was born. I'm Amanda Coolidge, which is Rob's surname, but they're both my dads – it's not like Rob's my real father and Sadiq is just his husband.'

'And what about your mum, you know, your birth mother.'

Wow. Most people take the time to lube up a bit before going in hard and deep on this one. I actually have to stop myself laughing at Kirsten's directness.

'I mean, are you still in touch with her?'

'We're kind of in touch. I mean, I've met her a couple times, but

73

she's from California. She lives in Santa Barbara. She's kind of a hippy but she's pretty cool.'

'But is it weird, you know . . . ?'

Kirsten lets it hang. Even she doesn't want to put a name to quite everything, it seems.

What? That she didn't want anything to do with me, so she gave me up to be raised by gays, no less?

'It's not like I was left missing something I never had. I've got my parents. My dads are my parents.'

Why do people find that so difficult to understand?

'So was it a surrogacy thing?'

'Kind of. She'd known them a long time. She was doing them a big favour. I'm sure money changed hands, as she's a total mess about that stuff. Never had a proper career, that kind of scene. I mean, she's a character and all, but I know who I'd rather have been raised by.'

'No, I get you, totally. My mum was a fucking nightmare. She couldn't be bothered with me most of the time. The only thing worth a damn that I got from her was a lesson in how not to raise my own kids.'

'You say "was". Is she . . . ?'

'Dead? Oh, no. But I don't have nothing to do with her, and I'm not letting her near Arron either. My sister still sees her but I just cut her loose. I'm like: fuck her, she's not worth it.'

There is a steeliness to Kirsten's expression. Not what you'd call grim determination, more like a calm but unshakable resolve.

It strikes me that there's more to Kirsten than I had assumed. There's no side to her either. I find that refreshing. She comes right out with what she's thinking, no worrying about how she's coming across, no bullshit and no posturing.

I reckon it's small wonder her husband is laying low if he's gone behind her back on something, but equally I can't help questioning why he would dare to deceive her in the first place. He talked about toasting whatever this deal is with Champagne. I guess the pay-off would need to be very high if Kirsten's wrath is part of the ante.

74

2002

Rory

Svetlana came out of the en suite, a towel wrapped around her and a cloud of steam following her from the door. The image composited two of the things he desired most right then, though there was only one Rory could do something about. He leaned over to the bedside table and lifted the stubby remains of the jay he had nipped last night.

'Open a window, would you?' Rory said. 'My mum and dad will be up and about, and I don't want to be dealing with any shit from them if they smell this.'

'They're in the other villa,' Svetlana said, ignoring his request and rubbing her wet hair with a smaller towel. 'And we are at the back of the house.'

'You'd be amazed at their detection range when it comes to something they can criticise you for. They could sniff it out at any distance.'

'So would not it be pointless to open the window?' she countered. God, he loved that accent. 'And would not it be wiser to keep the smoke in here? Anyway, is it not a little early to be smoking that stuff?'

'There's no way I'm getting through another day with my extended family without something to take the edge off.'

The obvious rejoinder would be 'so why did we come on holiday with them' but they both know Svetlana couldn't ask that. She knew why they came here, and it was about her needs more than his.

On reflection, he decided not to light up right now. He might need the edge. He put the jay back down and propped himself against the pillows.

Svetlana let the bigger towel drop and reached into the suitcase for fresh underwear. The mere sight of her caused him to immediately get hard.

She glanced over and noticed that he was tenting the single cotton bedsheet. Rolled her eyes. There was humour in it but also an acknowledgement of a mutual frustration. They were sharing with Marion and Ken and their kids, and it was always so quiet outside: no traffic, just the wind whipping along the coast from Sagres and the constant crash of the waves on the rocks only yards away. Indoors, every human noise seemed to carry through this place: adult conversations and children's shrieking, so he and Svetlana knew they couldn't make any noise. Also, there were no locks on the bedroom doors. Anyone could just walk in, and Hughie and Lia wouldn't think there was ever any reason not to barge in on their uncle Rory. It's not like Marion would have told them not to, and even if she did, they knew that the word 'no' never really meant much coming out of Marion's mouth when it was directed at them.

They would have to choose their moments, otherwise he was going to end up with a worse case of blue balls than a Catholic priest at Disneyland. It was going to feel all the more acute with Svet wandering around in bathing costumes the whole time.

He decided to service the only need he could right now: coffee.

Rory walked along the hall towards the big open-plan living room and dining area that dominated this end of the villa, the tiled floor cool under his bare feet. He loved the feel of that, like he loved the feel of the grass under them too. He wouldn't need to put on a pair of socks again until he was dressing for the flight home.

He gazed ahead through the wall of glass formed by the four sliding doors onto the patio. He could see Marion and Ken sat out there, reading. Across the grass he could see Mum and Dad too, outside the other villa. Mum was sitting cross-legged on a lounger with Niamh perched on the other end, playing with a ball. Dad was at the table, head in a book. Should have been his passport photo.

He felt a twinge of anxiety at the sight, knowing what lay ahead. He had felt Svetlana's eyes on him yesterday, as though urging him to make an overture. She didn't understand. He needed to warm things up gradually over a few days, establish some family rapport and goodwill before plunging on with the hidden agenda. In this family, it was always about playing the part and doing the dance, a complex process of ritual, obligation and strategy. Maybe they did things more directly in the Ukraine. Certainly, Svetlana had been dealing with people who did things very directly. That was the problem.

Rory felt his right foot slide involuntarily beneath him, causing him to almost lose his balance and yanking his attention back to his immediate environment. He had slipped on something, a smooth object skidding between his heel and the tiles. He looked down. It was a CD. There were CDs everywhere, scattered all across the floor, while over on the sideboard against the wall he could see the empty cylinder in which he had brought them here. The cylinder itself had once housed a fifty-pack of CD-roms bought by his flatmate Danny. He had been about to chuck it out when Rory claimed it to transport a music selection for the holiday, aware there was a half-decent CD player in the second villa.

When he first came here as a teen, he used to make mix tapes and listen to them on a Walkman out by the pool. He spent ages selecting the tracks for two C90s, cuing up the tape and recording with care. Now he could bring fifty albums, though he missed the ritual. Danny burned CD compilations all the time, boasting how it took minutes, but his music was all that moronic Ibiza trance shit. Danny always ripped his CDs as soon as he bought them, meaning he always had a digital selection at his disposal, while Rory could never be arsed.

He could hear his dad scoff at his laziness, telling him how a small investment of his time at one end would have paid dividends in the long run.

He heard a clatter and looked up. Hughie had come scampering in from the patio and looked mildly concerned to find Rory standing there. Hughie glanced to his left, Rory following his gaze. He saw that the kid had his Ninja Turtles lined up on the couch and figured he had been using the CDs as frisbees, or maybe more like shurikens.

Rory picked up the CD he had stood on. His weight and the friction of the slide had put a crack in it, rendering it useless. It was an advance sampler of *Untouchables*: the new Korn album. Had to be a good one that got ruined. Still, at least it hadn't cost him anything. That was the upside to working in a record shop. Among the downsides were the money, the customers and the parental disappointment, but this last was a constant anyway: like microwave background radiation, it felt like it had been there since the beginning of time.

Rory was wondering whether it was worth saying anything to Hughie when Marion walked in, empty coffee cups in her hand, blithely slaloming the discs as she headed for the kitchen. Rory was aghast. It was like this shit was invisible. He guessed that if she acknowledged it, she had to do something about it, so pretending not to see was a lot less trouble. Yeah, that was Marion.

Rory let out a loud sigh and broke the CD with a crack, so that Marion would notice as he dropped it quite demonstrably into the kitchen bin. He wanted to force her to confront that there was damage, not just mess. He knew he was a striker going down in the box after minimum contact, making the most of it because otherwise the infringement would go unacknowledged. He felt a bit of a dick for doing it, but equally, another part of him remembered his younger self being scolded for apparently not valuing things. 'Easy come, easy go,' his dad would say witheringly, if he lost a football or left his bike outside in the rain. He got guilt-tripped if he put a scratch on a new toy, or didn't put it back in its box perfectly. Yet it seemed his nephew was allowed to wantonly wreck stuff with impunity.

'What happened to that?' Marion asked.

'I stood on it.'

She seemed blithely content with this explanation, so he had to be clearer.

'I forgot to check the floor for Korn albums.'

Marion looked around, as though the mess had just suddenly materialised.

'Oh, I'm sorry. Let me help you clear them up.'

This wasn't what he was asking. Marion acted like her children's personal slave sometimes. Sometimes.

'It wasn't me who was throwing them around.'

Marion got it now. She sighed, looking pissed off, as much at Rory as at her son.

'Hughie, why did you throw these all over the room?' she asked.

'I was aiming for the turtles.'

Rory suppressed a smile. He had to give him props for that answer.

'These are Uncle Rory's CDs.'

'No, they're throwing stars.'

'These aren't toys,' she told him. 'They're for playing music.'

Hughie's face took on a familiarly stubborn glower.

'They're not. They're throwing stars.'

There was a pause. Marion looked to the floor, perhaps contemplating her initial strategy of picking up the mess herself. Then she looked to Rory, and a shudder ran through her. She emitted a grunt of frustration, but it was the prelude to a more toxic emission.

'Oh well, I suppose they are throwing stars,' she said to Hughie, her tone dripping sarcasm. 'You would know better than Rory what they are, wouldn't you? I mean, Rory works in a record shop and they belong to him, but I'm sure you must be correct and Rory must be wrong, wouldn't you say, Hughie?'

The kid just stood and fumed, but he looked as confused as he did angry.

'I only wish you were correct a bit more often when you're at school. Then maybe I wouldn't have felt so embarrassed looking at your jotters on parents' night. Perhaps if you played a game that involved *counting* Rory's CDs, you might get a few more of your sums right in future.'

Rory now wished he'd kept his mouth shut and just cleared up the CDs himself. He had been pissed off and consequently forgot what was most likely to happen. Rory had heard it said that everybody knows best how to raise someone else's children, but he was nonetheless damn sure his sister was particularly crap at it. Marion had two disciplinary strategies. One was to act like nothing was wrong, then when pushed, the other was this. It was equally useless, but at least with the first way there wasn't an accompanying air of poison.

She didn't get it from the wind, either. Monkey see, monkey do.

Even more than Rory, Marion had been constantly subject to criticism and sarcasm; principally from Mum, as Dad was seldom paying attention. As the oldest child she was given the most responsibility, which left her open to being sniped at when she mishandled it. Rory didn't know if it was nature or nurture: if she was born ill-equipped to deal with the mantle or if her confidence was shot from the drip, drip of scolding and disappointment.

'So are you going to help?' Marion asked. 'Or would you rather we were just scrabbling around on our hands and knees, doing it all for you?'

Hughie didn't answer. He was still confused, although there had to be a big part of him thinking: 'Well, yeah. Result.'

Hughie picked up one of his turtles, made it fight with another one, acting like he was already immersed in playing another game.

Marion gave Rory a look as if to say: What can you do?

Yeah, that was Marion all over the back. Inexhaustible in her will to surrender.

I've tried something reliably counterproductive and I'm out of ideas.

Rory was thinking about that joint he didn't light. He had a connect in Albufeira. He just hoped the guy could supply enough to get him through this fortnight.

Marion bent down and began picking up CDs. Rory crouched alongside her, feeling guilty about the whole mess. It was a perfect Temple family moment. He examined each one as he placed them on the spindle. Mostly they looked okay. Minor scratches that might have been there anyway. Between the two of them they cleared up about forty while Hughie busied himself with the equally pressing task of engaging Raphael and Donatello in a square go.

Svetlana wandered past and into the kitchen, which gave on to the living area via a wide hatch that served as a breakfast bar. She fixed herself a bowl of cereal and poured a glass of orange juice. Rory was pleased she skipped coffee: it looked like there was only enough for one cup in the glass jar beneath the filter machine.

Marion stood up again, but the war wasn't over. She had summoned the energy for one more defeat.

'Come on, Hughie. Why don't you show Uncle Rory you're sorry for throwing his CDs by helping him finish clearing up?'

Except the kid wasn't sorry, and nor should he be. His Uncle Rory had been a dick.

'Just leave it,' Rory said quietly.

'No.'

Because now this was about something between Marion and Rory rather than Marion and Hughie. A wise move: she had chosen an easier opponent.

Hughie was still acting like they weren't there, playing with the turtles. Raphael was his favourite, of course: the hyper-aggressive one with a short fuse.

Svetlana put her juice and her cereal on the table and sat down, offering Hughie a smile as she did so. Early indicator the kid might be gay: it was the only way a male could fail to respond positively to that face.

'So you don't care about Uncle Rory?' Marion persisted. 'You don't care if his music gets lost and broken? Come on: there's only one CD left. Put it back on the stack and put the stack back where you found it.'

They were down to the symbolic token gesture and yet the kid looked more determined to resist than he did at the prospect of clearing up the whole mess. The task had changed but the stakes hadn't.

'I mean it, Hughie. You threw all of them around and I'm only asking you to put back the last one.'

'Come on, Shugster,' Rory said, invoking the name that could sometimes make Hughie feel like he and his uncle were best mates.

To Rory's surprise and relief, this melted his resolve. Hughie picked up the last CD that was sitting on the couch in front of a prostrate Michelangelo. He carried it over to the table, where he placed it carefully on top of the others: four dozen-odd CDs once again stacked around the spindle.

'See?' Marion said.

No, Rory thought. Don't crow. Don't rub it in. But Marion couldn't help herself. She had learned from the best.

81

'Not that difficult to act like a civilised human being, now is it?'

There was a little spark of ignition behind Hughie's eyes. It travelled down to his hand and he violently slid the cylinder of CDs along the table towards his mum. It caught Svetlana's cereal bowl a glancing blow, tipping the contents onto her lap, while catching her orange juice square. Rory stepped instinctively as the glass shot past him and shattered on the tiles. Reflex proved his enemy, his left foot coming down upon a stray shard.

'Ah, ya fucker, ye.'

There was a moment of stillness as everyone took in what had just happened. Hughie was the first to respond, throwing himself face-down on the couch and bursting into tears.

Rory lifted his foot and turned it over. It was bleeding but the cut was small. He stepped very carefully away from the rest of the debris.

Marion turned to face the sliding doors and called out to her husband, her tone implying like she had called twice already.

'Ken, it's about time you got in here and dealt with your son.'

Rory recognised the eschewing of proper nouns as pure Celia. You always got defined by your role when you were being reminded of your responsibility.

Rory hobbled back towards his bedroom, figuring he had better clean the cut and get a plaster on it before dealing with the wreckage. He was spotting the floor as he walked. Something else to clean up. Jesus. Fucking weans.

If there was an upside to the fact that he and Svetlana would be struggling to get a shag on this holiday, it was that it massively reduced the chances of them accidentally becoming parents.

Rory was always careful about contraception, but if he was ever tempted to take any chances, he only had to think of Marion's two, and now he also had the cautionary tale that was his little sister. A disastrous combo of inexperience, curiosity and experimentation with family-friend boy-next-door Calum had seen her up the jaggy at sixteen. Of course, Sylvie had not even been able to take the sensible, rational course of action of getting rid of the thing soon as, while it was a microscopic bundle of rapidly dividing cells. Not in the house of devout Catholic Saint Celia.

Rory's mother was, as they said in the west of Scotland, Tim to the Brim. She had raised her kids accordingly, though it hadn't stuck with any of them once they grew up. Celia by contrast seemed to have become more hardcore the older she got. Was she making reparation for a wild youth? he sometimes wondered. He didn't see how she could have espoused such piety while being a sex symbol back in the early seventies. That said, he was wary of ascribing her values on the basis of the character she played. Just because she ran around in skimpy outfits on TV didn't mean she wasn't prudish.

Either way, it hadn't been a fun feature of his schooldays to hear his classmates tell him how they'd 'seen your mum's tits and bush in that vampire movie'.

Give Celia her due though: she had been open and upfront about her daughter becoming what the tabloids called a 'gym-slip mum' (a term simultaneously leery and judgemental, which was the tabloid mentality in microcosm. And what the fuck even *was* a gym-slip?) Having written all those articles about raising a family, promoting her 'traditional common-sense values', it might have seemed embarrassing, but Celia had incorporated the whole story into her columns. How they had dealt with the shock and how they were welcoming the child into their family. How it had brought them all closer together.

Unusually for Mum's family myth-making, this was even true. It had certainly rendered Celia fairly indispensable to Sylvie at a time when she might otherwise have been making her mother redundant by going off to university. Sylvie still had plans to do that, theoretically at least. From what Rory could surmise, the goalposts kept moving: she could go after the baby reached this stage, reached that stage. Nursery was the latest.

Rory was aware of Marion following him down the hall. He figured it was ostensibly to apologise but mainly to get clear while she left Ken to deal with Hughie. Or rather, left Ken to be familiarly ineffectual so that she could later hit him with a whole load of sarcasm about how feeble his actions had been. And Ken would soak up the abuse like a sponge, no hint of defence or retaliation. He was the last person in the world Rory would offer weed. Ken was already so unflappably laid-back, he feared that if the guy ever had a few tokes he might stop breathing altogether.

Rory was approaching his bedroom when Lia beat him to it, giggling as she appeared from across the passage and hurtled through the door ahead of him.

'Lia, dear, stay out of there,' Marion told her. 'You mustn't go into Uncle Rory's room right now.'

'Never mind,' Rory said, aware Lia wouldn't listen anyway. 'She's barefoot. It's best she's in there until we clear up the broken glass.'

'Good point. Lia, stay away from the living room, honey.'

Following the sixth-sense instinct that drew children below a certain age to the source of greatest danger in any given room, Lia went straight to the bedside table on top of which he had dumped a load of his stuff. She immediately picked up a tiny clear polythene bag full of pills.

Rory bit back the pain as he sped up his pace, hoping to grab it from her before Marion saw. He didn't make it.

'What are these pills for?' Lia asked. 'Are you unwell, Uncle Rory?'

Marion was right beside him, eyeing the bag. From his own reaction they both knew he couldn't pretend it was ibuprofen or paracetamol. He wasn't going to be able to pass off the twist of powder next to his tobacco tin as Alka-Seltzer either.

'I was, but I'm feeling better now,' he told Lia.

Her interest waned and she headed for the en suite, drawn by Svetlana's vast assortment of hair and bath products.

'Jesus Christ, Rory,' Marion said, quiet but forceful. 'Not only have you brought this stuff here, but you've just left it lying around where any of the kids could pick it up?'

'It's my room. They're not supposed to be in here.' He knew how lame this sounded.

'These things look just like sweeties to children. If you hadn't hurt your foot and come back here, Lia might have been eating these right now.'

'Guess it's a good thing Hughie broke that glass then. Otherwise his sister might have been totally loved up and rooting through my CDs for a Happy Mondays album.'

'Don't joke about this,' Marion warned. She had unexpectedly found herself on the moral high ground and she was going to make the most of it.

'Oh, for fuck's sake. Lia knows they're pills, you heard her yourself, so she wouldn't have eaten them. Mum couldn't get me to swallow half a junior Disprin when I was a kid.'

Marion glanced contemptuously from the bag in his hand to the items scattered atop the bedside table.

'Yes, I remember. But you've certainly made up for it since.'

2018

Amanda

I'm sitting on my bed, scrolling my laptop when I hear a babble of voices and the slam of a car door. Kirsten has opted for an early night, declaring herself beat shortly after we finished our takeout pizzas, which I had driven out to collect as soon as Arron was confirmed asleep. It has been a long day, and I'm learning fast that it's wise to grab some Zs while the kid is down. However, I've barely had a chance to get online in days, and the time difference means I'm not feeling sleepy.

I go to the window and look towards the other villas, not getting too close to the glass as I don't want to be caught looking. It is unlikely they'd notice me staring from across the pool though: they are too intent upon the latest new arrivals, a man carrying a baby. I wonder if the mom is one of the women already here.

I watch the exchange of hugs and kisses. It's more than just long-time-no-see: there is genuine emotion out there, tears and mutual comfort. I remember that for these people this is not so much a vacation as a wake. To my surprise, it seems the ice maiden from the pool is part of the group, as she was dining with them on the patio, and she appears to be staying in the same villa as Celia. She must be a friend of someone in the family rather than a relative though, as she has remained seated and is not partaking in the current round of touchy-feeliness.

I'm kind of freaked by the notion that this is Max Temple's family right here. The man was a legend, but so much so that I had never thought of him as a flesh-and-blood person, just an iconic figure and a body of work. He seemed to have been more of a public figure in the UK than in Canada, where I only knew him through the internet.

He wasn't someone I ever fantasised about meeting, but now I have this weird feeling, arising from the awareness that I *would* have met him – probably fangirling embarrassingly in front of him right now – if he hadn't just died. It is like a glimpse into a parallel reality, what I might otherwise be doing at this moment in a different timeline.

His was a name I saw cited on a daily basis. He was a respected psychology professor for much of his academic career, but since the early 2000s had become a high-profile debunker of conspiracy theories.

He was best known for giving his name to Temple's Law, which was not his own coinage but a quote of his that became an early viral meme. It stated that: 'A conspiracy theory collapses at the point where it requires greater complexity than the official explanation.'

I hadn't merely seen a few Temple quotes on Twitter, however: I read his work extensively, quoting from it in high school essays and more latterly in my videos. It was an invaluable weapon to have in my intellectual armoury because conspiracy arguments were everywhere these days and it wasn't enough to merely counter the fallacies.

From climate change deniers to 9/11 truthers to anti-vaxxers, when the facts were against them, a conspiracy theory was like turning on godmode. It couldn't be defeated, and in fact took any evidence you threw at it and transformed it into proof of the opposite. For instance, it should have been the end of the line for the Birthers when the state of Hawaii produced Obama's long-form birth certificate, but instead they claimed the document was a forgery and took it as further proof of how far the conspiracy went.

'When they win, they win,' Temple said. 'And when they lose, they win too.'

Temple's work didn't merely debunk conspiracy theories but explored what he called 'the intellectual short-circuitry of the human condition that leads to such theories taking hold and persisting'. That was why I was admiring of him, not to mention grateful. Without such a meta reading of the whole thing, you could go crazy with exasperation.

With his words so familiar, it feels oddly frustrating to now have this pseudo connection to the man only after his death. I watch Temple's bereaved relatives congregate around the patio, people to whom he was something else altogether. Inevitably, my curiosity leads me back to my laptop. I can hear Sadiq talk about it being creepy to search the internet for personal info on people you don't really know. Must be a generational thing. To me and my friends, it's second nature.

There's a ton of obits, tributes and retrospectives at the top of the search page, but even from the previews next to each URL, it is apparent that to a section of the British media, Temple was primarily of interest for another reason. Merely from the briefest glance, my eyes alight on repeated instances of the word 'tragedy', combined variously with 'family', 'holiday' and 'granddaughter'.

Something tightens in my chest as I open one of them, as though I am clicking on a live story and afraid of what will be revealed. It's from the day after his death, headlined 'Tot tragedy prof dies'.

May the British tabloids write all my enemies' obits.

I scan hurriedly, learning that 'Temple's eighteen-month-old granddaughter Niamh drowned at the family's holiday villa on the Algarve'.

Jesus. That's right here.

Automatically I look to the window again, where the underwater lights of the pool are aglow yards from the group gathered on the patio. How could they ever go in there again, or even set eyes on the thing without seeing *that*? But then I read another article which states that the kid fell into the sea, having slipped through a clifftop barrier.

I search again, this time for stories about the tragedy itself. I sort by date, wanting to see contemporary coverage rather than retrospective. There are some really old links to early newspaper online editions and the BBC website, where the first mention appears. The headline is 'British toddler feared drowned in holiday accident'. That was before the kid's death was confirmed and before the identity of the family was discovered. It became a bigger story after that.

The next article refers to 'Niamh's devastated parents Sylvie

Temple (18) and Calum Donnelly (19)'. I cross-refer to another piece to confirm. Niamh was eighteen months, so Sylvie would have been only sixteen when she had her. I think about how hard it's been just helping out with someone else's baby. I can't imagine what it would feel like to know that responsibility is for keeps.

Interest had built in the ensuing days, and soon enough I'm looking at art: intrusive long-lens paparazzi shots of the family walking through an airport. Because Temple had been on TV, his family were fair game to the British tabloids, who were apparently just as horrific as I've heard. These assholes were no doubt telling themselves what they were doing was journalism, when really it was just gatecrashing someone else's grief (though I can hear my dads' voices asking what I am doing right now).

I look at a picture of Max Temple pulling a suitcase, staring ahead with a dark expression. I had only seen headshots and TV interviews, talking-head stuff with him sitting down. I didn't realise he was so tall. Suave too, but unmistakably academic, like he could have been a professor at Hogwarts. I click to enlarge images of a glamorous woman I recognise as Celia, and what is obviously a younger version of Marion.

Then I find a picture featuring a chubby girl who sticks out from her skinny parents walking alongside her. She doesn't look like she could be eighteen – she would get carded everywhere – and yet the caption identifies her as Sylvie Temple. In the shot, all the others have their heads down, fixed on getting through the gauntlet of press and photographers. Sylvie is staring right into the lens, her expression challenging, almost defiant. That is when I realise who I'm looking at: this is the skinny ice maiden.

I instantly feel bad about thinking of her that way. If you lost your kid like that, damn right you would be cold and shut off. Part of you would never recover. And you definitely wouldn't want to make chit-chat with some other teenage girl who's got a baby in her arms.

I often get ragged on by my friends for being judgy. Judge Coolidge, they call me. I figure maybe they got a point.

The press interest largely peters out after a few days, though there is a strain within the media and beyond that seems determined not only to milk the tragedy, but to look for a deeper story beneath it. That is where something familiarly unsavoury begins to fester. Temple was known as the hammer of the charlatans, a *bête noir* of conspiracy theorists, so there seems a perverse inevitability that his personal tragedy should be mined for conspiracy theories of its own.

What had given the conspiracists an in was that the kid's body was never recovered. They seldom need much, and that allowed them to speculate that Niamh being supposedly lost to the sea was so that her body could never be examined, and the 'true' cause of her death never revealed.

I scroll down a list of blogposts and tabloid articles. I feel kinda guilty about looking, what with the subjects of this squalid speculation and innuendo sitting only yards away, but I can't help myself. I'm compelled to find out more, though I know that this unhealthy curiosity is what the conspiracy peddlers thrive upon.

Some theories focus upon the parents' youth: two under-pressure teens who might not have been coping: one of them lost their shit and shook the baby, then the manner of Niamh's death had to be covered up. Others speculate about abuse or neglect, with the same end result: the body had to be disappeared and the drowning story fabricated to conceal the truth.

There has been a resurgence in discussion of the subject following Temple's death, people reheating their bullshit from all those years ago. I can't help but get the sense that some of these assholes are avenging themselves retrospectively upon an opponent they could never defeat. It's not the biggest spike, however. That appears to have come five years after Niamh's death, with the abduction of a little girl named Madeleine McCann from a holiday apartment not a half hour's drive from here. I didn't know anything about that. I don't think it was a big story at home in Canada, though I can't be sure, as in 2007 I was too young to be paying attention to the news. Clearly it was a huge deal in the UK, and a section of the media there has never let it go.

That must have been just awful for the Temples, reviving so many painful memories and being doorstepped by reporters all over again.

90

If I get talking to them, I'd probably best not mention that I want to be journalist.

The conspiracists' perverse logic even incorporated Max Temple's scepticism into the narrative. He had given over his own grand-daughter to a child abuse ring and he was committed to discrediting conspiracy theories because he was part of a conspiracy himself. Presumably one involving covering up the existence of time travel, as he had come into the public eye on this subject several months before the death of his granddaughter. They were drawing lines from Niamh through Madeleine McCann, right up to Hillary Clinton and Pizzagate. It was so offensive and cowardly. For years they had been sniping ineffectively from the shadows, and now they were kicking his corpse.

I find myself gazing at the same image again and again on page after page: the one of Sylvie staring back at the camera, as though calling out the media for their intrusion. Sylvie is calling me out too for my voyeurism. I feel kinda sleazy.

I recall Temple talking about the buzz we get from thinking we've discovered secret knowledge, something the powers-that-be don't want us to know. It's an illicit thrill, but one you need to keep feeding.

I decide it would therefore double the insult to his memory if I read another page, so I close down the laptop.

For now.

2018

Ivy

Ivy picks up her mobile and tries Jamie again. It was engaged before, only a few moments ago, but she has spotted her mother glancing this way and she wants to send out her own engaged signal. She knows she can't hide behind her laptop all day, but she's happy to see how far procrastination can take her.

She's not sure she's ready for this. She's back at the scene of the crime, wondering why she decided it was a good idea to come here. She didn't go to the funeral, but was caught off-guard by the idea of seeing everybody in Portugal instead. She instinctively felt there was some kind of process to be observed, which required her once again being in the presence of her family. It was a woolly notion, clouded by emotion and sentiment when she made the decision and booked the flights.

Closure, that's what somebody on the outside might say she was looking for, and they'd be wrong. There is no closure for what happened here. She knows that what is truly needed is forgiveness, but forgiveness requires penitence. Guilt has to be admitted. Complicity, deceit, dishonesty, sins of the flesh, sins of omission: in this family, there's plenty of culpability to go around. But some have more to be guilty about than others.

She begins answering an email so non-urgent she would most likely have just deleted it if she was back in London. She's looking for anything that will take her away from the here and now, because all morning she's had this growing fear that she's about to cry, and that if she starts, she'll totally lose it. It's being at the villas that has truly brought it home to her that he's gone.

His presence is all around, memories of him haunting every inch of this place. Maybe this is why Mum was so insistent that they come here as a form of memorial. It forces them to contemplate the reality and permanence of his absence.

Ivy had barely seen him – seen any of them – in years, but throughout it all she always knew he would be there if she chose to pick up the phone or to go and visit. She had been paralysed by conflicting emotions. The same turmoil that made her want to pick up the phone, made her want to go visit, was also what meant she just couldn't face it.

She is haunted not only by her father but by the ghosts of her own emotions: the people she used to be in this place. She first came here when she was still in primary school, and part of her would always be that girl; or at least part of her would always be looking for that girl.

Marion is hunched beneath a sun umbrella, dangling Hugh's baby daughter Emily so that her feet are splashing in an inflatable paddling pool. Hugh's wife Maggie hasn't joined him on the trip. He says it's so she can get a little break from childcare for a few days, which all sounds terribly modern and noble, but Ivy wonders if there's more to it. Hugh is up for some big academic post in America, which will involve uprooting his family, and maybe his missus is not so delighted at the prospect.

Ivy's niece Lia arrived last night, completing the set for the 2002 family reunion. It is awkward being around her and Hugh, because Ivy has seen so little of them since they were children. She could have walked past Lia in the street two days ago and not recognised her. They're more or less strangers to each other and she's not going to pretend she has any intention of staying in touch with them once this sham is over.

Lia has just emerged from her villa, wearing a yellow dress and a frown. She must be twenty-one or twenty-two: Ivy can't remember when her birthday is, so she can't accurately calculate. She has gathered that Lia is studying medicine and has just finished her finals. Far more interestingly, she has also gleaned that Lia recently came out, and is in a long-term relationship with an older woman, a consultant obstetrician named Gillian. Ivy was pleased by this news,

93

but only because it had reportedly made Celia uncomfortable. Probably her biggest disappointment in her granddaughter since she was three years old and insisted on ditching the first syllable of her given name.

Lia makes a beeline for Marion, covering the distance in leggy strides.

'Mum, I need to take the hire car to the big supermarket at Lagos. I've come away without the adapter for my laptop.'

'I'm sure you can borrow someone else's charger,' Marion suggests.

'It's not a charger, it's an AC power adapter.' Her tone is scolding and impatient. 'There's nothing else compatible.'

'I was thinking of going to get some things from the supermarket myself,' Marion says. 'If you wait a wee while, we can go together.'

'I need it *now*,' Lia insists. 'I'll be there and back before you'd even be ready to go.'

Marion shrugs.

'OK. Do you want your dad to drive you?'

'I've had a licence four years, Mum.'

'Yeah but it's the right-hand side.'

Lia makes a scoffing sound and gives a withering eye-roll.

Yeah. *Now* Ivy recognises her. She was a pushy little madam back then too, and it doesn't look like any life experience has much chastened her.

She does seem kind of jumpy about something, though. When they ate last night, she came across as distracted, her mind permanently elsewhere.

Maybe it's the exam results, maybe it's something else.

Marion is on granny duties right now so that Hugh can have a lie-in. Emily kept him up half the night, her bawling echoing around the place, like Ivy didn't have enough triggers for painful memories.

Ivy feels surrounded by fucking babies, in fact. She saw some teenager from the other villa wandering around with one, looking knackered and overwhelmed. It turns out she's a nanny, but the image was enough.

The baby belongs to a bottle-blonde gym bunny she has learned is actually Vince Reid's new wife. When Ivy saw her, she just assumed

94

the place had changed hands. She's less than half Vince's age, and not so much a trophy as a consolation prize. Anybody marrying so inappropriately was clearly hurting for a life he never got but somehow thought he was due. He was a middle-aged man leeching off someone else's youth, but then Vince always did like them young. She remembers standing out there in a bikini when she was about fourteen, feeling self-conscious because he was always staring at her tits.

Vince's ex-wife Laurie had died last year, she heard. She is thinking about her when Jamie finally picks up.

'I thought you were on holiday,' he says. He doesn't sound like he's caught out: more like he's disappointed but not surprised.

'I'm never on holiday, Jamie, you know that. I may leave the country, but that's a matter of location. Have you had any contact from Flint Associates?'

'I haven't heard from them, no. Were you expecting them to get in touch?'

'I ordered a full work-up on Jane Astley. I hoped we'd have something by now.'

'Jane Astley. I see. Well, nothing so far.'

There was a pause after he said the name. He didn't know she had ordered this, and he was taking in the implications. Flint Associates were private investigators. They were doing a 'background profile' on Jane Astley, which was the industry euphemism for digging up as much dirt as they could possibly find. It didn't mean Ivy had set the dogs on her, but that part was what usually happened next.

'Keep your eyes peeled. If anything comes in, I don't want anybody else seeing it. I don't want anybody else even knowing I ordered it, do you understand?'

'Yes, ma'am.'

His tone is unequivocal now. He is still hoping she is hedging her bets, and as long as nobody higher up finds out that she's already set the wheels in motion, there remains the option to stop them.

'I'm still formulating a strategy on this. I need to know it's viable before we can go to the client and recommend this course of action.'

'Of course.'

Everything about this is on a knife edge. The client is one of the biggest the firm has: the retail conglomerate DKG. The corporation's logistics arm suffered a fire at one of its distribution warehouses in which two workers died. Both of the victims were young women on minimum wage, zero-hours contracts: photofit martyrs for anyone wanting to depict DKG as corporate villains. Ordinarily it would have been easy enough to put out a statement about respectfully waiting for all the facts to be established, while decrying those wishing to make political capital out of a tragedy. Unfortunately, a former employee had come forward, claiming to have warned the company several years ago about potential hazards and inadequate safety practices at the very same distribution centre. The whistle blower, Jane Astley, claimed to have been ignored, and in fact forced out for being a troublemaker.

'And what is your vision for the strategy?' Jamie asks.

'We have to change the narrative. Make it about trade union intransigence and unworkable health and safety culture. Move the debate. We get some friendly columnists to talk about how this has created a cry wolf problem – too many rules, people not knowing which ones are important or applicable. Half of them make no sense or get in the way, so that when somebody points out a genuine hazard, it can get lost in the noise.'

But that's not really what he is asking. He wants to know how Jane Astley fits into Ivy's strategy, because he is afraid of the answer. As he should be.

Sir Jock Davidson knows that there are two paths the Cairncross Partnership can present to DKG. One is to recommend they go for complete transparency. Bring in external independent investigators, welcome their findings, admit to any failings, and accept the consequent opprobrium, fines and punishment. Demonstrate that change is under way and that a different culture is being engendered within the company.

The other path is the one Ivy is working on.

These days, the role of corporate PR consultant is sometimes compared to that of priest and counsellor: explaining codes of conduct and advising on best behaviour. It sounds very worthy, but in practice it means that the clients want you to make moral decisions for them: or rather, make immoral decisions for them so that they can absolve themselves of responsibility. They want their counsellor to show them they can get away with this.

That's why Sir Jock and the board are pretending to be conflicted, when what they really want is for Ivy to take this on. That way they can lie to themselves about their own morality, about what they truly wanted. But just as importantly, they can show future clients what she is capable of, boast that they have someone so ruthless as an asset.

And Ivy is happy with all of the above.

The world of spin and manipulation is appealing when there is something about your own past that you can't bear to contemplate. It gives a sense of control and reassurance that you can conceal the darkest of truths and people are only too willing to go along with the lie if it serves them too. In the aftermath of every tragedy, every crime, there is an opportunity to sell a version that everybody wants to believe, a version they *need* to believe. She learned that a long time ago, right here.

Rory emerges from the villa, a *pain au chocolat* in his hand: breakfast on the go. Another sight to take her back: her brother staggering out looking bleary-eyed, several hours after everybody else has got up, though on this occasion it's down to the time difference, as he just flew here from San Francisco. It conjures another ghost of her emotions: how much she adored her big brother once. Mum and Dad were always on his case, acting like he was letting them down in small ways and in very big ones, but she found his shambolic nature comforting.

Their criticism of Rory was like water off a duck's back, she always thought, wrongly. It gives an ache to see him: a mixture of warmth and regret. She gets the feeling it's mutual. They've missed each other, but they both know why their lives have been spent apart. When she looks in his eyes she wonders how much he knows, and she suspects he's always asking himself the same question of her.

He wanders over and sits himself on the lounger next to her. She doesn't mind, except that Mum takes it as the cue she's been waiting for to come and join too.

'I hear you've got a new woman,' Ivy says. 'Didn't bring her though.'

'She's not that new. Kiko and I have been together almost four years now. She's got a lot on at work right now. Thought it was simplest if I just came out here myself.'

'What does she do?'

'She works for a tech start-up. They developed a tracker app for monitoring urban traffic patterns. It's a big thing in city management. All way over my head.'

'So, a woman with an actual job, even a career?'

He smiles at her, squinting against the sun, taking his licks. He knows Kiko represents quite a catch following the series of flakes, nightmares and freak-shows he has shacked up with down the years. A keeper, which is presumably why Rory decided he wasn't going to subject her to the Temple family shitshow, in case she bolted when she belatedly discovered his true provenance.

'I'm punching above my weight, no question.'

He seems happy as he talks about Kiko, albeit happy in that Rory way, which seems simultaneously sad.

'And what are you doing with yourself these days?' Ivy asks.

'He's working in a rehab centre,' Mum replies, insinuating herself into the conversation.

It's another moment to take her back. She recalls how Mum would often butt in when somebody asked Rory that same question. *He's working in a record shop. He's working in a pub.* There was something unmistakably passive-aggressive about it, judgement in her tone and in how she arrogated the right to answer for him. *You can answer for yourself when you've got something worth answering with,* was the subtext.

'It's an outreach programme downtown. We've got a massive homeless population, most of them with mental health issues, dependency problems.'

There was years' worth of complexity in that answer. Mum already knew what Rory was doing but he was answering as much for her benefit as Ivy's. *No, Mother, still no soaring career for the Temple scion, but I'm doing important work.* Important to him in particular. It sounds to Ivy like he's found a way to serve his penance.

'But never mind that, sis,' Rory says. 'You changed the subject before I could ask what about your love life.'

He's trolling. Like she's going to give him anything while Mum's sitting here.

'At best it's only ever a sex life,' she says, hoping to savour her mother's discomfort. 'But I've been working in PR too long to make the mistake of disclosing any details that can be used against me.'

'Fair enough,' Rory replies, acknowledging that she has headed him off.

She hasn't headed herself off though. The question has made her think about L, again.

Every time her phone chimes, she is hoping it's a message from him, even if it's just to say fuck you.

She doesn't want to admit that she's missing him. That she knew she would.

'I'm for a dip,' Rory announces, getting to his feet.

He ambles over to the pool, diving in without breaking stride, leaving Ivy alone with Mum.

'And how are things at work with you?' she asks, a pointless non-question. This is how it's done: a tentative dance around some inconsequential matters, like a parlay in no-man's land before hostilities inevitably commence.

'Busy.'

Portugal was always the place where things came out, tensions that had boiled up, or issues nobody had been prepared to broach at home. Being at the villas made it easier to be open, away from everyday surroundings. She wasn't sure why; maybe the lack of domestic chores and mundane routines provided a platform, an uncluttered stage. But it wasn't the case that what was said at the villas stayed at the villas. Things said here could not be unsaid. Just as things done here could not be undone.

It was here by this pool that she had told her mother she was pregnant. It just felt safer: as though she could talk about her life in abstract on holiday, her circumstances in temporary suspension. There was never any escaping what lay at the end of the return flight, though.

'Busy,' Mum echoes. 'Yes, I assumed you must have been.'

This is Celia's way of bringing up the fact that Ivy didn't come to the funeral, because she's not going to say that directly; not yet.

'It's strange there's this whole world of yours that we know nothing about,' she says.

'It's the nature of the area of PR I'm in, that it's not just confidential, we sometimes can't even say who our clients are. If people recognise our hand, we've failed.'

She pulls this off quite naturally, pretending that it was specifically the world of her work Mum was talking about. Celia isn't going to go along with it, though.

'I just mean that you live this separate life, and we miss you. Sorry, I said *we*, I keep saying *we*. I'm so used to talking on behalf of your father and me.'

'Hard to break the habit of a lifetime,' is Ivy's pointless non-answer.

'It feels weird to think there must be all these people who see you every day, who must know you better than I do these days, and who have only ever known you as Ivy. It's like you are who you are to us right now, but you'll become someone else again when you go home. Do you actually have a passport in that name?'

She maintains a calm expression, though this query boils her piss. They've been over this so many times, but when Mum doesn't like something, she refuses to accept it. She just pretends that it's news to her or keeps asking the same question in the expectation that the next time she'll get the answer she wants.

'Yes. I've told you this before. I had my name changed legally. I didn't want my whole life being defined by what happened to Niamh.'

Mum wears a wistful expression, a familiar look of reverie and regret.

'Those damned newspapers were so mercilessly intrusive,' Mum says. 'Especially after the Madeleine McCann thing.'

That wasn't why she changed her name, but Ivy doesn't correct her. Besides, it is quickly becoming clear that the wistful expression was not precipitated by a solemn contemplation of what had befallen her daughter. Mum has started talking about how the ramifications affected her. That's the thing to remember with Celia: it's *always* about her. And if it's not, she'll find a way to make it about her.

'That was what did for my career as a columnist. It's not as though I could have changed my name, because so much rested upon what the readers knew about me from reading about my family life down the years. I was defined by one thing, like you say. I became what they would now call a tainted brand, even though it was through no fault of my own. For the sake of my dignity, I had no choice but to fade quietly from the limelight.'

Ivy has the discipline not to scoff. Fading quietly is an idiosyncratic interpretation. She remembers the tantrums, the threats to sue, the how-dare-theys, and the blame, of course: the beloved, beautiful blame.

Mum is quiet for a few moments, watching Rory swim back and forth. She glances towards the paddling pool, where Marion is still entertaining little Emily. To the untrained observer, it might look like a great-grandmother surveying the generations of her family. Ivy recognises instead that she is making sure nobody is in earshot. The dancing's done.

'You didn't come to your father's funeral.'

It's a statement rather than a question, but that doesn't stop it from being an accusation, a challenge. Ivy is ready for it, though, and she's got a killer answer.

'Which funeral?'

Mum tries to act like she's confused by the question, but there is a moment of alarm in her face that she is not fast enough to conceal. She may have been an actress, but she's not always good without a script.

'Which . . . ? I don't . . .'

'Somebody ratted you out. I got an email telling me the details.'

Celia had gone against her atheist late husband's wishes and organised a secret Catholic funeral service over his remains. Ivy

101

suspects her name was added to the email chain by mistake, but she knows it will mess with Mum's head far more if she thinks she's been betrayed. It must be killing her that she can't even ask by whom, as that would be an admission she knows what her daughter is talking about.

'Don't worry, the others don't know,' Ivy says. 'It would only cause them hurt if they were to find out. So best that the truth of it stays hidden, huh?'

Their eyes lock briefly. It's the second time in a few moments that Celia has failed at pretending she doesn't know what Ivy is really talking about.

'I meant the memorial service,' Mum says. 'Yours was a conspicuous absence.'

'As it would have been a conspicuous presence. You know why I didn't come. I've gone to great lengths to protect my privacy. I didn't want to leave a trail of breadcrumbs.'

She dearly wants to tell Mum the real reason she didn't come to the memorial. She wants to scream the reason, but they've been here before, so what purpose would it serve? Dad's death hasn't changed what lies between the two of them.

'And that was the only thing you cared about?'

'What else should I have cared about?'

'For one thing, what you people in the PR world would call the optics. What kind of message does it send that you didn't attend your own father's funeral?'

'The only message I cared about sending was "leave me alone".'

'And that's exactly my point. You are the one who is letting your life be defined by what happened to Niamh. Or rather, by running away from what happened to her: acting like she never existed, like you didn't have the life that came before.'

Ivy silently seethes, too messed up to formulate a response.

'I can still see her sweet little face,' Mum says, gazing meaningfully out to sea, behaving as always like she knows she's framed in shot. She says this as though the shock of it might dislodge something from the depths of Ivy's mind, the implication being that Ivy *can't* still see her face, that she never thinks about her.

And what really stings is that Mum's right. Ivy has spent the past sixteen years trying to forget about the life that came before, trying to pretend Niamh never happened. But that's to protect the part of her that has to live with it. It's one of the reasons she became Ivy and left Sylvie in the past. There is a woman inside Ivy who thinks about Niamh every single day and wishes it had all been different. But there is also a woman inside her who understands her true nature, and that woman wouldn't change a thing.

The conspiracy theory allows us to hold on to our autonomy. It tells us that we can be experts too, we don't have to listen to what we're told, we can find the answers we're looking for only by journeying down the road less travelled.

Max Temple

2018

Amanda

I feel like crap but the sunshine and warmth make me believe I can at least get through the day. I've been up for seven hours already and it's not even lunchtime. Barely a minute has passed without thinking about when I can get back to bed, except that I know tonight could be exactly the same. If I was this tired in the Toronto winter, I would barely be able to function, but the brightness of the colours and the sight of the sea beneath a perfect clear blue sky are tricking me into feeling at least halfway conscious.

I'm trying to read an interview with Lauren Mayberry on my phone, but I've read the same paragraph about four times and the words won't stick in my brain because I'm so tired. I think I'm gonna need a vacation to get over this vacation, which is when it hits me that I've signed up for months of this.

I want to cry, but Arron is threatening to beat me to it. He's starting to get that grizzly way I already recognise: restless and dissatisfied. How can he even be awake? The kid seemed to sleep almost as little as I did last night. I was up to him over and over, the crying starting again every time I thought he was settled, until I was unable to sleep because I was on tenterhooks waiting for it. A couple times I even got out of bed to respond before realising the sound was coming from one of the other villas, where they had one of these merciless little demons too.

I hear Kirsten come back in from the car. I've barely seen her this morning. She went off first thing to the gym at a hotel in Praia Mexilhões, where she has purchased a temporary membership, then after her shower she headed out again to the supermarket.

She walks outside to where I'm seated on the tiled terrace, shaded by an automated canvas awning.

'Rough old night,' Kirsten says, acknowledging that she is at least aware.

'Oh yeah.'

'Welcome to my world.'

Except it appears to be my world instead now, I want to say.

'Is it always that bad?'

'Not always. Half the time it's worse. I wanted to get a professional nanny early doors, but Vince was grumbling about the money, like always. Then he changed his tune and said he would organise something. Should have known he was organising something on the cheap. No offence, I just mean . . .'

'None taken. I understand.'

Kirsten takes out her cell phone and places it down on the table in front of me.

'Speaking of Vince,' she says, pointing to the screen.

There is finally some communication from him, in the form of a text.

Sorry, maddest thing. I got stopped by police at the airport and questioned about a client. It's sub judice, so I can't discuss it. It's been a nightmare. It's not done either, so I'm not clear to leave the country yet. Hoping to get the okay soon. Phone has almost no charge, hence the text. I'll call tomorrow.

'Got that last night,' she says, her thin-lipped expression not giving away how she feels about it, especially behind her sunglasses.

'Well, at least you've got an explanation,' I suggest.

'Bollocks I have. He's lying. He thinks I'm bloody stupid. Saying it's *sub judice*, so he can't give any details. How convenient. "Phone has no charge" my arse.'

'He does say he'll call tomorrow. I mean, that's today, right?'

'We'll see.' She doesn't sound convinced.

Arron is squirming in his bounce seat, the previously half-hearted beginnings of a cry becoming more committed.

'Listen, you were a trouper last night,' Kirsten says. 'You can go back to bed for a bit if you like.'

'I don't think I'd sleep now,' I reply, figuring I would just lie staring at the ceiling in a state of exhausted frustration.

'Maybe after lunch then, an afternoon nap.'

The prospect of this rallies me.

'Why don't I take him a little walk in the harness,' I suggest.

'You sure?'

'Yeah. I'd like to have a look around.'

'OK, but let me get him creamed up and stick a hat on him.'

Arron responds to being lifted, his humour instantly improved by activity. Kirsten dabs the sun cream on him liberally, in a way I interpret as intended to convey her belt-and-braces approach to the issue. Then she helps get him strapped up, his head leaning against my chest.

'Wouldn't he like to face forward, so he can see?'

'It's not good for his spine. The harness doesn't support him right if he faces that way. Plus, you'll find he nods off if his head's snug against a warm body.'

I get what Kirsten means when I start walking. There is something comforting about the warmth of Arron's little form pressed tight like that, despite the wetness of his drooly mouth. The rhythm of my steps causes his head to bob gently, which seems to have a hypnotically calming effect.

I have only one destination in mind. I want a look at what I've heard – and, significantly, read – referred to as the clifftop path. I take the long way around, feeling oddly self-conscious due to the presence of the people by the pool, as though they can read my intentions and my unwholesome curiosity.

The trail is screened from the complex by a hedge, broken at intervals where it abuts paths leading from the two Temple villas. What lies on the other side is hardly a clifftop at this point, though there is a sheer drop of nine or ten feet straight down into water. It continues like that eastwards until it flattens out near the beach at the village. Westwards it just keeps climbing steadily higher along the coast.

The water is calm today, lapping against the rockface in gentle splashes. It's clear and still enough to see fish darting in and out of shadows. It's also clear and still enough to see the jagged ridges of stone that lie beneath the surface. Nobody would be having fun jumping off of here, and even if there weren't death-trap rocks under the water, there isn't any place to climb back out. Fall in here and you'd have to swim all the way to Praia Mexilhões or a quarter of a mile around the ever-rising headland to the first inlet.

I can imagine how scary it must look when it gets choppy. Even yesterday, when it wasn't exactly stormy, the sound of water crashing against the rocks had been a constant. I've been googling our location. We are only a few miles from Sagres, one of the extremities of mainland Europe: the end of the world, once upon a time. It's where the Mediterranean meets the Atlantic, and where any two large bodies of water flow into one another, there are powerful tides and currents.

I look at the bundle strapped to my chest, his eyes struggling to stay open. I think of how fragile that little girl would have been, how quickly her tiny body would have been dragged out to sea.

Yet I can't repress the inquisitive impulse in my brain that says: Yeah, but was she really?

It formed before I could stop it. That's what is so insidious about conspiracy theories: as soon as an alternative explanation is offered, it becomes immediately more interesting than the given one. It's like when you're on the bus and someone else's book or magazine instantly becomes more interesting than the one open on your lap. Plus, there is the added allure that while the accepted version is something settled, the alternative seems live, developing, a story still awaiting its season finale.

A baby falls into the sea, drowns or hits her head and gets swept away by the tides, never to be seen again. That's all there is to think about: a sad, tragic death by misadventure. Whereas, the notion that the body was really disposed of somewhere else lets everybody write their own version.

It isn't simply about coming up with an alternative explanation, though. To get your ad-hoc bullshit some traction, you need to start by picking holes in the credibility of the official story, and from what I skimmed last night, the conspiracy theorists were convinced that the baby could not and would not have walked so far, especially in the dark.

I could see the lights last night, bathing the entire complex in soft colours, from the driveways to the clifftop. It's possible they were a recent addition, but the ones out here next to the path look identical in design to the lamps sunk in the concrete surrounding the pool, which had to have been installed when the place was built.

Light or dark, the tinfoil milliners made it sound like the toddler would have had to embark upon some epic journey to reach the clifftop. At ground level, the villas are almost as much glass as stone, sliding patio doors designed so that you're inviting the outside in. I can see that the nearest of those sliding doors gives onto a bedroom, only a few yards to the gap in the hedge. From being around my cousins – Sadiq's sister's kids – I am aware that if you take your eye off a toddler for ten seconds, it's alarming how far they can get, as well as how quickly they can place themselves in potential danger. If Niamh had got out through the door I'm looking at, it could have been as little as twenty seconds between her leaving her bed and hitting the water.

But I'm forgetting the heads-I-win-tails-you-lose logic of the CTs. It doesn't matter if their doubts are unreasonable. Not everything in their hypothesis has to add up: it's always about picking holes in the official one. They're 'just asking questions'. JAQing off.

I read that there was no way an eighteen-month-old could have climbed over the barrier. One guy had even managed to source a photo of this spot, pointing out that the fence was around four feet high. As far as he was concerned, this single image was checkmate for the official version. In truth, the only thing it proved was that he was ignorant of what the world looks like to a child that size. The barrier comprises three parallel series of wooden beams, the lowest of which is about a foot from the ground. You don't have to climb over a fence when you can climb under it.

Standing next to it now, I look down and notice that there is a wire mesh between the ground and the lowest beam. Unlike the

111

lights, I suspect this is a more recent addition. It makes me think of safety legislation that only manages to pass through the political system after a tragedy: a measure often named in tribute to the person whose death it came along too late to save.

Instinctively I take out my cell and snap a picture of the barrier, figuring I can use it if I write a piece or record a video about this. Then I become aware of a shadow in my peripheral vision. When I turn, I find Sylvie Temple standing a few yards away, staring at me. I pocket my phone and take a step away from the railing, involuntarily emphasising the very thing I'm afraid I was caught looking at.

'Hi,' I say, trying to sound casual and friendly. 'It's Sylvie, right?'

The words have barely left my mouth when I see a flash of something in the woman's face that tells me I just pissed her off. I suss it way too late: I shouldn't know her name. Or maybe I'm just being paranoid. Sylvie couldn't know who I have or haven't spoken to, so it might have been Celia or Marion who told me, or Kirsten.

And yet.

'It's Ivy, these days,' she says, her face neutral but her eyes cold. 'Been doing a bit of googling, have we?'

I feel my cheeks burn. If there was a window for pretending I don't know what Sylvie's talking about, I missed it.

'And photographing the fateful spot, I see. What's your angle? Is it a morbid curiosity, or are you checking the veracity of the official account?'

I think that if I didn't have Arron strapped to me, I'd be considering throwing myself over the edge right now.

'It's not like that,' I say. 'Totally the opposite, in fact. I was a huge admirer of your father and his takedowns of conspiracist thinking.'

Again I feel like I just said the wrong thing. Maybe bringing up the woman's dad right now was a further act of intrusiveness.

'But you've been researching the local history, right?'

'I just . . . realised I knew nothing about Max Temple the man. I read an obit which mentioned it. I'm Canadian. I had no idea about what happened. I'm sorry.'

Sylvie lets the silence linger and the awkwardness grow. She doesn't say 'It's okay' or offer any kind of acknowledgement, and we both know that's her prerogative.

Eventually she speaks.

'What's his name?'

'Arron.'

'He's Vince's? Vince and his new . . . ?'

'Wife. Kirsten. Yeah.'

'And you're the nanny.'

'Kind of. I'm not trained or anything. Just helping out for bed and board, sorta thing.'

'Wouldn't trade you. It's a hard shift.'

'I'm learning that.'

Sylvie lets another silence endure, though this time it seems more reflective.

'Niamh liked throwing stones off of here,' she says.

I feel a weird tension, amazed that Sylvie is sharing something regarding the dead daughter I read about, but wary of what this could be the lead-up to.

'I practically cleared this path picking up every stone I could find. She loved to see the splashes, but to do that, somebody had to hold her up. Because of the fence.'

She fixes me with a stare, like she's demanding: Do you get it?

I swallow. I don't know if I'm supposed to say anything.

Sylvie picks up a stone, turning it over between her fingers. I worry for a moment that she's about to throw it at me. Instead she tosses it over the side. We both hear the quiet splash.

'My mother sent me down to say we're all having some lunch, and you should come and join.'

2002

Sylvie

Behind her in the en suite, Sylvie could hear the thunder of water filling the bath, while from outside there was the gentler splash of bodies in the pool. The sliding doors were open, but as far as she was concerned, there might as well have been a force field delineating a mystical barrier between two worlds. The people on the far side of it were on holiday, relaxing and enjoying themselves in the pleasant warmth of the early evening sunshine. On this side, she was imprisoned, and her latest parole hearing had not gone well.

Niamh was on the floor of Marion and Ken's bedroom, chewing on the corner of her omnipresent purple blanket while Lia read to her from *That's Not My Train;* or rather pretended to read from it, mostly reciting from memory. Sylvie and Calum had been billeted in the same villa as her parents. Just like back in the day, Marion and Rory got to be in the second villa, while Sylvie was just along the hall from Mum and Dad. Far enough for noise not to carry if you were quiet.

She was giving the baby her bath in the other villa tonight so that Lia could 'help', though in truth, any kind of break from the relentless routine was to be welcomed. When you were expecting, people told you about the joys and they warned you about the dangers, making it sound like a roller coaster of polarities and extremes. Nobody told you how soul-crushingly bored you would be most of the time, watching the seconds tick slowly by, stuck in a developmental stasis while life as you used to know it continued for everybody else, just beyond your reach.

Some nights the sound of the bath running would cause Niamh to lose it, as she knew it was the beginning of the process that ended with bedtime. This evening she was too distracted by the presence of her cousin, so Sylvie was grateful for that much.

Outside, Calum was in the pool, playing some kind of piggy-in-the-middle ball game with Hughie and Ken. Ostensibly the rules were as standard, but for the adults the true skill was in convincingly screwing up so that Hughie didn't kick off at things not going his way. Calum had cottoned on to these rules without being told; in fact, in general he was showing more patience and rapport with the ever-combustible Hughie than he ever did with Niamh. He was staying in the middle, faking failure after failure. Eventually, however, one of Hughie's better throws took a weird skim off the water and landed in Calum's arms by accident, precipitating a familiar response. Hughie turned purple, refused to go in the middle and stormed out of the pool.

His father watched him leave with a patient smile. Marion would have gone chasing after him, either to comfort him or to tick him off depending on her mood, though both were fools' errands.

Ken climbed out of the pool and began towelling himself dry. Sylvie allowed herself an indulgence, reckoning he wouldn't be aware of her gaze from inside. Ken had a nice body, toned and muscular, a man in ways that emphasised Calum was just a boy.

She wasn't the only one to be aware of it, either.

'Oh, Ken, while you're on your feet there, would you mind putting just a dab of sun cream on my back?'

Mum was lying on a lounger, turning over so she was face-down and unfastening her bikini top. What was that about? Sylvie wondered. It was almost seven o'clock, so the sun wasn't strong enough to warrant a cream top-up, and she had chosen this exact moment to flip over? Plus Dad was sitting out too, why didn't she ask him? It wasn't that she was shy of rousing him from his book at any other time.

Mum never went topless but Sylvie noticed that she always seemed to be showing off her cleavage whenever there was a younger man around. She could be sitting in the shade in a sundress all morning, then she would whip it off and sit out in the sun in her bikini if the pool cleaner or the gardener showed up.

Ken ambled over and obliged as asked, rubbing some cream between Mum's shoulder blades. She moaned with exaggerated satisfaction. It was gross. Poor Ken. He was always so obliging, so patient. Sylvie wondered how he put up with Marion's high-maintenance oscillation between hectoring and neediness. When Sylvie was younger she had fantasies about stealing him away from her sister and making him a better wife.

With the pool otherwise empty, Calum took the opportunity to swim some lengths. He must have clocked up a mile's worth over the course of the day, when he wasn't reading. It was the same when they came here in April, during the Easter holidays. It appeared that looking after the baby was her responsibility in accordance with some unwritten law, and everybody else seemed cool with it. Sure, he took his turn now and again, something easy, like taking Niamh to the path to gather stones and throw them over the barrier, but that was all.

What bothered her was not merely the division of labour but the assumptions everyone made that she ought to somehow like it. All her human needs had been subverted by her duties as a mother and she wasn't supposed to mind because it was her natural role.

Recently at home she had sat playing with Niamh on the living-room carpet for a solid forty minutes while Calum and his uni friend Alan chatted on the settee.

'I'm just spellbound by this natural rapport you have with your daughter,' Alan said. 'It's amazing to watch how content you are, sitting there with her, totally at peace.'

It took all her restraint not to shout: 'Are you fucking crazy? I'm bored out of my tree. I am hating this. Every second drags. Every. Fucking. Second.'

It ached to think of how she might otherwise be in lectures or seminars instead of watching the minutes trickle past, feeling like her intelligence was being eroded by a chronic lack of intellectual stimulation. And the really depressing thing was not only what she was missing out on right then, but the awareness of how little a life she might end up leading.

Calum had just finished his second year studying law. Sylvie had been reassured by her mum that she would still get to go to university, but there was always a reason why now wasn't the right time.

She had brought it up again this afternoon. It didn't go well.

'Niamh will be able to go to a nursery after first term,' Sylvie suggested, when she and Celia were still seated at the table after lunch. 'The Montessori place takes them at age two.'

'That's still a whole term to get through first, and even then, the Montessori's hours wouldn't cover your timetable, to say nothing of the fetching and carrying. Calum's parents both work full time, remember.'

As if she could forget.

'I was hoping you could help out with that. You would actually be doing less than now if she was at nursery.'

'I've got a lot on, and I might have a lot more coming up.'

She didn't specify what, but she didn't have to: she had already outlined the paradox. Mum was happy to be playing an active role in Niamh's life, as long as Sylvie did what she wanted. But if Sylvie wanted to exercise some autonomy, then the assistance that autonomy relied upon would be withdrawn.

She realised it was hopeless. Mum loved the power this situation gave her, and she wasn't going to surrender that, especially not now. Celia was pretending otherwise but Sylvie could tell it really pissed her off that Dad had become the famous one in the house. She was always afraid of being outshone, which was why she did such a number on her first daughter. So now it was important that she had this hands-on grandmother role she could write about in her columns, but even more crucial was that she got to keep Sylvie in a little box.

'Then there's the studying – how much time would you have left to spend with Niamh in the evening after having been away from her all day? Not much, I would imagine. She deserves better than a mother who always has one eye elsewhere.'

'And what about what I deserve?' Sylvie had asked, frustration giving her a voice that she nonetheless knew to be a waste of breath.

Mum had fixed her with a look that feigned pity, as though Sylvie did not understand, but in truth it held only scorn.

'You *got* what you deserve. That's what you need to accept, and the sooner you accept it the sooner you will know some contentment and see the richness of what you have.'

'I deserve a chance at life, at education. I don't want this to be what defines me.'

'*This* has a name: Niamh. This is a person. And motherhood is a life. I gave up my acting career to be a mother, remember.'

Knowing her bridges were already burned, Sylvie had lashed out.

'You gave up your acting career because you couldn't get arrested. There's a thing called the IMDB on the internet, Mum, and it says you hadn't worked for two years before Marion came along.'

She saw a flash in her mother's eyes. Celia remained calm but there was ice in her manner thereafter. It didn't do to mess with the mythology.

'I'm afraid this was the only way you were ever going to learn some responsibility, Sylvie.'

'So you're content to see your daughter as some kind of cautionary tale?'

They'd been over this before, like when she first announced she was pregnant. It brought out Mum's censorious, prudish streak, which managed to coexist inside the same woman who constantly sought to manipulate people with coquettish behaviour that was becoming more inappropriate and less dignified with every passing year.

'Certainly there's too much emphasis on sexual gratification in our modern culture, but that's not what I'm talking about. You were spoiled, that's the problem. Honestly, you spent so much of your upbringing being Daddy's little girl. You had him wrapped around your little pinkie, doing whatever it took to grab his attention, expecting him to do everything for you. You never could accept that he was a busy man with a lot of people demanding his attention, so it was important that you learned you can't solve all your problems by batting your eyelids, flashing a smile and expecting someone to come to your rescue.'

Sylvie was temporarily paralysed by the realisation that her mother could have been talking about herself; and by the retrospective reve-lation that whenever Celia was voicing criticism, she was usually describing her own behaviour. It ought to have given her a killer comeback, but she was disarmed by the fact that what her mum just said was nonetheless true. She grew up worshipping her father, and a part of her still did. That was her undoing.

Spoiled. Yes, that was a literal description.

'It's important to learn there's a price to be paid for your behaviour,' Mum went on. 'You brought this upon yourself in more ways than one.'

'What's that supposed to mean?'

'Oh, come on, Sylvie. You're always creating dramas around you. Like that phase when we kept finding you drunk and being sick when you were fourteen. Or when you swallowed those pills and we had to take you to hospital. The doctor called it a parasuicide, said it was very common in attention-seeking teenage girls. As ever, you gave no thought to what it might do to the people around you. Just so long as you were the centre of the drama, that's the only thing that mattered.

'When you got yourself pregnant I couldn't help but see it as merely the latest episode, except you failed to anticipate that this one couldn't simply be apologised for and forgotten about. So now you've found yourself in not so much a grand melodrama as a twenty-four/seven soap. And yes, a lot of it is going to be boring and dull and a bit of a drudge, but maybe that's the antidote you've subconsciously been looking for.'

Sylvie just had to sit and listen, filled with a familiar mixture of boiling rage and abject helplessness as her mother laid down what sounded like a life sentence.

There had been a time when she believed pregnancy was a way out. Instead Niamh had become the human manacle that meant she could never escape.

Sylvie returned to the en suite where she checked the bath's temperature with her elbow. It was fine, though the water level was higher than she intended. She had been daydreaming and become distracted. She felt hungry now, which she understood to be a Pavlovian response to the sound of the taps running. It wasn't merely the anticipation of an imminent meal, but the best part of the day, when Niamh was tucked up in bed.

Hopefully she wouldn't reappear ten minutes after, just as Sylvie was finally getting a seat and some time to herself. That was a new thing since they arrived Portugal. At home, if she didn't feel like nodding off, she would cry until someone went in (usually Sylvie). But the cot here was a travel version, and Niamh had been utterly delighted to discover that she could now climb over the sides.

On the first night, she kept doing it not because she needed anything, but simply to show off that she could. Calum had quite disastrously laughed at her executing this manoeuvre, thus guaranteeing multiple repeats. She had done it at least twice every night since.

Sylvie turned off the taps. Niamh hadn't responded to the sound of them being turned on, but as was sometimes the case, she did react to the sudden silence: no crying, but rather a giggle and an exit on unnervingly rapid feet. It was a game: it's bath time and Mummy has to chase me. Sylvie failed to anticipate it and was still getting used to how fast Niamh could move. Last time she was here, at Easter, she was just cruising the furniture, and a few weeks ago she was still doing the Frankenstein walk. Now she was a whippet.

Sylvie pursued her into the hall and watched her go barrelling through the slightly open door into Rory's room, sending it flying against the wall. Sylvie felt a moment of familiar anxiety at the distance between them, too far to immediately intervene. Doors used to be mere portals from one room to another: now they were finger-slicing hazards. She caught up and followed inside on apologetically quiet feet.

Within a second of entering, she was under no doubt that she had just intruded. Rory and Svetlana looked at her as though caught in a moment they did not wish witnessed.

There were chopped lines on top of the chest of drawers, dusty parallels testament to these not being the first of the day. There was no atmosphere of hedonistic abandon, however; rather a distinct air of tension. Two people getting out of it because they were having difficulty dealing with what was in front of them, or maybe what was between them, or both.

The chest was like a sideboard, long and deep but only two drawers high and thus the top was eye-level for Niamh, who was staring at a plastic bag of pills next to the coke. Most likely ecstasy, sitting there at an invitingly grabbable height and distance.

Sylvie whipped in and grabbed the bag as Niamh's curious hand reached for it. She still wasn't past the stage when they just put everything in their mouths. Doesn't matter if it tastes nasty either, they'll still give it a second shot to be sure. She and Calum had taken her to the beach at Praia Mexilhões yesterday and she ate some sand. After about ten minutes of her crying and Sylvie washing out her mouth with all the bottled water they had brought, the moment she put Niamh back on the ground she did it again. And back in April, she drank the paddling pool and gave herself diarrhoea.

Sylvie was pissed off that Rory had left this shit just lying around, but she didn't want to say anything. For one, he could hit back with the reasonable response that it's his room and Niamh's not supposed to be in here, but mostly she doesn't want to be that moany mother, going on and on about her child's safety being everyone's responsibility. She had always hated that in Marion when her two were little, and didn't want Rory to see her the same way. She still wanted him – wanted someone – to see her as the girl she used to be, before she turned into this.

On top of all that, she was kind of embarrassed by the awkwardness of what she'd stumbled into. It would have been easier had they been shagging. It certainly didn't take any sixth sense to detect that there was an atmosphere in the room. There had been something coming off the pair of them the past couple of days, over and above the smell of hash. She suspected it was related to the fact that Svetlana was so conspicuously out of Rory's league. This wasn't to deny that her brother was a reasonably attractive guy, but he was hardly a man of prospects. His girlfriend looked like a supermodel, or a porn star at least, albeit one from a skin-flick about an Eastern European gangster's moll. There was something hard about her, beneath a very smooth surface. When Sylvie first set eyes on Svetlana, all she could see was how attractive she was. Consequently it had taken longer to notice that she was older than she first appeared. She had a good ten years on Rory, Sylvie reckoned.

Niamh proved she had greater situational awareness than her

mother: she recognised that Sylvie was momentarily distracted and seized the opportunity to bugger off again.

Sylvie retreated, closing the door properly. By the time she turned around, Niamh had vanished once more. The game was still on.

She called her name, because yeah, that always worked.

'Niamh?'

Nothing.

Sylvie wandered through to the living room, where she found only Marion clearing up CDs. Again. Hughie had taken to firing them about the place like frisbees.

'Where is she?'

'Lia?'

'No, Niamh.'

'I thought they were both with you.'

'She won't have gone far,' Marion said breezily. Words of rank hypocrisy from someone who had always overreacted any time her kids strayed from her line of sight. When Hughie was a toddler, she had regarded Marion as everything she would never want to be in a mother. That was before she discovered a far stronger candidate for that role.

She heard a loud splash from down the hall.

'Oh, Jesus.'

Sylvie felt something seize her any time Niamh did something like this: unexpectedly disappear or head directly towards potential danger. She was amazed at the strength of her instincts, while appalled by how little control she had over herself. When she saw those pills, her hand had reacted before her conscious mind had even processed it. Because the truth was, deep inside there was a part of her that was ambivalent about the danger: a part that knew if something terrible happened to Niamh, everything would be simpler. That part never got to take charge. Maternal instinct had the wheel and there was a big sign next to her saying 'do not distract the driver or stand forward of this notice'.

She hastened through Marion's bedroom to the en suite, where the first thing she saw was Lia looking pleased with herself despite the water all down her front. The second thing she saw was Niamh face-down in the bath with her head submerged.

Sylvie whipped her out of there, grateful that she had instinctively checked the temperature before turning off the taps. Niamh was spluttering and coughing, her little eyes wide in fright and surprise.

'Fucking hell, what were you thinking?' Sylvie scolded.

Lia got a fright, physically shuddering in recoil at the ferocity of Sylvie's tone. She glanced towards the doorway where Marion had appeared, and promptly turned on the waterworks in a dependable act of self-defence.

'I was giving her a bath like you said I could.'

Lia threw her arms around Marion's legs for protection, like Sylvie meant her physical harm.

Would Niamh ever look for that from her? She always had this fear that, deep down, Niamh sensed her ambivalence and knew she wasn't a good mother.

Sylvie held her daughter close. Ironically this was one of the few incidents to which Niamh was not responding with tears.

'Baf, baf,' she said, reaching towards the tub. There was probably sufficient distraction, having so many people around. Plus, she did love being in the water, loved to make a splash. She resisted the onset of bath time, then once in she would resist coming out of it.

Still, that didn't change what Lia had done.

'Baths are dangerous to a baby. You could have drowned her. You could have scalded her.'

'Why do you do it if it's dangerous?' Lia asked.

Sylvie wasn't getting into the nuance here.

'You just don't do this unsupervised. You're six, for God's sake.'

'She didn't mean any harm,' Marion said. 'And you don't usually run it so deep.'

Sylvie was exasperated but also arrested by Marion's patience and devotion. Marion was a real mother. Everybody talked about her being too indulgent of her kids, but she'd run into a burning building for them, take a bullet for them. She'd do anything to protect them, no matter what it cost her, no matter what they did.

2018

Amanda

I see that Kirsten is already seated at the big table on the Temples' terrace as I follow Sylvie between the villas. Kirsten gets up as she sees us approach, observing Arron with some satisfaction.

'Told you he'd nod off. I'll get his seat.'

'It's fine. Best not disturb him. Just as long as I can sit.'

'Gets heavy after a little while, doesn't he?'

'He's beautiful,' says Celia.

'They all are when they're asleep,' Marion observes, bringing out a bowl of salad to place down alongside a plate of cold cuts and cheeses. 'Do tuck in,' she adds, sitting down.

'Aren't we waiting for anybody?' asks Kirsten. She looks around at the one person not at the table, a hipster-looking guy reading a book on a lounger by the pool.

'No,' Celia answers. 'My grandson Hugh has gone to Praia Mexilhões so that my great-granddaughter can have a little paddle on the beach, and Marion's husband Ken has gone to visit the castle at Silves with my granddaughter Lia.'

Celia glances towards hipster dude.

'My son Rory has not long eaten breakfast. He's on a different time zone. It feels like that's been true of him his whole life, but on this occasion it's because he's recently flown from San Francisco.'

I wonder at Celia's answer. It's helpful to have a breakdown of who's who, but it strikes me as oddly grandiose. Celia defined everybody according to their relationship to her, like she was laying down a matriarchal marker.

'And will Vince be joining us at some point?' Celia enquires.

It sounds polite enough, but I detect something in it that's not merely nosy, but pointed. Judgy.

'That remains to be seen.'

'I'm still trying to work out how you can miss a plane when you're already in the departure area,' Marion says with a chuckle.

'If anybody could manage it, it would be Vince,' Kirsten replies, though she doesn't elaborate regarding his texted excuse. 'Good thing I've got Amanda here to help me out.'

Marion pours me a glass of water from a jug topped with lemon slices, acknowledging my difficulty in reaching across the table with Arron attached.

'Kirsten was telling us you're Canadian,' Celia says. 'How is it you came to work for her and Vince? Was it an internet thing? Or is there a family connection?'

'Kind of. One of my dads knows Vince from way back.'

'One of your dads?' Celia repeats.

Hoo boy. Here we go again.

'I have two fathers. Two gay fathers. Double prizes,' I add in a sing-song voice, trying to sound breezy so that it doesn't get awk.

'I didn't mean anything by it,' Celia says. 'I'm just curious. I'm not judging anybody.'

Which is something people only say when they're judging somebody.

I can feel tension around the table, though maybe I'm projecting and it's just me. I'm still feeling rattled by my encounter with Sylvie, who hasn't said a word since.

'I mean, they've obviously done an excellent job in how they've brought you up. It's just . . .'

Here it comes.

'I think every child, especially a girl, does need a mother.'

Celia has a wistfulness to her tone, like she's offering some kind of undeniable but sorrowful piece of truth or wisdom.

I strain to keep my voice measured as I reply. I'm a guest at this woman's table, and I've been raised – by my two dads – to be polite. (Also, duh, I'm Canadian.)

'I have a mother. It's just that she's not in my life so much.'

125

Celia puts on a cloying smile, saccharine and patronising.

'But that's precisely my point, dear. I know it's not politically correct to say, but there's a reason marriage and parenthood works best between a man and a woman.'

I want to respond, but I worry I'll go into a rant and everything will be awful after that. Besides, it's not like I'm going to change this woman's mind. Nonetheless, it pisses me off that Celia thinks she has laid down the last word on the subject.

Except she hasn't.

'Not everybody would say that having a mother is a gift,' Sylvie says.

At first I think it's a gag to cut through the atmosphere, but the ensuing chill at the table tells me otherwise. My other mistake was thinking Sylvie might be weighing in on my side. In fact it has nothing to do with me. I am just the ball, and the game is between these two.

'Kirsten tells us you're starting university,' Marion pitches in, bidding to move things on.

'She's going to be a TV presenter,' Kirsten adds.

'More like a reporter. I'd like to go into broadcast journalism. I have a YouTube channel.'

Why did I say that? I chide myself. I'm totally off balance. What if they go look it up?

'Well, if you want to be a journalist, you should speak to Syl . . . to *Ivy* here. She's the expert.'

'You're a journalist?' I ask, unable to mask the surprise in my voice. It seems an unlikely career choice for someone with her experience of the media. Unless the expertise Celia is referring to is just that, meaning my stated vocation would be another way I have painted a target on myself.

'No,' Celia replies. 'You could say she's the opposite of a journalist, so she knows all about how they operate.'

'What's the opposite of a journalist?' I ask.

'Nick Robinson,' says Marion. It's a joke, one I don't get.

'I'm in PR,' Sylvie states flatly, in a manner not intended to encourage further enquiries.

'Yes. The journalist tries to find out what is really happening in the world, while Ivy helps rich people cover it up. Isn't that right, dear?'

Wow, I think, reeling. There was a whole lot going on in that little exchange. Bereavement has brought these people together physically, but the cracks must run real deep if they can't contrive to cover them up in front of a stranger.

'That's one way of looking at it,' Sylvie says. 'I won't pretend I don't derive a degree of satisfaction from frustrating the efforts of reporters. They're a largely despicable shower. "The best lack all conviction while the worst are full of passionate intensity." Gormless automatons mindlessly processing press releases and cobbling together stories from exchanges on Twitter; or twisted muckrakers with an inappropriate interest in other people's business.'

Sylvie isn't looking directly at me but I know I am the one being addressed. Coming on top of Celia's patronising bullshit, I've hit my limit for polite passivity and I feel a powerful urge to stand up for myself.

'A journalist's interest in other people's business isn't inappropriate if they might have something to hide.'

I realise immediately how this sounds. It wasn't my intention, but I can't back down without drawing attention to why and thus making it worse. Anyway, I'm pissed and my point stands.

'Ah, see, that's where you overestimate the role of journalists and underestimate the power of what Ivy can do,' Celia says. 'She is the kind of PR consultant you come to *after* the damaging truths have come out. Facts and evidence aren't even half the battle any more.'

I feel a hard kernel of rage forming inside. Sylvie has been sneering at me from the moral high ground since our encounter on the path.

'You're talking about corporate reputation laundering,' I say. I keep the anger from my voice but I'm not going to have my journalism aspirations disparaged by someone who does *that* for a living.

'We prefer the term "strategic corporate communications".'

'Call it what you like, it's the same bullshit. I want to work in journalism because I believe in bringing information into the open. Not letting corporations decide what the rest of us are allowed to know.'

Sylvie looks calm, but patronisingly so. *Poor child, how little you understand.*

'And once the information is in the open, that's where my work begins,' Sylvie tells me. 'Facts and evidence are not the same thing as objective truth. Everybody tries to shape their message. Sometimes what I work on is a matter of helping people understand what a company is really doing, and avoid misconceptions that can make them unnecessarily concerned.'

I decide to show her what I understand.

'And it just so happens that helping people avoid misconceptions involves faking grassroots campaigns and dictating talking points to tame journalists, is that it? Do you mean "misconceptions" like climate change? Or that tobacco is harmful? Facts and evidence aren't objective truth, sure, but they're not to be brushed aside by flooding the zone with shit. I mean, in this era of fake news, isn't the practice of neutralising hard evidence and making up your own reality an insult to everything your father stood for?'

There is a moment of silence as I realise what I just said and to whom. My closing remark seemed an absolute clincher as it rose logically from my mental processes a few seconds ago, but as soon as it left my lips it turned into something crass.

Celia appears momentarily taken aback, Marion paralysed by the awkwardness, eyes on the table. Sylvie, for her part, regards me like she wants to crush me under her heel. She opens her mouth to reply, then seems to take a moment.

She composes herself, and when she does speak she is calm. She is even smiling, but in a professionally polite, coldly corporate way.

'I really hope you get what you want,' she says. 'That you become a campaigning journalist or the head of a protest movement. It would make my job easier, because it would be a cinch to turn the public against you. People don't like shrill, hectoring crusaders, and that's why *I* love them. The optics are a gift. It's easy to make your client look dignified when their critics are losing their shit. Plus, you're so sure of your moral righteousness that you're easily blindsided by nuance. It comes as a shock that anybody else would have a different point of view.

128

'Perception is everything. Very few things are as black and white as people might assume. I'm working right now on helping change perceptions of a political regime – I can't say where – but its reputation is utterly skewed right now because of its position regarding FGM.'

'Is that to do with genetically modified food?' Celia asks.

'No,' I correct her, feeling something freeze my insides. 'Female genital mutilation.'

'Well, female circumcision is the less loaded term for it.'

'Less *loaded*?' I splutter.

'Yes. That's the first battle we have to fight: people assuming that morally and culturally, it's a done deal. We need to move the debate into an open space. Pro-FGM Muslim women are being intimidated out of the whole discussion due to an assumed cultural superiority on the part of white, western feminists.'

I fight to control my tone, mindful that Arron is still asleep on my chest.

'You're planning to astroturf women's voices in *favour* of FGM?'

'Just to get the ball rolling. My strategy is essentially to copy-paste some of the positions regarding the burqa and niqab. We need to make people wary of jumping in with both feet in case they are accused of being racist or culturally insensitive.'

I have to take a sip of water as my mouth is dry with anger. The worst part is that I can imagine this strategy working, muddying the waters enough to slow down progress and leech momentum from campaigns on the issue. It is utterly depressing, but worse than that, it's shameful.

'I can't believe that anyone with a functioning conscience would even consider this. But as a woman, how can you . . . ?'

I can't even. I don't have the words.

Sylvie looks at me utterly calm, her expression still the same: professionally polite, coldly corporate.

'You say you can't believe I would do this, but you do believe it, otherwise you would have realised I'm lying.'

Jesus Christ. It hits me like a freight train. She had been toying with me the whole time, like a cat with an injured bird.

'For God's sake, Sylvie,' chides Marion. 'There was no need for that.'

129

Sylvie doesn't even acknowledge her sister. She only has eyes for me.

'I wanted you to understand that what you assume of people's motives and morals can make you vulnerable to being misled.'

I'm grateful for the warmth and the audible soft breaths of the sleeping baby strapped to me, because it is compensating for the paralysing chill of anger and humiliation that has me in its grip.

'Not for the first time, I can only apologise for my daughter's rather strange sense of humour,' says Celia.

Sylvie's expression remains calmly neutral, clinically emotionless following her takedown of me, like it was a professional hit.

I say little as everyone moves on from the awkwardness, or at least conspires to pretend to: polite chit-chat over salad. I answer when spoken to, compelled by social etiquette to collaborate in the charade but keeping my answers brief. I need the headspace to process what just happened, and to contemplate what kind of person humiliates a guest like that. I don't believe I have the greatest of spidey senses, but I have seldom been around anyone who made me feel so instinctively uncomfortable from the get-go.

However, the words of the man missing from this table echo in my head.

'We should be wary of first impressions, because they can inform every subsequent impression. Once an idea has taken hold, particularly when it is an idea that gives comfort or security, or that reinforces our understanding of the world, it is very difficult to shift. We find it very difficult to believe something bad about a person we have already decided we like, or of whose behaviour or ideology we approve. And equally we find it very easy to believe something bad about someone when the values are reversed.'

I remind myself of what Sylvie has been through, what that might do to a person. If you lost your baby daughter, some part of you would be damaged irreparably, a part that loves, that cares, that feels.

Then I recall that image of Sylvie staring defiantly down the camera lens and can't help but wonder whether that part of her was already damaged, or missing in the first place.

2002

Rory

'She does not want that child.'

Svetlana had a sour look, speaking soon enough after Sylvie had left for Rory to fear she might still be in earshot. He didn't want his little sister to hear anything hurtful, particularly as he knew Svetlana was only having a pop at Sylvie as a proxy. Her true target was Rory's relationship with certain other members of his family.

'How can you say that? She's just young, dealing with a difficult situation. It's natural she's showing the strain. I don't think you can judge when you've not been a mother yourself.'

He instantly regretted saying this, and not just because he feared an escalation. Svetlana didn't seem wounded by it though, or perhaps she just wouldn't let him see it if she was.

'I grew up in a large family. Lots of children, lots of mothers, mothers younger than her. She does not want that child. You argue, defend her because she is sister and you feel sorry for her. But you know the truth also.'

Rory didn't want to catch her eye, for the admission she would see. His gaze alighted instead upon the drugs on top of the chest of drawers, seeing it through Sylvie's eyes. Marion had already complained about him leaving gear out the other day. He had got a bit of a fright when he saw Niamh reaching for the bag of pills, but he would have to admit much of his dismay was an instinctive response to someone else trying to grab his stuff.

He normally kept it out of sight, mainly so that it wasn't a temptation to his flatmate Danny and his pals. Rory wondered if he kept leaving the gear out because subconsciously he wanted it seen, though it wasn't his sisters he was thinking of. When people keep telling you you're a disappointment, you perversely want to prove them right, fling it back in their faces.

Svetlana stared at him accusingly. He knew what was coming. Niamh and Sylvie's interruption had been only a temporary respite.

'We have been here four days now, and still you do not ask.'

'It's all about timing. It will help if they've got to know you properly, formed a relationship.'

'Your family makes you unhappy. I do not know why you want them to get to know me. The sooner we get the money, the sooner we go somewhere else, and you will not need to deal with all of this . . . *otruta*.'

Sometimes she genuinely didn't know the English, but Rory suspected that occasionally Svetlana liked to resort to Ukrainian for emphasis. It forced him to ask, so there could be no question of what she meant.

'What is *otruta*?'

'It is like . . . from a bite.'

Yes, there could be no question of what she meant. Not in this household.

'Poison.'

'Yes. That is the word.'

'You don't understand. Yes, there is . . . poison. But I have to play the game. I haven't come here on the big family holiday for a couple of years. My absence has been noted and marked, and my mum has been on my case about it constantly. They come here several times a year, and I get guilt-tripped in advance of every occasion. That's why I agreed to stay the whole fortnight. I have to pay my dues.'

Rory was concerned but not surprised that his discomfort at being here should be so obvious. He wondered if it was as clear to his family as it was to Svetlana that he was merely playing the part of the dutiful, loving son, rather than actually living it.

But then, that was the whole Temple dynamic in microcosm. They all played at being a dutiful, loving family: a *tableau vivant* both orchestrated by – and performed for the benefit of – Saint Celia. It was bound up in her faith and yet was a miniature religion in itself:

132

the Grand Sacrament of Family. These holidays and other gatherings were very much like Sunday mass: a series of rituals the devout had to go through, the content of which was banal at best and offensively hypocritical at worst, and if any of it ever had meaning, it had been long since lost in time. Everyone had to turn up and go through the motions, but nobody could admit to anyone else how empty it felt, how bored they were, or how they weren't really connected to it by anything other than an indoctrinated sense of obligation and the inertia that dragged you into always doing what you've always done because you've always done it.

Still, for once his family weren't the biggest problem in his life right now, and certainly the shit Svetlana had been through – and was still dealing with – put it into perspective. Poor little privileged western white-boy waster that he was.

Rory wasn't fobbing Svetlana off with an excuse: they did have plenty of time, and in fact they had to spend that time to guarantee a result. Nonetheless, he could understand why she was anxiously impatient, why they were having the same conversation over and over again.

'These people are not patient, Rory. And the longer it goes on, the more interest they will add to the debt.'

Maybe it was the drugs, working in conjunction with the sight of the glinting sea and the clear horizon, but Rory felt an enticing sense of possibility and wondered, why don't they just disappear?

'When we get the money, couldn't we just run with it instead?'

'They will find me.'

'How could they? We could go anywhere. Australia, Thailand. Come up with new names for ourselves.'

'Believe me, they will find me. Find *us*, and when they do . . .'

She didn't complete the sentence.

'I cannot live with this hanging over me. That would not be freedom. You have always known freedom, Rory. You grow up in UK. I grow up with KGB. After the Soviet Union fall, much in Ukraine get better, but KGB never go away. They just become gangster. Humans are just flesh to them. People call it trafficking, but they are slavers, like in history. Some slavers capture slaves, some sell slaves, and some transport them from one country to another. But they are all slavers, then as now.'

He could see the weight of the years when she spoke this way, pondering distantly whether anyone in his family had noticed the age difference and what they might read into it. He did the arithmetic and worked out what age Svetlana had been when the Wall came down. He wondered what her childhood had been like, what kind of teenager she had been. And inevitably he thought about the married life she was living at a time when his biggest worries concerned exam results and Nintendo high scores. Lives so far apart that neither would have believed they could ever converge.

They had come from such diverse backgrounds, but they quickly recognised something in each other. In their different ways they had each escaped from their pasts, but now they didn't know what they wanted from their futures. They were both failures, chronic cases of wasted potential. Disappointments to themselves.

Svetlana had been married to a football player, some superstar who maybe wouldn't have adorned so many posters or got so many endorsement deals if people had known how he brutalised his wife, and how effective he was at making her believe it was her fault. She still did, still regarded it as her own shortcomings that had caused the marriage to fail.

Svetlana was understandably loath to map out every station on the journey, but with her self-esteem shot to hell and her family abandoning her for blowing her ride to the top with Golden Boy, she had ended up in the hands of the slavers, as she called them. She was working as a prostitute, albeit a high-end one. They had drawn her in with the promise of freedom and travel, facilitating her moves from city to city: Budapest, Prague, Munich, London. That was where she had met Rory. She was working off a debt that would never diminish, especially as the traffickers were also her dealers.

Rory realised that she had a record of being drawn to flawed and destructive individuals, not relishing what that said about him. Maybe that was why he was so determined to break that cycle: for both of their sakes. He had the opportunity to be the one who would help her start again. They could both start again.

She needed thirty thousand euros to buy her way out once and for all. Rory didn't have it, of course, but his father did, especially after recently becoming famous and having signed this big book deal.

He had come here to ask for it, but as he found himself explaining to her over and over again, it was going to be a long game.

Rory heard a splash, like someone jumping into the pool, except it seemed to come from down the hall. It was followed by the thumps of rapid feet, then anxious voices: Sylvie giving out to Lia, Marion trying to calm the situation.

Svetlana flashed him an expression that claimed some kind of vindication.

'Marion, she love her children. No question. But the other one . . .'

Svetlana shook her head.

2018

Amanda

I switch on the aircon and close the sliding doors as I watch the group retreat along the road towards Praia Mexilhões. I stand close to the unit and let the cold air play on my skin. I need to cool down in more ways than one.

Kirsten is pushing Arron in a buggy, Celia and Marion walking just ahead. They are going down to the village to take a walk on the beach and maybe grab a coffee. Kirsten had asked if I would prefer to come along or to have a little quiet time alone. I didn't need to think about my answer.

I'm in a horrible mood and I know I shouldn't be around people. I hardly ate anything, which hasn't helped my state of mind, but I was just so angry during lunch that I couldn't face putting anything in my mouth and swallowing it. It all tasted of nothing, and I hated the sense that Sylvie was observing me, by turns amused and scornful.

I feel pissed at everybody though, not just that skeletal ice-queen bitch: Celia for being a nosy busybody and judgy homophobe; Marion for being so insipid; and Kirsten for being so confoundingly calm regarding her husband failing to turn up on this goddamn vacation.

What's with that?

Their whole relationship seems kind of weird, in fact. I thought I had a handle on it when I first arrived at their place and took in the age difference. I saw a middle-aged lawyer past his prime who had married someone young, cute and uncomplicated, thinking she would do as she was told. Equally I figured Kirsten as none-too-bright but with cynical street smarts: a clothes horse who had nabbed herself a sugar daddy. The problem with my gold-digger hypothesis is that I would have expected more gold. The house was pretty modest, a seventies-looking semi in the burbs, and right from the get-go I heard Kirsten moan about how penny-pinching Vince is.

When I learned Vince had a villa in Portugal, I assumed he must be wealthy, but it turned out to be pretty much the only thing he got in the divorce from his first wife. She had been a lawyer too, Kirsten said, and clearly a better one, as she had burned him pretty bad in the settlement.

'Vince is always just about to land some big deal that will make him rich,' Kirsten said last night. She sounded scornful. I had wondered if she was getting bitter that she might have backed the wrong horse, and yet the more I learn about Kirsten, the harder it is to imagine she didn't know what she was getting herself into. She had been his secretary, so she must have had the measure of Vince before she married him.

I know I would benefit from an afternoon nap, but equally I am aware there's no chance of falling asleep while I'm still so mad. I've barely stopped shaking from my anger over Sylvie's FGM rope-a-dope stunt for humiliating the stupid little teenager.

What kind of psycho does something like that to a stranger, a guest, over lunch?

I grab a slice of cold pizza from the fridge and wash it down with a Coke while my laptop boots up. I usually find some distraction in my favourite channels, but as the first page loads and I read the video descriptors, it all feels kind of remote and irrelevant. A couple days ago I was composing responses in my head, thinking I might film something on my phone if there was time, but not only can't I think straight any more, the issues don't seem to matter either. So what if some incel dick-dribble parroted another cookie-cutter talking point?

Almost automatically, my hand takes the cursor to the history bar and reloads some of the conspiracy sites I had foresworn. Within seconds I am confronted by that photo again: Sylvie Temple defiantly staring down the camera. I felt creepy and voyeuristic the last time I looked at this image, but that was before I got to know the real thing. The picture seems striking for different reasons now. Who feels defiant at a time like that?

I think of our encounter at the clifftop, Sylvie implicitly accusing me of tragedy tourism. Okay, she was probably right, but wasn't it weird to be making that assumption, to be bringing up the subject straight away? Wasn't that a little defensive? A little suspicious?

As I surf the sites, I find repeated reference to contemporary reports mentioning how Sylvie didn't seem all that emotional over the loss of her child. They're not just talking about a single photograph either. I find quotes from Portuguese officials remarking how cold Sylvie seemed, while a retrospective tabloid interview with one of the policemen describes the whole family as being strangely evasive. The piece is carefully worded so as not to give explicit voice to outlandish claims, the journalist focusing more on the fact that Niamh's death happened during a party. It is heavily insinuated that the family never told the whole truth, in order to conceal irresponsible behaviour and possibly outright neglect.

Nevertheless, I can't help thinking that nobody ever got a backhander from a journalist for an interview that confirmed the official version. In fact, as I scan the forums, where the bloggers are less constrained in their theorising, I find myself deconstructing every claim, every assertion. And what's really weird is I'm hearing the deconstruction in Max Temple's voice. I'm recalling things he said on videos, or in some cases merely imagining his voice as I remember pieces I read.

Sylvie Temple killed her own baby because she couldn't handle being a mother and wanted to go to university instead. She got rid of the body and then made it look like the kid had wandered off, or she drowned the baby in the bath then tossed the body over the cliff so that it would wash up the next day, except the tides never brought it back to shore.

It was Calum, Niamh's father, in a 'shaken baby' case. He went too far in his rage at her constant crying and killed his own daughter, so he had to disappear the body before anyone found out. He drove along the coast and disposed of the evidence while everybody was drunk or sleeping.

One of the young kids killed the baby by dropping her in the pool, either by accident or playing a game, and the adults had to cover it up because they were busy partying instead of paying attention.

Depending on the cause of death, some theories have it that the body had to be driven away and buried, other scenarios sticking with the thrown-in-the-sea hypothesis.

A conspiracy theory does not even necessarily require a conspiracy. It is an unsupported alternative explanation that usually falls foul of intentionality bias, whereby motive is ascribed to mere happenstance.

Another blogger notes that Rory Temple's girlfriend, Svetlana Gruskov, later wound up in jail for travelling under a false passport. This part is actually verified, linking to a newspaper report revealing that her real name was Tatiana Livchenko and she had connections to Ukrainian gangsters. Less supported is the claim that she infiltrated the family and stole the baby to order for people traffickers.

'I'd like to know who "discovered" the kid's blanket by the clifftop,' one blogger states, 'because they're the one who framed the whole drowning/accident narrative.'

A reply to this post disagrees, insisting the real killer could have planted the blanket in that spot for the same reason. 'It looks more convincing if someone else discovers the evidence and draws the conclusion independently.'

Conspiracy theories don't gain much traction purely on hypothesis: there have to be anomalies, apparent inconsistencies with the official version: the white Uno in the Paris underpass, the witness reports of shots from the grassy knoll.

I read multiple references to a witness in a villa along the road, who saw a car being driven past his place in the direction of the village around half past eleven, then saw another vehicle heading towards the Baia Serena complex ten minutes later. He couldn't say for sure if it was the same car, as it was too dark to identify the model, but he noted that the Serena villas lie at a dead end. He was also adamant that he saw a woman at the wheel, though admitted he only got a decent view the first time.

Nobody at the Baia Serena complex would admit to having driven anywhere that night, and though this was noted with great significance by the theorists, I had to admit it was hardly a smoking gun.

I've been here a few days and have seen several cars drive to the villas and turn back, discovering the road doesn't go where they thought. It is hardly a stretch to suggest the witness might have remembered their journeys the wrong way around.

The order of events frequently gets jumbled as we reassemble our memories, creating versions that people want to believe, or which give them that buzz of being in the know, of discovering occult knowledge.

It doesn't just seem like I'm hearing Max Temple's voice: it's like he is defending his family from beyond the grave, and specifically warning me off entertaining these unworthy thoughts about his beloved daughter. And yet my instincts keep telling me that Sylvie is hiding something, and not just because she was mean to me. Why would she be going in so heavy at the mere possibility I might be taking an interest in what happened down at the clifftop?

Even more pertinently, what was the story with this vibe between Sylvie and the rest of her family? She was literally apart from them most of the time, sitting on her own.

Celia had been sore about the fact that Sylvie went back to the solitude of her lounger as soon as she had cleared her plate.

'You'd think she could spare more than twenty minutes, seeing as it's the first time we've all been back here together since . . .'

She had stopped herself there. Celia didn't say since when, since what, but she didn't have to. Clearly there was some serious history here, an ongoing tension evident from the terse exchanges I had witnessed at the table.

I think about the fact that Sylvie changed her name, another symbolic act of distancing herself from her family. I wonder whether it isn't only the conspiracy theorists who have suspicions regarding the Temples and the official version.

2002

Sylvie

Sylvie felt the mattress shift as Calum rolled over, moving closer behind her in the dark. He smelled boozy, despite brushing his teeth. He had been hitting it pretty hard in that short golden period as an adult human being between Niamh finally settling down and the onset of total exhaustion. She couldn't blame him. It was always tempting to prolong it, to eat some more, drink some more, enjoy conversation that wasn't about nappies and bottles, but they never knew what was awaiting them in the night, or how early Niamh might wake up in the morning.

She had made that mistake last night and paid the price all day.

'Hey, do you hear that?' Calum asked.

She listened closely. There was only silence other than the sound of the waves hitting the cliff wall.

'What? I don't hear anything.'

'Precisely.'

He cupped her breast. She could feel his erection pressing the small of her back.

'Niamh's sound asleep,' he said.

'Yeah, but my parents aren't. It's only just gone eleven.'

'We can be quiet. Plus it's not like they don't know we do this. Or at least *think* we do this.'

There was an edge to this last remark. It had been a while, she knew that, but that wasn't all her fault.

'I just want to get some sleep. Surprised you're not more tired, after all the swimming you did while I was chasing about after Niamh.'

He ignored this dig, but he rolled away and his tone turned from horny to huffy.

141

'I'm trying to work out what I did wrong, Sylvie. You used to be all over me. You wanted to do it all the time. I'm beginning to think what you actually wanted was to be pregnant. You liked the idea of having a baby – until you got one. Now you don't seem to like either of us very much.'

'Well, I didn't exactly land Dad of the Year. You know, if you want to get physical, it helps if you're actually present.'

The three of them were 'living' in what ironically was referred to as the granny flat. Her late grandmother, Max's elderly mum, had lived there when Sylvie was growing up. It was an extension to the house with its own separate entrance, though the privacy and autonomy that suggested were, she had come to learn, purely symbolic. The current granny – Celia – now lived in the main house, and it was the younger generations who were boxed off.

Sylvie's accommodation was a physical embodiment of her allotted role. Her feelings, behaviour and decisions were never her own. She was merely an appendage to the greater ideal of the Temple family, with its matriarch the keeper of the sacred flame. Effectively, she had never left home, but nor had Calum. Eighteen months on it still felt as though it was a temporary arrangement, like a series of sleepovers; or be-kept-awake-half-the-night-overs.

He was still getting to go to uni, getting to lay down plans for his life. 'It's for all three of your futures,' was the phrase Mum used. This was to drill home why Sylvie was supposed to be satisfied by this, even though she couldn't lay down plans the same way. At least everybody had backed off on pressuring them into getting married. But Calum was coming 'home' fewer and fewer nights. He sometimes crashed at friends' places on campus after working late at the library, or stayed at his parents' house along the street, so he could study in peace. His mum and dad were allowing him to retreat into his single state, still their little teenage boy like before Sylvie did this to him.

Maybe that was fair. But Sylvie didn't have the option to regress.

She thought back to what Celia said earlier, or more specifically how she said it: she had 'got herself pregnant'.

Nobody had ever been able to do that, not even the Blessed Virgin. There was an angel involved there, according to the myth.

A visitation.

Sylvie had choices, off-ramps she never took and was now seeing regretfully in the rear-view mirror. She could have had an abortion. She knew that. Mum couldn't have stopped her. It wasn't what she wanted then, however. She had her reasons, confused and naive as she could now see. The same reasons as she hadn't wanted to put the baby up for adoption. Calum was right, though: she didn't want to be a mother any more. There was a time when she thought it would be a means of defining her own life, away from the family. Instead it just let the tentacles coil ever tighter around her. No wonder he was trying to wriggle free.

In his parents' eyes he was still the golden boy for doing the right thing, though nobody really made clear what the wrong thing would have been. That was Calum's parents, though. They weren't judgemental and if they were disappointed in him, they never let it show.

Calum was almost literally the boy next door. They had grown up on the same street, close childhood friends who drifted apart when puberty brought its changes, but she had sought him out in recent years because he was tender and caring. He was a few months older than her but younger in so many other ways. She thought he was manipulable, and she was right, but in her grand plan she would have been the only one doing the manipulating.

She didn't love him. She didn't even fancy him (though she was no catch herself these days, getting heavier and heavier), but she did feel sorry for what she had done to him. He was such a sweet guy, or at least he had been once. She feared all of this was turning him into something else.

He placed a hand on hers and squeezed it gently.

'I'm sorry,' he said. 'I don't want us to be like this.'

In that moment she caught a glimpse of a better time: a different version of him, a happier version of her. She couldn't say whether it was a glimpse merely of her past, or of a possible future. But she did know that in either case, that better time existed in a place where they weren't parents.

Sylvie turned around and slipped her nightie over her head, pulling him to her. She hated how her body looked and hated anyone seeing it, but she enjoyed the feeling of his skin against hers.

As she felt his hands about her, she closed her eyes and didn't see Calum any more. She imagined the hands were Ken's. She ran her fingers along his skinny arms, picturing instead Ken's taut and wiry frame, and as she pulled him inside her, she pictured Ken's shy smile, his dusty blond hair, his bottomless patience, a masculinity that was calm and tender and nurturing and strong. For the first time in ages, she thought she might come.

Then she heard it: crying from down the hall.

They both froze, both tensed up, taken out of the moment like only that sound could.

A rational voice told her they could both ignore it – maybe even *should* ignore it – at least for a little while. But her instincts compelled a response, setting off signals in her body and her brain that could not be ignored. That voice was screaming like those super-piercing burglar alarms intended to drive out the intruders.

'Fuck,' she said with a sigh.

Sylvie pulled her nightie back on and climbed out of bed, the crying growing louder as she opened the door. She turned on the hall light and started as she found Niamh standing right in front of her, only a few yards away. Sylvie had known she was able to get out of her travel cot, but she was sure she had closed the bedroom door. Niamh definitely couldn't reach the handle yet. Maybe the door hadn't been closed properly.

She walked down the hall and picked her up. She read recently that once they were walking, you should walk them back to bed. It was in some parenting book or magazine article, she couldn't remember which: she'd read so many, hoping for something that would make her feel more like a mother. This particular advice had seemed well-argued in the cold light of day, but right now she didn't have the energy or the patience for anything other than the most direct method.

Niamh's tears dried quickly from the comfort of physical contact. Instead it was Sylvie who found herself weeping in sheer desperation as she sat there in the dark, remaining with Niamh until she went back to sleep. In one way she was grateful for the time it took, because she didn't want Calum to see her like this. She wasn't sure why.

She left on very quiet feet and closed the door. She noticed that it didn't quite catch: that was the problem. The metal strike plate was slightly warped.

She returned to her bedroom, where she expected Calum to be asleep. Instead, she heard running water in the bathroom. She hoped he had wanked himself off in there and wasn't holding out hope for resuming activities. When he emerged, it took the briefest look at his face to tell her that his thoughts were far from libidinous. His expression was over-wrought.

He sat himself heavily upon the bed, as though his limbs were a burden.

'What?' Sylvie asked, already feeling her hackles rise.

'I can't handle this.'

He was acting exaggeratedly pathetic and it was pissing her off. She had just comforted one baby to sleep, so whatever pity might be left in the tank was reserved for herself.

'Handle what? This holiday's the most time you've been in her immediate vicinity in weeks, and even then you've hardly been with her. You've spent more time playing with Hughie than looking after Niamh.'

He nodded, a glazed look in his eyes. He wasn't disputing it. He wasn't really listening either, just talking.

'I kept thinking once we got through the really hellish early months, the longer it went on the more I would grow into feeling like a father. I'm still waiting. I was never ready for this. I never wanted it. I was pressured into it because I had already let my parents down by getting you pregnant. I didn't want to let them down further by being a dick and abandoning my responsibilities. But now when I look at Niamh, I don't feel love. I just see this thing that has ruined my life, this thing that seems way too high a price to pay for a couple of shags.'

He sighed.

'I want my life back. I want to be a teenager, an adolescent, a student. I want to get drunk and stupid and fuck around and fall in love and fall out of love. I want to be able to make more than one fucking mistake.'

Sylvie stared at him, waiting for him to meet her eyes. He had mostly been speaking to the floor, afraid to face her.

'Don't you think I feel that way too?' she asked.

He frowned, looking exasperated.

'I know what you're coping with, but it's different for you. You're her mother, the one who gave birth to her. You've got this natural connection.'

Sylvie opened her mouth, gaping in outrage at his misconception. She wanted to rip into him for it, but she was silenced by the awareness that he was right in a way he didn't even realise. She and Niamh did have a greater connection, but that only made it all the more frustrating that she didn't feel the way everyone else seemed to think she should.

'I'm afraid of who I'm becoming,' Calum said. 'I'm afraid of the thoughts I have. I want to run away: that one pops into my mind a dozen times a day. Head off to Cyprus or Ibiza or somewhere, get a job in a bar and just become someone new. But there's worse. What really scares me are the thoughts of what I might do if I get so desperate that I lose control. I lie awake sometimes asking myself what would be easier: if Niamh was dead or if I was dead.'

Finally he looked at her, seeking an acknowledgement or a response. She got the impression she was supposed to be shocked. Instead it was a weight off her shoulders to know that Calum felt the same way she did.

'Part of me knows I would miss her if she was gone from my life,' he said. 'But not as much as I miss being myself.'

Sylvie knew she would miss Niamh too. But she could live with missing easier than she could live like this.

2018

Celia – Marion

When Celia looks back at the catastrophe that took place here, she regards the true watershed moment as the arrival of the police. Yes, the panic and growing desperation of the night before remains horribly vivid on the rare occasions she opens a crack in the door behind which that memory stays locked. But that is the memory of something that by its very nature is blurred and indistinct: a haze of emotions, a time of flux and turmoil, with everything in the balance. It was a time when nothing had yet truly changed for sure, and thus a time of not knowing what to feel.

The arrival of the police, approaching with the dawn, was when it all became irrevocably real, bringing home that the worst had indeed happened. It no longer felt like a situation within and among themselves, a crisis that could somehow be resolved or contained. When the authorities became involved, she understood that it was all out of their hands: that Niamh was out of their hands and would never be back in them.

That was the beginning of the end for the family as she knew it.

Behold, children are a heritage from the Lord, the fruit of the womb a reward. Like arrows in the hand of a warrior are the children of one's youth.

That is how Psalm 127 puts it.

Generations that gathered together so often, so close, so intertwined. Only after that morning did what was once whole begin to fracture.

That was when suspicion crept in. When poison seeped in.

And God forgive her for saying it, but that poison ultimately derived from her own daughter: not just in terms of what happened

147

to Niamh, but Niamh's very existence. If Sylvie hadn't got herself pregnant, things in the family would have all gone so much better. For sure, there would have been ups and downs, people moving on with their lives, but there would still be closeness and love.

It is the most painful thing for a mother to accept that there is something corrosive and destructive about your own offspring.

Sylvie is over on the far side of the pool right now, sitting apart from everybody as usual. It is almost eleven. They are supposed to be gathering and heading out to this ceremony for Max in about five minutes, yet she is still on the bloody phone. She has shown up here physically but it is as though she is making a point by barely engaging with anybody, and when she does it's unpleasant, like that business with the Canadian nanny.

Celia hadn't specified a day for the ceremony and had contemplated delaying because she suspects Sylvie will head home again as soon as she feels her obligations are discharged, having paid the minimum dues. Unfortunately, Celia can't afford the delay because Lia is only able to come out for three nights. And besides, what would be the point of making Sylvie tarry if she was acting like she didn't want to be here?

This morning's is to be a simple ritual. They are going to walk along the path to the bench at the tip of the headland. Max always loved the view from there. They will each say a few words and then scatter the ashes, letting the wind take them out to sea. It is the final of three ceremonies to mark Max's passing, preceded by the funeral service everyone but Sylvie had attended, and the secret one that Sylvie had somehow found out about.

Celia had got her parish priest to carry out the Catholic funeral rite over Max's coffin the night before the official service at the crematorium, as Max was an atheist and it was against his express wishes. The others would not have understood, but ironically Max would.

She used to banter with him that she would do precisely this if he died first.

'It would be kind of a side bet on Pascal's Wager. And by your own argument, you won't be caring at that stage.'

148

'A fair point,' he had conceded, though admittedly he thought she was joking.

It was an aspect of the unique harmony of their relationship that he could be outspoken without making Celia feel her faith was being got at, and she never asked him to hold back in his writings and lectures on account of her sensitivities. Reciprocally, he allowed her to raise the children in her faith without complaint and without undermining Church teaching. He knew it meant more to her that they should be brought up Catholics than it meant to him that they shouldn't. That is why she would always smile when she heard him described as a 'militant atheist'. And equally, when she encountered genuinely militant atheists, she would wonder why they couldn't be more like Max: respectful and tolerant while getting their point across, yet waspish and merciless when confronting cant and hypocrisy.

He would have been so happy to see the holiday they were having now: four generations of the Temple family gathered once again at the villas, the way it should always have been.

Celia's not naive. She knows that families grow and spread, that they all have their own lives, but in the past – before it happened – they were happiest during those times when they all came together in this special place. She wants everybody to remember this, and to see that it can be that way again. It hurts that it took Max's death to make it happen, but she has come to accept that it was the only way.

Marion watches Lia fussing over her baby niece – Marion's granddaughter – and feels a glow of something whole, something healed. She has felt so much tension about everyone being here, so many potential conflicts and pitfalls that it sneaks up on her how pleasant it is to be around so many of the people she loves.

Hugh is adapting well to parenthood. She always sensed his wife Maggie would, but had her worries over Hugh's patience. He's surprised her though. She never would have imagined him so contentedly taking on solo dad duties while Maggie caught up on things back home. He seems better at compartmentalising, channelling that more fiery and uncompromising side of himself into his work. That's going well too, with him in contention for a post so prestigious she gets sick thinking about it.

Lia is doing great too, having secured a position at a major teaching hospital starting in August; though again Marion gets butterflies when she thinks about her imminent finals results. Mum visibly swells whenever she gets to talk about her granddaughter becoming a doctor. Celia is less thrilled about the fact that Lia recently came out as a lesbian, though she won't admit she's uncomfortable with it. Mum's always had that prudish streak. She talks around the subject, saying things like: 'I remember Lia sitting there playing with dollies, talking about what kind of man she would marry when she grew up. Just shows you can't predict these kinds of things.'

Marion takes a seat next to Mum, who is surveying the scene like she's taking the register, sending disapproving glances towards where Sylvie is still talking on her mobile. This is a big day for Mum. Everyone is here. She has reunited the family, geographically at least. But then, when was such unity ever anything but superficial, an illusion of a close family painted over the truth? Maybe this is as close to united as any family truly gets: everybody living at close quarters for a while: the Waltons' Fantasy, as Rory always referred to it.

Hugh emerges from the house, laughing about something as he stands next to his wee sister. Marion can still picture them both standing in the same spot as children. She can see how they've changed and how they haven't.

She thinks of the sniping and criticism she took for the way she raised them, how indulgent she was accused of being. Unavoidably, she thinks also of the guilt she has always carried. Part of it is survivor's guilt that it wasn't one of her children who died. But primarily it is guilt over what she knows and kept to herself. Despite all of it, however, she only has to look at them now to know she wouldn't change anything. Her job was to raise them and protect them, and she has succeeded. They're here and they're thriving.

Nonetheless, it is impossible to look at them in this context without seeing the other ghost at this feast, and to wonder at the life Niamh might otherwise have led.

She takes in how Mum is regarding Sylvie even now and recalls with concealed distaste the uncharitable thoughts Mum occasionally voiced about the tragedy.

'I sometimes console myself with the thought that perhaps God knew what was best for that child,' she once put it, implying that being raised by Sylvie would have been literally a fate worse than death.

She made it sound like wistful musing, but it was driven by a bitterness that was as enduring as it was sincere. Mum never forgave Sylvie for what she'd said about Dad. There was no question Max was hurt, but he had the strength to brush it off as just Sylvie being Sylvie (and Sylvie had been Sylvie turned up to eleven in the preceding years). By contrast, Mum had hung on to it, creating a retrospective narrative in which everything bad that followed had flowed inevitably from this one appalling moment.

But awkward and shameful as it was to admit, it did make a sort of sense. Bad things did keep happening around Sylvie, and when Niamh died, though they were reluctant to acknowledge this, it didn't go unnoticed how emotionally muted her response had been. Calum's too, to a certain extent (though was it sexist to expect Sylvie would feel it more?). Either way, Marion couldn't help but think there was an element of relief inside both of them. Sure, there were tears, but dear God, if it had happened to one of hers . . .

'She really doesn't care, does she?' Mum says, hearing Sylvie laugh as she chats on the phone. 'About her father, I mean.'

'She came, didn't she?' Marion responds by way of defending Sylvie, or at least defusing Mum's anger.

'She's here physically, but that's as much as you can say. Truth is she left this family a long time ago and there's no bringing her back. She won't even bear the family surname or the name we christened her. Why did she choose Ivy anyway? I've been puzzling that one for years.'

'Didn't she have a doll called Ivy when she was little?' Marion asks, a hazy memory bubbling up from a time when she was more concerned with OMD and Duran Duran.

'No, that was Slyvie,' Mum replies.

151

How could she forget. The name had derived from an early attempt by Sylvie to write her own name, the transposition roundly mocked by Mum. She was always so hard on the girl. Mum would insist she was merely 'holding her youngest to a high standard' (itself a dig at her older siblings for their under-achievement), but Marion blamed this for Sylvie's attention-seeking behaviour, in particular towards Max. It escalated over the years, a confused little girl desperate for affirmation, finding herself in competition with a narcissist for her father's affections.

'No clue what the Roan part is about,' Mum goes on. 'But it's not random, you can guarantee that.'

'No,' Marion agrees. This is why Sylvie is cut out for PR. She understands that layers of meaning can be inferred from any message, some of it unintentional, and some of it encoded. 'It must mean something, to her at least.'

'Oh, it will have a hidden significance that it amuses her not to share. But the real intention is to make us wonder at the puzzle: it's another subtle way of making her the focus. Sylvie always finds a way to put herself at the centre of the drama. There was the vegetarianism, the drinking, the over-eating, the under-eating.'

Mum sighs, anger gathering on her brow. When she speaks again, her voice is quieter.

'Then of course there was . . . *that.*'

2018

Celia

She places the urn on the edge of the cliff and bends down, delicately removing the lid. They all stand around for a moment, not quite sure what to do. It had been a solemn procession up here, passing in silence. The sun is already strong, the day unseasonably hot for early June. There is a light breeze offering some relief from the heat, but she knows they won't want to be out here for long.

Celia grabs a handful of the ash and casts it over the cliff, where the wind takes it. A dark cloud, dissipating into nothing: the essence of a great man rendered to dust, then gone completely.

She'd imagined she would have something profound to say at this moment. She had given it plenty of thought, but nothing worthy had come. It all seemed trite and inadequate. No words could capture everything he meant to her, and now that she is here, it feels wrong to even try.

'I'll miss you,' she says, but even that is lost as the back of her throat constricts and the tears begin to fall.

She feels Rory's arm around her shoulder, comforting her. Marion's too on the other side. It means a lot.

They all grab a handful in turn: Marion, Ken, Rory, Lia and Hugh, who manages the task with Emily cradled in his other arm. They each find something to say, something simple.

'Farewell, Dad.'

'Love you, Grandad.'

'Goodbye, Max.'

'Rest in peace.'

Several eyes fall upon Sylvie as she has not yet approached the urn. Once again, she manipulates the focus, makes it about her.

When finally she crouches by the cliff-edge, there are tears in her eyes.

Celia experiences mixed feelings at this display of sorrow. She is instinctively moved to see her daughter weep, but can't help but think it is too little, too late.

Sylvie says nothing as she casts a handful to the wind, then steps back from the edge, her eyes following the dust out to sea.

Celia lifts the urn once more and is about to empty the rest of the ash, but as she grips it she changes her mind. She puts the lid back on and decides to keep what remains.

There is an air of relief, the atmosphere lighter as they walk back down the path towards the villas.

'Hey, I saw that three of Dad's books are in the *Sunday Times* top ten after last week's sales,' Rory tells her, cheer in his voice but a sad smile upon his face.

'That's brilliant, isn't it?' suggests Marion.

'Yeah,' says Sylvie. 'You can't beat dying as a marketing move.'

People laugh a little too hard, to convince themselves that there was only levity in her intention. Celia knows otherwise. The barb was meant to wound, and she knows who it was aimed at. Sylvie showed Celia her true face a long time ago, and once seen it could never be fully hidden again.

She had just turned sixteen. She had been difficult throughout the holiday, bristling with spite and attitude, drinking when she had been told not to, and spitting venom about 'hypocrisy' whenever any of the adults had so much as a beer or a glass of wine.

She wanted to go with Rory to this pub down in Praia Mexilhões, the closest thing the village had to a night club. The arguments had gone back and forth for days, until eventually Celia relented – against Max's wishes – mainly because it would provide an evening of respite from Sylvie.

Sylvie did not respond with good grace, however. When she emerged on to the patio after dinner, dressed to go out, she looked like a hooker. She was wearing this micro-skirt of the sort Celia heard referred to as a pussy pelmet, and a flimsy, low-cut top with no bra. It was all the more appalling because she had put on weight and was spilling out of it in most unflattering ways.

Celia saw it for what it was: a conspicuous act of provocation, but there was no option to ignore it. They couldn't let her go to a bar looking like that, especially as she was also already tipsy. They hadn't given her anything with dinner, so she must have had a bottle stashed in her bedroom. She seemed on the cusp of being out of control, sending out all kinds of reckless signals, and someone was bound to take advantage of that. She was supposed to be going with Rory, but if he took his eye off her, perhaps to talk to some girl, who knew what might happen.

'I am not having you go out dressed like that,' Max said. One of those things you swear you'll never say as a parent until you find yourself saying it. There was anger in his tone, as he had been opposed to letting her go in the first place and this was her response to being permitted.

Sylvie's reaction was to pull her arms tight so that her cleavage was even more prominent, then to pirouette, the rise of her skirt revealing thong panties Celia had no idea she owned.

'What, am I not to your taste?' she asked Max.

It was horrible, truly horrible. She was baiting her father with a vulgar display of her own burgeoning sexuality, one of the hardest things for any parent to deal with in their daughter at the best of times. It made Celia uncomfortable in too many ways to describe. The sole consolation was that only Marion was present. Rory was still getting changed to go out inside the other villa, and Ken was putting the kids to bed.

'You're making a fool of yourself,' Celia told her, naively thinking the fear of ridicule would have some currency.

'Dad can't handle how sexy I look,' she said. She smiled as she spoke, but there was something bitter running through every word.

'You don't look sexy,' Celia replied. 'You look like a thirteen-year-old boy's idea of a prostitute. You really ought to aim a little higher.'

'Well, maybe I should have dressed up like Kurlia from *The Liberators*,' she said, addressing Celia with mock sincerity. 'Or get my kit off altogether, like you did in that horror film. It's the only reason anybody ever remembers you, isn't it? What you wore and what you didn't wear. At least if I flash my tits in a bar tonight,

155

it won't be something my children have to see twenty years from now.'

Celia felt blindsided by this, assailed in many ways at once. She fought to contain tears and anger, reeling at how hurtful her daughter could be.

'It was a different time, and I was a very different person,' she had replied. 'We all do stupid things when we're young, regrettable things that have greater consequences than we could possibly envisage. Perhaps you should be heedful of that. I was naive and full of myself once too, you know, but eventually I learned the meaning of self-respect, and it's about time you did too.'

'Self-respect?' Sylvie scoffed. 'You mean turning into a frigid old god-botherer steeped in her own self-righteousness? I don't know, Mum, maybe if you put on the old Kurlia costume and gave your husband a treat now and again, he wouldn't be fucking me.'

2018

Celia

The sun is high in the sky and the breeze has dropped. The heat feels oppressive when there is no shelter to be had from it: an angry ball of fire indifferent to those caught in its rays. That's what Sylvie was back then.

Celia recalls the momentary look of fear upon Sylvie's face, as though briefly afraid of the consequences of what she had just said. Then a spiteful determination came down again and masked it.

'It's true. He's been at it for years.'

It was as though the world stopped for a moment, and she felt like it would never be the same when it started turning again. Even now she can vividly recall the hurt, her surroundings swimming in her vision. And in the midst of it all, some rational, pragmatic kernel of herself trying to hold the centre, again taking solace from the fact that only Marion had been witness to this.

She remembers how Max moved to comfort her, even though he was the one who had suffered the most vicious wound. Perhaps it was his act of acknowledging the ways in which he had brought it upon himself by indulging her over the years, encouraging the worst of her behaviour.

'Good God, Sylvie, look what you're doing to your mother,' he had said. His voice was remarkably calm and restrained, but Celia could recognise the boiling anger beneath it. 'Is that what you want? Is your temper worth this? I don't know what's got into you tonight, apart from a whole load of vodka, but I'm going to do you the enormous favour of pretending the last few minutes didn't happen. You take that back and we will all erase it from our collective memories.'

She stormed off, of course, because when did Sylvie ever take something back? When did Sylvie ever own up to having done anything wrong? That is why all those companies are lining up to retain her talents: she is a genius at avoiding the admission of culpability.

Something changed after that. It was a transgression they couldn't get past, a line that was crossed, and Sylvie knew it. Celia found it hard to forgive, and Sylvie responded to that too.

Max forgave her, but that only made it worse. She was never contrite. Forgiveness can set you free, but when there is no contrition there can be no change.

That was why Celia sometimes thought Sylvie got pregnant just to hurt her and Max. They were the two people who had given so much to equip her to succeed and who would do anything to give her a future, yet she found a way to sabotage that – perhaps literally.

When they all had it out regarding the pregnancy – a memorably ugly afternoon – the distraught Calum swore he had always used condoms (like that made it okay he was having sex with their sixteen-year-old daughter). He admitted one might have split. Looking back, Celia wouldn't put it past Sylvie to have deliberately damaged the thing. She knew now how ruthless her youngest could be in the service of getting what she wanted, or what she thought she wanted: headstrong in pursuit of folly, and heedless of who she was hurting.

As they stride back down the slope, Celia wonders again what Sylvie thought about as she cast those ashes. Was she weeping for the girl she once was, for the memory of how special and important Max always made her feel? Or were her tears in regret that she had been too proud to apologise or to ask for his forgiveness?

Celia is painfully aware that the past few years had brought forth first a trickle and then a torrent of horrific revelations. Women who had stayed silent for so long because they feared they would not be believed. Victims who feared the power and the vengeance of those they accused, and the forces ranged to protect them.

The MeToo movement had chimed at the very heart of her. Having been an actress, she remembers all too clearly what it was like: having to sell yourself on the basis of your looks as much as your ability, and consequently being treated like a whore. There had been lucky escapes, and there had been occasions when she wasn't so lucky, convincing herself afterwards that it had been something else, something consensual or something she had precipitated through her own conduct. She's read that victims blame themselves because it at least gives them a sense of control.

The message of these awful revelations is one she understands: that we have to be prepared to believe unthinkable things, prepared to believe the victims, no matter who they accuse. But though it is politically uncomfortable to say it, the inconvenient truth is that there is a corollary to this, which is that it is therefore all the more unforgivable to claim you are a victim when you are not, for not only is the false accusation a despicable act, but it is also a grievous insult to all those who have truly suffered.

That is why she alone has never been able to let it go, and why she has been haunted by the further ramifications. Because if Sylvie could lie about something as serious and evil as that, it begs the question of what other lies she has told.

What other deeds she might be capable of.

They are almost at the villas now, approaching the section of the barrier where the wire mesh had been installed. She notices Sylvie briefly slow and cast a glance down at the spot where she had lost Niamh.

Celia had lost a daughter long before that.

She can see now that there was never going to be any tearful reconciliation on this holiday. But maybe she can reconcile herself to the fact that Sylvie is gone: that she has become this Ivy Roan person and that Ivy Roan will no longer be a part of the Temple family.

Celia could live with that. She can appreciate the riches she has in the others who are now gathered about her, here in this beloved place. She has lost Max, but for the first time in so many, many years, she has found peace. What had been rent asunder is now once more whole. Everything that had begun to fracture in the dawn of that horrible morning is finally healed.

They cut through the gap in the hedge and proceed towards the pool, Ken and Marion leading the way. They are holding hands, which prompts a pang of she knows not quite what. Wistfulness? No, more like resentment. It is something she and Max will never do again.

Then they stop still in front of her, and Celia clutches a hand to her chest as she sees why.

A spectre. An echo.

There is a police car parked in the drive, almost exactly the same spot as sixteen years ago. But this time she can see no officers. Instead it is the young Canadian girl, Amanda, who is walking towards them across the grass, the baby Arron clutched in her arms and a numb, stunned look on her face.

'It's Vince,' she says. 'He's dead.'

PART TWO

Proportionality bias is the instinctive notion that a large outcome must have had a large cause. It is why we find it hard to accept that a princess can simply die in a car crash or that a lone sniper can take down a president. In a world that seems frighteningly chaotic, we crave a sense of order, and paradoxically we would rather believe malevolent forces are exerting control than accept that no one is. It's why the boys in *Lord of the Flies* dreamt up The Beast.

Max Temple

2002

Vince

The early morning light seemed cruel, its brightness brashly invasive and the vivid colours it painted utterly inappropriate. Vince felt like it should be a day for rain and low skies, for weather to match the mood, but maybe they were getting what they deserved: the sun acting as a spotlight for an interrogation, telling them all there would be no hiding place.

Apart from the sight of the police car, there was no physical indication of how much had just changed, of what turmoil was going on inside each of these three villas. It was a beautiful morning, but it was going to be a horrible day.

He and Laurie sat a few feet from each other at the dining table. He had a mug of coffee in his hands. She was nursing a glass of clear fluid. He hoped it was water. He hadn't seen her pour it but was aware there was a bottle of vodka sitting on the sideboard behind her. Vince had been pleased to note that she had eased off her consumption in recent days, but he feared these circumstances might send her over the edge again. And by 'these circumstances', he didn't just mean what had happened to Niamh. He meant what had happened before that too: circumstances that were entirely his fault.

That said, she had been hitting it hard last night way before she saw what she saw. That litre bottle was full yesterday, and now there was only a quarter of it left. What he really feared was the cops coming here and smelling it off her before they were across the threshold. They had been called out to the villas over an apparent accident, but there was no question that everyone would be under suspicion regarding how their conduct might have contributed to the situation. A kid goes missing while everybody's getting pissed and, in some cases, getting . . . No, it didn't look good.

Vince could see one of the police officers standing just inside the patio doors of the villa opposite, asking questions of the drained and dazed individuals inside. He wondered what lies the Temples would tell, and what reasons they each had for telling them.

He felt worn-out, his insides all churned up and his piercing headache sharpened by every photon of the sun. It wasn't like the kind of hangover you woke up with, blearily coming around from oblivion several hours after a party had finished. These were the symptoms you only felt when something awful brought the revelry to a sudden close, and what followed was not sleep but tension and dread. He had experienced the temporary sobering effect of fear and panic as everyone rushed around in growing desperation, then the adrenalin and the alcohol had soured inside him, their effects no longer useful but slow to abate.

Feeling sober when you were still drunk was not good for your judgement. Thus it was taking Vince a while to sort through his recollections, as it was hard to piece together a clear picture without knowing for sure which recollections to trust.

He was wary of one factor in particular skewing the image, which was that something gut-wrenching had already happened before it was discovered the baby was missing. It was like a foreshadowing of what everyone was about to feel: a sudden jolt yanking him back from hedonistic abandon.

Laurie had seen him in the midst of what he was doing. No room for nuanced interpretation or an impassioned plea of 'it's not what it looks like'. The look had lasted barely a second, and she had walked on without saying anything, but it was irreversible. That moment of eye contact had given him a glimpse of consequences that had not yet arrived but which were now inevitable.

Only afterwards did he realise the significance of what *he* had seen in that moment too.

Vince stared across the pool upon a scene of incongruous tranquillity. He could see Calum sitting outside at the big table, Rory leaning against the wall alongside him. Vince wondered what must be going through the kid's mind. Poor bastard was still just a teenager. He had been struggling to accept the reality of being a father, but he would surely trade it in a heartbeat for the reality of having just lost his daughter. All those thoughts of frustration and ambivalence would have vanished, and too late he was understanding the value of what he once had.

Rory's girlfriend Svetlana was sitting on the edge of a lounger by the pool, sipping from a bottle of water. Even now she still looked like she was in a perfume ad, except she wasn't blankly gazing into nothingness: she was staring fixedly out to sea.

Inside, through the open patio doors, he could see Celia doubled over on the couch, shaking with sobs. Max was sitting with an arm around her, but she looked lost in a private world of misery. Vince wondered if guilt was making it worse: torturing herself with thoughts that this might not have happened if she hadn't been doing something she wasn't supposed to. The type of irrational accusation you make of yourself when you've otherwise gone unpunished for a different sin.

Everybody looked numb and beaten. There had been no rest, only hours of harrowing helplessness followed by the dawning acceptance that the situation was as bad as it appeared.

Only the children had slept: Marion's two. They hadn't emerged from their rooms throughout the whole horrible process, from Sylvie first raising the alarm, through the frantic search, to the harrowing realisation that the worst had indeed come to pass. He had heard it said of some kids that they could sleep through an earthquake. Certainly the earth had shaken beneath Hughie and Lia. Their world had been transformed and they had no warning of what they would be waking up to. It would make no sense. Baby Niamh was alive when they went to sleep, and there was a party going on. Everybody had been happy, in their eyes at least.

Vince remembered his own incomprehension at his dad's gloominess and temper, his frustrating inability to predict what would set him off. At least these two would have an explanation they could relate to for why the grown-ups were sad and distant, and in time it would improve. Growing up, he never had a clue what had made his father so angry on any given day. But the hardest part was that there was never anything he could do to make him happy. Vince knew that if you were working all the time, you had a bit more insurance against being accused of uselessness. But that didn't mean you were doing the work right.

Vince often found himself up at this hour because Laurie complained if she found him busy on the laptop, so it was a chance to get some work done before she rose. They were on different schedules here as much as at home. He used to kid himself that they would lie in and have sex when they came over here, but he'd long since given that up as a fantasy.

At such times he could feel like he had the whole complex to himself. The only other people up this early were kids, and the older ones were usually inside watching TV. At most he might see whichever parent was tasked with the first shift of looking after the baby.

This time yesterday, he had seen Sylvie taking Niamh for a carefully escorted walk around the garden, glazed-eyed with boredom and fatigue yet permanently vigilant, her eyes never straying from her charge. Her gloomy and exhausted expression had been occasionally punctuated by momentary panic if the kid looked like she might do something dangerous, and occasionally by a warm smile if she did something cute. She had smiled in a way that suggested the child had surprised her, and that her reaction surprised herself.

Sylvie had trailed her around the pool a couple of times, trying to keep her amused while everyone else slept. Then Niamh had led her in the direction of the clifftop path. She liked going there to throw stones and see the splash.

That was a place none of them would ever look at the same again.

It was Marion who found the blanket, snagged on one of the wooden crossbeams between the path and the drop. She came into the house clutching it, looking hollowed out. Her hands had shaken as she stood and held it out to Sylvie, saying nothing, her voice choked. It was as though she was inviting everyone to infer the significance so that she wouldn't have to articulate it herself. But she was never going to be spared that, because nobody wanted to give voice to what they truly feared, as if that in itself would somehow make it manifest.

'Where did you find it?' Sylvie had asked.

Because the discarded blanket on its own didn't mean anything definite. But when Marion answered, it felt like the end of hope.

When Sylvie discovered the baby was missing, the first place everyone rushed to had been the swimming pool. It was as though they had forgotten there was a vastly greater and more dangerous body of water only yards away. Now that Marion had reminded them of it, their conclusions were inescapable. Until then, there had remained the possibility that at any second Niamh might crawl out from an overlooked hiding place within one of the villas, or emerge from somewhere unexpected in the garden. That was the moment when all those possibilities ended. That was when they knew they had to call the authorities.

There was a coastguard boat out there right then, patrolling back and forth. There would be officers down at the beach and others searching inlets along the coast, but none of them was expecting to find anything other than a tiny body. Everybody knew this was over bar the questions and the blame.

He glanced at his wife. She noticed and looked back, holding his gaze. They had been sitting there for close on an hour, neither of them uttering a single word, but they both knew that had to change, and soon.

Vince finished his coffee and put the mug firmly down on the table like he was calling a meeting to order.

'So, before the police come knocking,' he said, 'do you want to talk about what we saw?'

2018

Ivy

Ivy retreats to her room, the same blank-walled chamber she has always stayed in when she comes here. She knows nobody will intrude upon her once the door is closed, making it technically a place of privacy, but not of sanctity. A haven no longer inviolate can never be a haven again, but it's all she's got, and she needs time and space to process everything that has unfolded in the past hour.

Creepy Vince RIP. Dead in his office, appropriately enough. He had eventually worked himself into that early grave everyone else had picked out for him.

His absence had felt conspicuous, but maybe that was just her. She was used to feeling his gaze upon her whenever she was here. She had always wondered how much he knew, what he might have seen. Now she will never know for sure, but she isn't ready to think about him, not while there is still the residue of her father's ashes upon her fingers.

She goes to her en suite and turns on the tap to wash. She places her hands beneath the stream and sees the grey dust streak the basin before vanishing, diluted and carried down the drain. That is when it truly hits her that he is gone. That is when the tears start, and a tiny little trickle of memory becomes a deluge.

She thinks of the man her family is mourning, and of the man the wider world has lost. But her tears are over memories of a man only she truly knew. The man for whom she would have done anything. The man she had worshipped.

The man who first raped her when she turned sixteen.

It was not a watershed moment either: by that stage it was almost a perverse rite of passage, a station on a journey that began when she was still twelve. She thought for a long time that it began when it did because she had reached puberty, but then she realised that it coincided with both Rory and Marion leaving home to go to uni. Marion stayed at home until her final year, but Rory flew the coop as soon as he could, and once they were out of the house, there were two fewer people around who might notice.

She sometimes wondered if it had happened to Marion too: maybe that was why he waited until she had left home, as she would know his habits. But then she realised that if it had happened to Marion, she would have done something to protect Sylvie. At the very least, she would have spoken up when she found out about Sylvie's accusation. Instead, she was as incredulous as Mum.

It figures. Dad never seemed to be very interested in Marion.

That was the man whose ashes she enjoyed casting to the wind and washing down the drain. An eminent psychologist who built a career exploring the mechanics of conspiracy theories, but whose true mastery lay in his command of gaslighting. It was from him that she learned just how big a lie you can sell the world.

Conspiracy theorists are first and foremost engaged in trying to convince themselves, willing dupes in the act of their own deception. It's not hard to sell a lie to people who are desperate to buy it. Gaslighting is thus a far trickier art to master, but Max Temple was a virtuoso.

Conspiracy theories always need an official version from which to diverge, but with gaslighting, there can be no official version. When it came to how Sylvie was abused, there was no consistent narrative, no consistent version of anything, because an official version would give her something to anchor herself to, or something to react against. Max disoriented her so completely that she didn't know what to believe or who to trust, but just as importantly, nor did she know what to disbelieve or who to distrust. She had no certainty, no conviction about anything, and she became utterly reliant upon Max himself because his version was the only point of reference she had.

She was constantly trying to make sense of it, deconstruct it; deduce how it had changed from the previous account, calculate how it diverged from what she thought she knew. She didn't even have a consistent lie to reject or fantasy to cling to. Reality was permanently in flux and the past was constantly being rewritten.

It took a year for her to say anything to him, because it felt like it was a new normal before she was really sure what was going on. There was never a place to make her stand, no line to be drawn in the sand when the sands were permanently shifting.

Whispers in the dark. A fearful heart, beating so fast at her first attempt to broach it.

'Dad, I don't think we should be doing . . . you know . . . those things any more.'

'Doing what things?'

'You know. Things we sometimes do.'

'I don't know what you're talking about.'

'Touching me. Me touching you.'

'Oh dear, Sylvie. This is a father's great fear, but in a way I'm glad you brought this up. It is a documented phenomenon among pubescent girls, you know: girls your age and older. They can sometimes blur the lines between fantasy and reality or dream and reality, things that they imagined happening as they lay in bed. Particularly sexual things because they are at that sensitive and curious stage in their development.

'It's where the phenomenon of the poltergeist comes from. It is always associated with teenage girls, a means of explaining away strange behaviour that derives from this blurring of imagination and reality. Sometimes the fantasies are things they are afraid of, and sometimes they are things that they deeply want to happen.'

She was told this by a voice of compounded authority: that of a professor of psychology and the author of textbooks on the subject, but also the father to whom she looked for wisdom, advice and guidance on every confusing thing she encountered. He used her own defence mechanisms against her: the disassociation that took her out of the moment during the abuse, and the denial that tried to rewrite the past for her own protection. He knew it was comforting to believe it hadn't really happened, and he played upon that in order to keep her confused as to what was real.

172

But even that was not the official version, because there could be no consistent truth. It is confusing even now to remember what happened when and in what order. She can't easily construct a narrative of it, and that was his intention. Everything was so gradual, so fluid. She could actually tell herself it hadn't happened, it had been a dream or a fantasy, at the same time as telling herself she was the one who had instigated it and thus it was her fault.

'I wish you hadn't made me do that. You're so persuasive and you take advantage of my weakness. You're such a special girl that I always want to give you what you ask for and to please you in whichever way you desire. But a father shouldn't spoil his daughter.'

He made her believe it was her idea, something she wanted. And the really difficult part to deal with, even now, is that sometimes that felt true. She enjoyed the physicality, the intimacy of having this exclusive access and closeness with her father. She craved his attention and his approval. But there was something much harder to deal with: a source of confusion, guilt and shame throughout most of her life. How could she enjoy it if she didn't want it?

It took years for her to understand that her body did what it was designed to, and that there were processes and responses in play over which she had no control.

He knew that too. He used it all. And of course, it had to be their secret.

'We mustn't let anyone else find out. They won't understand. Your mother would be very hurt by it. She would be very angry with both of us.'

He was wasting his breath, as there were so many fears preventing this: fear of how they might react; fear of her father finding out she had told; and greatest of all, the fear of not being believed. Consequently she'd have found it impossible to tell anybody, especially her mother. But how she wished, how she so deeply wished that her mother would find out independently, would read the signs and come to her rescue.

That was how she learned that there is something worse than not being believed.

Sylvie always put her bedsheets in the basket on the morning after. She felt compelled to wash it all away, that was part of it, but it was a coded message. She could smell the semen off them, so surely her mother could too. She wanted her to start asking questions. That would have been the easiest way for it to come to light: the investigative impulse would come from her mum, who would then act to protect her daughter.

But nothing happened.

In an attempt to force the issue, one day she stood over her mother as she loaded the washing machine. She said nothing, though she wanted to scream the truth. Her mum became aware of her presence as she handled the sticky sheet. Their eyes met.

To this day, she can still picture the expression of disgust and anger, all of it directed at her. She understood the true bitterness in her mother's rebukes about her showing off, grasping for her father's attention.

'Acting coquettish.'

She was fourteen.

What she failed to anticipate was that her mum *did* read the signs but refused to accept the reality of what she was confronted with.

It was the beginning of this weird duality whereby Celia pretended it wasn't happening, while simultaneously blaming Sylvie for the fact that it was.

The feeling of betrayal was probably the hardest thing of all, prompting her to keep asking herself: 'What was so awful about me that my mother wouldn't save me?'

Celia's entire world was constructed around her myth of being the perfect mother to a perfect family. Ivy has read about it since and discovered it to be textbook behaviour of the narcissistic parent. Anything that threatens to challenge the myth will be met with a combination of denial and hostility.

Nonetheless, Sylvie saw a glimmer of hope even in her being ignored: a way she might discourage Max.

'I think we might have to leave off,' she told him. 'I'm worried Mum is becoming suspicious. She was putting a washing on today and I'm sure she noticed something on the bedsheets.'

It didn't work. He didn't leave off, and he had a warning for her, one she couldn't ignore.

'You need to be more discreet, and if your mother was ever to ask, you mustn't tell her anything. If she got really angry, she might overreact and go to the police. She wouldn't realise the consequences of what she was setting in motion. The whole family would be ripped apart, can you imagine? Mum's been on TV and in films, she's got a career as a columnist, so the media would be all over it. All over her, all over me, all over you. Marion, Rory, everybody, the whole family's lives would be ruined, and for what? Just because people wouldn't understand these little moments we have, how special our relationship is.'

This was the part people didn't understand when they wondered why abusers didn't tell anyone. It was always easy from the cheap seats. They didn't get what it looked like from the inside: that years later, it remained impossible to speak out because you were still looking at your abuser and your family from the perspective of a child.

It wasn't like she didn't try to send out signals. That's what the drinking was about; that and a search for oblivion to blot everything out. She hoped that somebody would put the pieces together, ask a few questions. For a time, she ate next to nothing, an act of self-destruction born partly out of self-loathing and partly in the hope that people would wonder why.

When a friend of her mum enquired as to her looking thin and pale, she remembers Celia remarking that she was probably starving herself for some boy. And when Marion mentioned it, Mum told her Sylvie must have been reading about anorexia.

'It's just the latest attention-seeking gambit.'

She was right about that much. It was attention-seeking like a distress flare is attention-seeking.

She went from starving herself to over-eating. Her mother was slim, whereas Marion was always a little heavier. Maybe Sylvie being skinny was why he went to her and not her older sister. She reasoned that maybe if she became fat, he wouldn't want her any more. That didn't work either, though. She would say this much for Max: whatever he saw in her was more than skin deep.

And all the while, nobody on the outside noticed anything was wrong.

'The enemy counted on the disbelief of the world,' wrote Elie Wiesel, a survivor of the Holocaust. The myth of the perfect family, cemented weekly in Celia's columns, presented a façade nobody was minded to look behind. For who was going to make such an accusation against Max Temple, a respected academic increasingly famous for debunking outlandish claims?

Ivy rinses her face, washing away the tears, then pats herself dry with a towel. She looks in the mirror, the same one in which she had to face herself on so many mornings after. Holidays were always particularly bad. She is not that person any more, not that helpless little girl.

It's time to get back to work. That's an arena where she's not helpless but someone to be feared. Poison Ivy? You better fucking believe it.

She lifts her phone to resume what she was discussing with Jamie before she got hauled away to take part in the ceremony. It was regarding the fire at the DKG logistics warehouse, and their whistle-blower problem.

'I chased up on a few things while you were busy,' Jamie reports. 'There's been developments on a number of fronts, but I don't think you're going to like any of them.'

'Try me.'

'OK. DKG have confirmed that they do have an email from Jane Astley regarding the inadequacy of their safety arrangements, and there is documentation of the procedures that were in place at the time. It all confirms her story.'

'It's not a problem. DKG can destroy all surviving documentation and delete the emails from their server. We can say the hard copies were lost in a move between offices, and that there was a massive purge of old data or a catastrophic server failure.'

'Yeah, but that doesn't change the problem: Astley has copies.'

'She has nothing if we wipe the paper trail. We say they're forgeries, mocked up by an attention-seeker with a grudge. She can't prove they're genuine without DKG's originals to compare. What else?'

Jamie pauses a moment, digesting her comments. She can tell he's in Jiminy Cricket mode.

'It's Liam Sneddon.'

Sneddon was a DKG employee who snapped a load of pictures on his phone before the scene was sealed off. Nothing showing the victims, as that wouldn't have been a problem: you can't show burnt corpses on the front page of a newspaper. When there is a deadly fire, at most there will be images of a smouldering building, and headshots of the people who died. Nothing to convey the true horror of the blaze.

That was why what Sneddon had captured was potentially so much worse. The part of the depot that got the worst of it had been full of toys. Ivy has seen these images: Elsa, Moana, Igglepiggle, Makka Pakka, all blackened, twisted, melted, lying on the wet ground like the corpses of little children. Ivy understands this stuff instinctively: there was something horrific about them that conveyed the ferocity of what the fire had wrought. They would become iconic, disastrously so. She had bought the pictures from Sneddon herself so that the purchase didn't go through the company books and thus wasn't ultimately traceable to DKG. She also bought the phone they were taken on, and Sneddon affirmed that there were no back-ups in a highly binding non-disclosure agreement.

'What about him?' she asks Jamie.

'He lied. He did keep back-ups. And he's having a crisis of conscience.'

'Is he trying to squeeze me for more?'

'The opposite. Now that the whistle-blower story is gaining traction, he wants to tear up the agreement and give the money back. The problem is that even if we don't agree, he can just leak the pictures anyway.'

'No he can't, and no he won't. Get the lawyers to scare the shit out of him. Make sure he understands that if these images ever see the light of day, he won't just forfeit his payment, I will bankrupt him. I'll take his fucking house. Let's see how much conscience he has when he's faced with ending up on the street and owing us for the rest of his days.'

'Understood.'

'Good. What else?'

'The investigator has got back with his work-up on Jane Astley. It's less than helpful.'

'How so?'

'It turns out she had a miscarriage just prior to when she raised her concerns, most probably resultant of domestic abuse by a violent ex-partner. It's just going to make her more sympathetic, and anyone going after her will look really bad.'

Ivy says nothing, weighing up what he just told her, and drawing very different conclusions. She can tell he's holding something back, too.

'Is that it?'

He sighs.

'No. The investigator uncovered a conviction for soliciting, but it was years before she worked at DKG.'

Oh, Jamie, she thinks. He really isn't going to last in this game. He was hoping the revelation about Astley's miscarriage would seem discouraging enough that Ivy wouldn't ask for the rest of the report. He really doesn't understand. It wasn't bad at all. It was perfect. The fact that she had also been a whore was just the icing on the cake.

Reputation laundering is not always about making an individual or an institution look good. Sometimes it's about making someone else look very bad. Nobody understands that better than her.

Her strategy is to go after Astley's character and credibility so that DKG can say this so-called whistle blower isn't a reliable source. They can push the line that nobody believed her back then because she had a track record for crying wolf. She was flaky, attention-seeking. She was emotionally damaged at the time, a hormonal wreck who wasn't thinking straight and needed counselling. If they ever really existed, her safety warnings may have been overlooked because they were interpreted as another cry for help.

Jamie is wrong about how sympathetic people are. It doesn't work the way he'd like to believe. Once somebody is outed as a victim, sure, people might feel sorry for her; but they also write her off as damaged, and they don't feel so concerned about all the subsequent bad stuff that might happen to her.

It is an unconscionable thing to do, Ivy is under no illusions about that, but it will deliver results. She knows what it is to destroy an innocent life in order to get what you want, and she also knows there's no truth so harsh that it can't be covered up if you're ruthless enough.

2018

Amanda

Arron looks all the tinier lying on the changing mat, his Babygro stripped so I can change his diaper. I've wiped him down and he is swinging his little legs joyfully back and forth, like he's just discovered they can do this. He seems as amused by this as he is by the gurgling noise he is making, his world full of innocent new wonders. The fragile little thing has no notion of the extent to which that world has just been altered. No idea that he will never know his father.

I guess that at least this way will be easier on him than if his dad died when he was five, or nine, or twelve. And you don't miss what you never had. I am proof of that. I grew up without a mom, and it's not like I feel I was neglected because of it. It's all about the love you get from the people who *are* there.

With that thought I glance across to poor Kirsten. She just sits there gripping her wine in one hand and thumbing her tablet with the other. She doesn't drink for ages then suddenly she'll take a big parched gulp, a striking contrast to the relished sipping I have witnessed before.

She's looking glazed but she hasn't cried, which I find kinda weird. She hasn't spoken since the cops left. Nice of them to send actual human beings out to break the news, I think. Better than just learning from a phone call. I wonder if that's a Portuguese or a European thing.

I slip a fresh diaper under Arron and fasten it. I'm getting the hang of this much, at least. Too bad everything else seems to be descending into chaos. I've been fighting off tears, not wanting Kirsten to see me cry because my sorrow wouldn't be for her or for

Vince, but myself. I am freaked out and a little scared. I'd only known him a few days, and in fact spent less time with him than with Kirsten, but Vince is the person who arranged for me to come to Europe.

I'm feeling every mile of the distance from home. Having finished high school and got into college, I had notions that I was on the cusp of being an adult, but right now I feel like a lost little girl somebody else should be taking care of. I'm not inclined to be quite so judgy towards Sylvie Temple either. The girl was two years younger than me when she became a mom. I'm starting to get how scared and trapped she must have felt.

I think of this time last week, when a contrary opinion by some MRA YouTuber felt like the most difficult thing I had to deal with in this world. But then, I only need to look across to the other family here to appreciate how suddenly everything you take for granted can change.

They say if you want to give God a laugh, tell him your plans. I don't believe in God, but I can see the truth of it. I had imagined a bright summer helping out a nice young family with a new baby, seeing a bit of Scotland, maybe visiting London then going touring in Europe before college starts in the fall. I don't know what's going to happen now. Will Kirsten make other arrangements, get proper help? Will I be sent straight back to Toronto? I don't even know what I want to happen right now.

I hear voices approaching outside and look up from the changing mat to see Marion and Celia walking towards the villa. Marion is carrying a big bowl of something. Looks like pasta.

I get to my feet and open the sliding doors for them.

'Don't get up,' Celia says to Kirsten. 'We just wanted to see how you were doing and to bring you something to eat.'

'Thanks,' Kirsten says, her voice hoarse and faint. 'I'm not hungry, though.'

'I know how easy it is to go without food at a time like this,' Celia replies. 'You think you don't want it, but you do need it. Trust me. My experience of this is all too fresh.'

Kirsten gives a blank nod like she's too weak to argue.

'I'll put this in the fridge,' Marion says, almost apologetically.

'Can I get you something?' I ask, like my parents trained me.

'Oh, not at all. Not at all,' she answers, looking at Kirsten rather than me. 'We're here for support, not to impose. You poor thing.'

Celia puts a hand on Kirsten's arm.

'You poor, poor thing. Do you know what happened? No, actually, it's not for me to ask. But if you feel you want to talk.'

'They found him in his office,' Kirsten replies. 'That's all they would say. Must have had a heart attack or something. They didn't give me any details.'

'And how are you holding up?'

'I don't know. I don't know what to feel. None of it seems real and they've told me stuff, but it's just words. I can't make sense of them. Vince weren't here in the villa this morning, same as he weren't here yesterday. That part's not changed. Now the police tell me he's dead back home and I'm never gonna see him again. I can't make it add up. I can't accept that he ain't gonna text me he's on the next flight and he'll be here in a few hours.'

Celia sits down beside her on the sofa.

'There is no making sense of it, believe me.'

'I just feel like it would be easier if I was there. If I could see him.'

'I was the one who found Max. He had a heart attack in his office too, upstairs in the house. I can picture it like it's still in front of me, and though I can recall everything I felt in that moment, it still makes no sense that he's not here right now, where he should be.'

I finish fastening Arron's Babygro and lift him up. Celia gazes at him, adoring and sad. I can see it in real time the moment it dawns on her what it means for the kid.

'Oh, the little soul,' she says, tearing up.

That's when Kirsten's dam breaks. She doesn't know how to feel for herself, but she can feel for her own son, and nobody's going to tell *her* that he won't miss what he never had.

She cries for a few moments, Celia comforting her and Marion on hand with tissues.

'I just don't know what I'm gonna do,' she says, sniffing. 'There's gonna be so much to sort out, so much to deal with. How am I meant to handle all this without the one person I rely on?'

'You've got Amanda here,' Celia assures her. 'And you've got us.'

'I need to get home, though. I've been looking up flights on my tablet but I'm really struggling here. The Glasgow and Edinburgh flights today have already gone and everything's full going back to Scotland tomorrow. I can't wait that long.'

'Then why don't you look at going back via Gatwick or Luton by yourself?' Celia suggests. 'Amanda can stay here with us and we can look after Arron for a couple of days, keep him out of the way while you deal with everything at home.'

I don't much like the sound of this, but the worst part is that I'm not being asked, and I know the decision is out of my hands.

Kirsten looks at Arron and casts a glance across to the other villas, making a reckoning.

'You'd be okay with that?' she asks Celia, not me.

I swallow. I feel sick.

'It would be the least we could do,' Celia replies.

I feel helpless as Kirsten packs her stuff, preparing to leave me here. She keeps offering thanks and apologies, which I am equally helpless but to brush off, saying it's nothing. I'm scared and I'm all messed up inside like no time I can ever remember, but it's nothing.

Ken carries Kirsten's suitcase out to his car and slings it in the trunk. He is driving her to Faro, as she would be in no state to drive even without the wine she's been necking. As I watch her walking to the car, I can't really believe she's going. Within minutes of making her decision, she had booked a flight to Luton leaving about four hours after she clicked Confirm. If it's on time, she will make a late connection to Glasgow and will be home by midnight.

A bunch of the Temples gather round to see Kirsten off, expressing their condolences. All except one. Okay, I haven't been with Kirsten the whole time, so maybe I missed that, but it wouldn't surprise me. Maybe that's unfair, maybe it's not. The rest of them come over as a caring bunch, and they all seem real close, but that just makes me appreciate all the more how much I'm missing my own family.

Kirsten stops halfway into the passenger seat and climbs back out again, taking Arron from me for one last hug.

'I just need a day or so,' she says, apologetically. It's not clear if she's saying this to him or to me.

I feel a tear well up as I watch the car drive away, red dust blowing in its wake.

'You okay?' Marion asks me.

'I could do with phoning my dads,' I reply.

'You go and do that. We'll look after Arron. We'll sort some dinner for you too.'

I hurry to the bathroom and give my face a wash, wanting to compose myself. It's stupid: I'm worried and need their reassurance and yet I don't want them to know I'm worried and need their reassurance.

Instinctively I try Rob first, as always telling myself that it's not because he's my biological father. It goes to voicemail. Shit. I call Sadiq. Same deal. I try them both again, twice more, still no replies. I check my watch, calculate the time in Toronto. Late morning. They'll both be at work, tied up in meetings.

A scared little voice tells me I know somebody who won't be at work, definitely won't be tied up in a meeting. I wouldn't normally entertain it. It feels ungrateful even thinking there's any role to be filled outside of what my dads provide, but I'm just feeling a little vulnerable right now. Far from home. Out of my depth. Everything falling apart. And now a baby to look after without its mother, surrounded by people I barely know.

I've had the number a long time, secretly copied from Rob's phone. I've never been able to bring myself to use it, though.

I dial. There is a long pause while it connects, then the tone pulses. I think about hanging up the longer it rings. I do the math: it's ten in California. Or is it nine?

Then she answers.

'Hello?' Her tone is wary. Her phone won't have recognised the number.

'Hey, Kara.'

'Who is this?' She sounds sleepy.

184

'It's Amanda.'

There is a pause. I'm not sure if it's because Kara is freaked to be getting this call or if she's still trying to work out who I am. Am I really going to have to say: 'You know, Rob and Sadiq's kid'?

'Oh, sure. Amanda. Is everything okay, sweetie?'

'Yeah, I just . . .'

I swallow because I don't want Kara to hear the emotion in my voice. I don't know why. I swore on a point of pride never to address her as Mom, because it would feel like an act of disloyalty to my dads. Also, an angry little part of me thinks Kara didn't earn the title.

Why *did* I call? I'm not going to pour my heart out about my situation, like I would to my dads. But we're speaking now, and really there's only one thing I want to know.

'I need to ask you something.'

'Yeah, go ahead.'

'When you were pregnant . . . no, I mean, after you had me, like, after you gave birth . . .' I swallow. 'Was there a time you thought about backing out of the deal?'

Was it hard to hand me over? Do you have any regrets? Why did you reject me? How could you give me up?

Kara sighs. Her voice is wistful but compassionate.

'Aw, sweetie. It's complicated. This is why in most cases of surrogacy the mother's identity is kept confidential from the child. To protect them both. But you know Rob and Sadiq, nothing according to the book, and little as you know me, you know I don't do things conventionally either. It was a big favour to good friends, and it's something we *should* talk about, but I don't think it's a telephone call kind of conversation, do you know what I mean?'

'Yeah,' I manage to say, though my voice is choking.

'Hey, you must have finished school for summer. Why don't you get down to California sometime before you start back?'

Tears are leaking out. I feel weirdly empty, as I have done every time I've spoken to my mother. It's like I'm holding back, like there are things I feel but I'm not allowed to admit to myself that I feel them.

I would never want to concede anything to the bigots who love going on about 'natural' families. What I feel isn't about instinct, it isn't about what I never had, but about what I know. Little Arron isn't going to miss a father he has no memory of, but when he grows up, Arron will know it wasn't Vince's choice to have no role in his life.

You don't miss what you never had, that is my mantra on this. Except that sometimes you do.

2018

Ivy

Ivy rests her arms along the edge of the pool, a satisfying ache in her limbs from having completed a hundred and fifty lengths. She is exhausted but that's what she was aiming for, so that she will sleep tonight. Exercise helps her sort through the shitstorm in her head, and it's too hot to go running. She doesn't normally clock up such a distance in the water, and she felt like quitting several times, but it's amazing what a motivator it is when the alternative is to interact with your family.

The atmosphere is muted and sombre. Nobody wants to be seen laughing and joking, cracking open Super Bocks and doing comedy dives into the swimming pool when the next-door neighbour has just snuffed it. It's a *show* of respect rather than anything driven by genuine emotion. Everybody's got to make like they cared about Vince for the sake of propriety: pretend everything wasn't weird and awkward for the past sixteen years; pretend they wouldn't have been massively relieved if he'd sold up and they never saw him again.

Which isn't to deny the news was a shock, or that it has taken some digesting. Mum is in her element because there's a crisis, while Marion is dealing with it the way she deals with everything, which is to lie low in the kitchen and cook another fucking meal. They have a guest for dinner, after all.

Awkward, especially after the words they had yesterday lunchtime.

She's pretty sure their earlier animosity is part of the reason Mum is taking Amanda under her wing. That and being able to tell herself what a warm, welcoming family the Temples are: how they are kind people who step into the breach to embrace a stranger in need.

Ivy by contrast wants to scream at the stranger to fuck off out of

187

the villa, fuck off out of the Algarve, fuck all the way off back to Canada. She wants the nosy bitch nowhere near her, and not just because another crying baby comes with the package, but because she is setting off alarms.

She has seldom felt so instinctively wary about somebody, and bitter experience has taught her to trust her instincts when it comes to these things. She's been through too much, made too many sacrifices to protect Ivy Roan from the sins of Sylvie Temple. And then the mere circumstances of being here had revealed her identity to this person: to an aspiring journalist no less.

That was why she had overreacted yesterday. The FGM stunt was harsh and she's not proud of it, but she could sense Amanda's curiosity and needed to send out a warning. The girl was probing and inquisitive, armed with the entitlement that comes from youthful moral certainty. It reminded her of herself once upon a time, which was how she knew that an effective antidote was to hit hard and early, knock the idealism out of her and let her know not to tangle.

She felt so exposed down at the clifftop when she saw Amanda crouching at the barrier, imagining what might be going through the girl's mind. Maybe she should have been ready for it. Ivy had prepared herself for being around her family in this place, but not for being around an outsider, someone new. It had sparked an unsettlingly vivid recall of how vulnerable she had felt around outsiders back then. It was like the cops could see right through her. The media too, as though they only had to look to observe the truth of everything she was hiding. That was why she closed herself off, suppressed everything she felt and wore a face of stone.

The great and bitter irony is that this insecurity and paranoia flies in the face of what she knows to be a deeper truth. Not only can people not see through you, but they don't even see what's right in front of them if they choose otherwise.

She glances towards the big table and recalls that infamous flashpoint when she was sixteen. It was a moment pivotal in Temple family lore, but not for the reasons it should have been. Not only did Celia instantly dismiss what her daughter was telling her, but another family myth was created, in which Sylvie had withdrawn the accusation. In some versions, she had apologised for it; in others she was too ashamed to ask forgiveness, all dependent upon who was talking and how they felt about it at the time.

Sylvie hadn't withdrawn it and she damn well never apologised for it, and Celia never forgave her for that. She knew the truth and yet she was angrier at Sylvie for not playing along than she was about her husband raping their youngest child.

Dad had acted all calm and dignified that day, stoic in the face of this grievous wound. He seemed more measured in his response to her accusation than he had been a few moments before when he was objecting to her attire. He hadn't liked the idea of his daughter looking like a slut if it was for someone else's consumption. He was pissed off because he had brought those things to Portugal secretly for her to wear, and to wear only for him: to dress up in so he could take them off.

He threatened to lose his temper over that, but he was cool and controlled as he spoke to her alone in the living room, once Mum had tearfully withdrawn to her bedroom and Rory had gone off to the bar in the village without her.

'You've made your mother very upset. I'm sure you'll regret what you've done and you'll feel very ashamed once you sober up.'

She remembered the room spinning, the backlog of the alcohol she had guzzled fast catching up. She felt disoriented and uncertain, but still defiant.

'Maybe,' she replied. 'But do you think she's upset that I made such an appalling accusation, or because she knows it's true?'

It was meant to unsettle him, but it didn't work.

Dad had given her a patient, confident smile.

'How can any of us be sure what is true?'

This wasn't just the usual denial and manipulation. It was a warning. And that night, he came to her room to drive the point home. Literally. She had no power, and reality was what he decreed it to be.

When they started having penetrative sex, it seemed inevitable: not some kind of watershed escalation, merely the next phase. Nonetheless, it troubled her to know she was no longer a virgin, that this part of herself had fallen to him. She had known it would but still hoped otherwise.

It first happened shortly after she turned sixteen. She doesn't know why he waited. She guessed he had a weird, twisted sense of propriety, and this way he could tell himself it wasn't statutory rape. He even pretty much convinced her that it was her own idea to move things up to the next level.

He had a vasectomy shortly before her birthday. He talked about it a lot in advance, made sure she knew. It was so she would understand that it was time to go all the way, and there would be no need to worry about birth control.

However, it turns out vasectomies aren't instantly effective. You would think someone who prided himself on being a man of science would have done the research and run the numbers. There can still be some viable sperm in the testes for a few weeks afterwards. And one strong swimmer is all it takes.

She thinks of all those obits and tribute pieces describing Max as Niamh's grandfather. They weren't wrong, but they weren't giving the full picture either. His true status was not so grand.

2018

Ivy

She hauls herself out of the pool and sits with her feet dangling in the water, heart still thumping against her chest from her sustained exertions. It's a fifteen-metre pool, so she's clocked up two and a quarter kilometres.

One strong swimmer.

Ivy has heard how other women go through a period of dread and denial when they find out they're unexpectedly pregnant, especially if they're only sixteen. But denial is often a response in people who haven't already had the worst happen to them. When she had learned she was pregnant, she knew it was for real, and forced herself to consider the paths before her.

She saw the abortion clinic, the consultations and the DNA test that would both lift her burden and prove her plight. But she also saw everything that would follow. Some of this, she knows now, was resultant of her father's gaslighting and manipulation, but some of it was not. She would be at the centre of a major scandal, her anonymity impossible given Max's academic profile. Her family would indeed fall apart, and despite there being proof of what had been done to her, Celia had made it clear she would not be seen as blameless. She would not be forgiven. She would be marked, shamed, detested, and utterly alone.

But there was a ray of hope in the midst of her fear, an opportunity deriving from her otherwise disastrous condition. That was when she took pains to rekindle her relationship with her childhood friend from along the street.

When she was a girl she used to play little games with Calum in which they were husband and wife. She used to say it was what

191

would happen when they grew up. They would get married and have a baby girl. Maybe in some hopeful part in her mind, she thought this was fate.

She knew he was a good person, a friend, someone who would do the right thing once he found out she was pregnant. But first she had to make sure he thought he was the father. She had to make everyone believe it, including and especially Max. Because if she had a baby, surely he could not come between her and her partner, the father of the child.

All this shit made some kind of sense back in the year 2000.

Poor Calum. He did nothing to deserve what happened to him. He was kind, good-hearted, caring and conscientious. But he was also seventeen years old, horny, and not going to turn down carefree teenage sex when it was being served up to him on a plate.

He was responsible, of course. Always used condoms. Even that first time when she pretended it was mutual exploration that was getting carried away. He had them in his bedroom, evidently purchased to familiarise himself ahead of the opportunity ever arising. Sylvie knew where he kept them, though. She secretly punctured several of them through the wrapper, keeping the needle hole small on the outside, but gouging away beneath the foil. Nonetheless, it took lots of attempts – lucky him – before the crucial occasion when he pulled out afterwards and his dopey come-face was replaced with one of concern.

Honest and decent, he hadn't attempted to conceal the discovery that his condom had split.

'I'm sure it'll be okay,' she lied to him.

Was it an evil thing to do? She often looks back and asks herself this, usually after a few drinks. She tells herself Calum was merely collateral damage, an unavoidable casualty of the only course of action available to her. But she cannot escape the fact that she specifically nominated him for this and did so because he was a good person. For that, she does feel guilty. Though not as guilty as she feels about what she put him through next. What she turned him into.

But how else was she to go from being a helpless and trapped little girl to being a cold-blooded bitch built to survive? It required a form of witchcraft, you could say. The blackest magic: a miraculous transformation that called for a human sacrifice. Because with every death there is the opportunity for rebirth. When Niamh died, Sylvie died too, and in that moment of execution, Ivy came into being.

Ivy. A name chosen so that she never forgot what made her the woman she is. IV: Incest Victim.

She threw away the name her parents gave her and took on one that stated what had been done to her. She knew they would speculate as to its meaning, though she also knew that even if they caught a glimpse of it, they would never admit to themselves that they had stumbled upon the truth.

And yeah, she'd read all the stuff about calling yourself a survivor, not a victim. A victim is weak, and to call yourself one is to define yourself by what has been done to you. There was no point in trying to sugar-coat it, though. She *was* at that point defined and shaped by what was done to her. Her survival mechanism was to own it, to build from it. To truly become the woman it had made her.

Women are expected to be nice. They're expected to smile, to be friendly, to make you feel comfortable, to make you feel that they like you. She can see through the absurdity and unfairness of this. It's a part that women play without realising how it has been forced upon them. Sylvie played it. Ivy doesn't. She was through having roles handed to her, whether they be handed to her by society or by family.

Which is not to say she can't be friendly or she can't be charming. It's important when dealing with clients, though it's not because she needs to show them deference and courtesy. Clients need to see that you can turn it on in order to demonstrate that you can turn it off, because there will be people they want you to intimidate on their behalf. There will be people they need to not like *you*, instead of not liking *them*.

As for her new surname, yes there was a hidden meaning there too, but nobody in her family was going to work that one out. It was for her alone to know. Ivy signified what had been done to her. Roan signified what *she* had done. Ivy was about being powerless.

Roan was about the act from which she had derived power. It was about seizing control. About being a cold bitch if that's what it took. Those four letters represented her great fuck-you to anyone who wanted to tell her how to behave, what her duties were as a daughter, a mother, what was expected of her as a woman. Roan signified slamming a door on all of it.

Ivy Roan is not merely her new name, it's her force-field, her armour. That's why she is feeling so vulnerable about the stranger in their midst, someone who had so evidently been googling the family name and therefore knew all about who she used to be.

She has largely dried off in the sun, her arms tingling from the endeavours of her lengthy swim. She walks across to her lounger and lifts a towel to her hair, glancing at her phone by instinct as she does so. She'd like to believe it's purely symptomatic of being unable to switch off from work, but there are some things she can't lie to herself about. She's still hoping to see that there's been a message from L. There isn't, but the thought of him suddenly sends a pulse of anxiety through her.

She thinks of the people close to her who chose not to see what was in front of them, no matter what she laid bare before them. Then she thinks of what she may have laid bare before L: how much she let her guard down, what she was inviting him to deduce. Subconsciously she was trusting in him, because deduction from the slimmest of evidence is pretty much his USP. It was something she never worried about while they were in a relationship, but which poses a massive vulnerability now that it's over.

She had these freak-outs during sex with him, a full-blown version of the minor panic attacks she had previously managed to keep the lid on with other partners. Ivy had feared it meant she was getting worse but can see now that it meant she was getting better. She was letting go in a way she never felt able before. Something instinctive had told her it was safe to freak out with L, safe to face the demons.

They had never talked about it. He tried once, but she brought the lid down hard. He must have put it together, but she made sure he knew it wasn't his right to ask.

How could she tell him that she always calls out L when she comes in order to ground her in the moment, to reassure herself about who she's actually with. She has these horrible memories of losing herself in what was going on, succumbing to the physical pleasure, then in the millisecond when orgasm began to recede, she would be jolted back with a feeling of revulsion and self-disgust that echoed and echoed for ever.

How could she talk about something like that? What would he see thereafter? She wouldn't be Ivy any more. She would be Sylvie, and Sylvie was pathetic.

It frightens her to think how much he knows. He could even know her real name, could have known it all along but never let on. What might he do with that information after what she did to him, after she dumped him in the cruellest way she could?

It is the answer to this that hurts the most. He won't do anything. He's a good man. That's why she had to spare him from her.

L. It was derived from his middle initial, but it had come to signify something else, secretly, only to her. Her L. Her lover. Her love.

Ivy is so lost in her reflections that she doesn't notice Rory's approach until he's right beside her.

'Hey.'

His voice gives her a start. She shudders.

'Shit, don't do that. Fucking ninja.'

'Sorry. Just checking in, making sure you're okay.'

'Why wouldn't I be?'

Her tone is a little pricklier than she intended, instinctively defensive.

'With what's happened today. Everybody's been thinking about Vince and rallying around Kirsten and Amanda, but it occurred to me, the sight of that police car . . . It really brought some things back for me, so I realised it might be, you know, difficult.'

Poor Rory. It was his curse always to care. Christ knows where he got it from in this family.

'Thanks, but I'm good, honestly,' she tells him.

This isn't true. The sight of the Portuguese police car had been

195

unsettling, deeply so to the part of her that's been waiting for a tap on the shoulder these sixteen years.

When she found out it was regarding Vince, she felt only a temporary relief. Her anxiety did not entirely abate, but was rather replaced with an instinctive wariness that something was amiss. It had stayed with her since, though she was unable to quite nail down the source.

'What happened?' she asks. 'Is there any news?'

'Nah. Amanda said the cops didn't give Kirsten any details. He was found in his office, so Kirsten's assuming a heart attack or something. When you see police though, you wonder if it's been something heavier, like suicide. I mean, it doesn't sound likely when he's about to go on holiday with a new wife and baby, but I guess you never know with these things.'

There it is: the thing that's been troubling her. Your husband dies suddenly: heart attack or even suicide, you're only getting a phone call. You're not getting a visit from the police to break the news, especially foreign cops if you happen to be abroad.

Ivy suspects a favour has been called in between the forces in two countries. The Portuguese cops had been sent here to witness Kirsten's reaction when they told her. Could have been to judge whether it seemed that big a surprise, or if she put on too big a *show* of surprise. There is no way of knowing what they were looking for, but that's the point: the very fact of the cops showing up to deliver this news means they know far more than they're letting on.

A notion forms in Ivy's mind, a way to find out more about what's going on. It's desperate, she knows. She wonders how much of it is provoked by her paranoid insecurity – her fear of being seen through – and how much is about fabricating a pretext simply to call. But either way, she knows she's doing it.

'I'm going inside,' she tells Rory.

She grabs her phone and heads back to her room, where she closes the door so no one can hear. The soundproofing in this place was never great. Voices carry: that's why she was sure her mum must have heard everything back then. Certainly, after her accusation fell on deaf ears, she made sure she was noisy, hoping to be caught. She

196

thought Dad might have told her to keep it down, but he never did. He understood that a combination of denial and Celia's myth of the perfect family constituted the best noise insulation known to man. She stopped once she realised he was merely getting off on it.

She takes a breath and dials, pressing a field marked with the single letter L.

He answers after two rings. She realises she isn't ready, but it's too late now.

'Ivy?'

There is surprise in his voice, though if there's anything else, such as judgement or anger, he is effective at hiding it.

She thought briefly about masking her number in case he didn't pick up, but in all honesty, she knew he would. It's why she knows he'll help right now too. He's a good person. Good people want to help you.

It's why they get hurt by people like her.

'Yes,' she confirms.

'To say I wasn't expecting you would be on my big list of all-time understatements, right below "Boris Johnson is not the most honourable of individuals" and "Finding your girlfriend in bed with another man can be a something of a . . . buzzkill."'

She wonders at the pause. Whether he was choosing his words or disguising that his voice had choked. She doesn't want to think of him hurting, though she realises that it would feel worse if he didn't.

She wants to say sorry, but she wouldn't know where to begin. And she doesn't want him to think she's looking for a way back.

'I know I've no right and I've no expectation . . . But I need to ask a favour.'

'Is it on behalf of one of your clients or is it just for you?'

'I told you from the beginning I would never ask you for anything on behalf of a client.'

'That was when we were going out.'

'My position hasn't changed.'

'Neither has mine.'

'I don't follow,' she admits.

He sighs.

'It means my judgement remains messed up when it comes to you and that consequently I'll still give you anything I can. What is it you need?'

2002

Celia

'*Obrigada.*'

The young girl behind the bakery counter smiled indulgently at Celia's use of Portuguese and handed her a brown paper parcel, the loaf inside pleasingly warm to the touch. She slipped it into the pull-along basket Max was dragging, and as she did so she became aware of that familiar feeling of being stared at.

She glanced in the direction of a couple passing the milk section and noted that they quickly looked away. A couple of decades in the public eye had taught her to recognise the signs. They were around the right age too.

She could hear their voices when she and Max turned into the next aisle, the pair of them not realising they were only on the other side of the shelving unit.

'Are you sure?' the woman said. 'I didn't get the best of looks. The counter was busy.'

'Deffo.'

Celia allowed herself a smile. She glanced to Max but he was miles away, in a world of his own, as usual.

'You should say hi, if you're such an admirer. You might never get the chance.'

'I don't want to bother anybody,' the husband replied. 'Especially on their holidays.'

He needn't worry, Celia thought. A little polite hello was always welcome from people who enjoyed her work, whether it be the sci-fi fans or more recently her magazine readers.

As they reached the turn, it was clear Max was planning to head directly towards the booze at the far wall. She took his elbow and guided him down the next aisle, knowing it would precipitate an encounter.

'I just need some tins of sardine pâté,' she said, confirming that the couple were now approaching from the opposite direction.

She recognised the ritual: the furtive glances, the moment of indecision, then an urging nudge from the woman. The man strode forward, the one who was 'such an admirer'. Going by his age and gender, she pegged him for a fan of *The Liberators*, though she did get letters from male readers of her columns too.

As was always her way, part of the meeting-the-public dance, Celia pretended she had no idea she had been recognised and was being approached.

'Excuse me.'

When she looked up, the man's eyes were on Max.

'Sorry to trouble you, but I recognised you from that Abby Cook programme and I just wanted to say I thought you were amazing. Seeing that charlatan get shut down was priceless.'

'Oh, thank you. Well, it's all part of the service.'

The man gave Celia a smile by way of greeting. She returned it politely but something inside her felt slighted, like it would have been better if he'd ignored her completely. He thought she was nobody.

'The number of times there's some arse down the pub saying the moon landings were faked, or banging on about aliens at Roswell. It was great to hear a proper scientific breakdown of it all.'

'Well, I can assure you the aliens at Roswell thing is gospel truth.'

Fanboy gaped.

'Just kidding.'

The man burst into sycophantic laughter. Pathetic.

'So, is it true you've a book coming out? Are you writing about just the moon thing or other conspiracies?'

The wife sidled up to her as Max went into his answer. She gave Celia a sympathetic smile.

'You must get this all the time,' she said quietly. 'Is it a pain being married to somebody famous?'

A response popped into her head: *'Oh, I think Max has grown used to it.'* It was a joke reply to a joke remark made by a friend shortly after the TV show aired. She didn't say it though, as the woman clearly had no idea who she was. Neither of them did.

She managed another smile.

'I'm getting used to it.'

He got recognised on the aeroplane over here too, some woman leaning over to make a complimentary comment as she made her way back from the loo. This was going to be the way of things now, Celia realised. And she was fine with that. She was absolutely fine with that. She was happy for him.

Just as long as he remembered the extent to which the Max Temple brand was enhanced by being Celia Wilde's husband. She was the reason he got the gig co-writing with Jason Cale – Danthos to her Kurlia – which was why he was on that Abby Cook programme in the first place.

And the great irony, of course, was that there really was a conspiracy in play that night. The director was in a snit with the producer over the show giving a platform to Toby Cutler-Wood, so he sent Max a copy of *The Apollo Conspiracy* in advance. He tipped off Max so that he would have all the right information fresh in his mind, which was how he was able to mount such a comprehensive dismantling of the moon man's arguments. The director also sent Max an email assuring him that as he would be in charge in the control booth that night, he didn't need to worry about being cut off.

Secrets of showbiz, folks. He wouldn't be telling his admirer in the supermarket *that*.

A few hours later, Max was holding court once more, this time in the villa. He was standing with his back to the open patio doors, blathering on about that bloody TV show and about conspiracy theories while everyone stood or sat around him sipping aperitifs. Celia was getting familiar with the effortless artifice of his manner: coming across as though he was somewhat bemused by all the fuss, an intellectual academic unimpressed by the vulgar trappings of showbusiness, and yet clearly basking in the glow. Always backing into the limelight.

'What really struck me about Cutler-Wood's book is that he and his ilk have the most astonishing faith in the power and reach of the implied conspiracists. The complexity of the things they believe to have been pulled off inevitably outstrips the complexity of whatever the conspiracy is supposed to have fabricated or covered up.'

It was a full house. Everyone was gathered around, even Vince and Laurie from next door. They were heading out to the village for dinner but changed their plans when Marion invited them across for drinks and a late supper. It was looking like a later supper than anticipated, Marion having got distracted by Lia earlier and falling behind on her cooking plans. Consequently Celia was a little tipsy, having had two gins on an empty stomach, and Ken was pouring. He was always heavy with his measures.

Svetlana was sitting nearest Max, hanging on his every word and batting her eyelids. Celia was pretty sure she'd undone a button since she sat down too. She wasn't the only one giving him rapt attention. Calum and Vince kept asking questions, and even the normally quiet Ken was pitching in.

'Weren't you nervous?' he asked.

Celia saw her opportunity and answered for him.

'Jason Cale and myself are old hands at the interview circuit, so between us we made sure Max was comfortable before the cameras. Not as comfortable as us, but then we had three series of *The Liberators* together. Oh, the tales I could tell you about that.'

She looked around the room, ready to field a question. There were no takers. She did notice Vince's eyes briefly light up at the prospect, but that was a given. The day he ever seemed uninterested, she had definitely hit rock bottom. If he had a question though, he was beaten to the punch by Ken, of all people.

'I meant, were you not nervous about going off the reservation, diverging from the format? I've never seen it happen on that kind of show.'

She consoled herself that maybe Ken had heard all her stories over the years, whereas Max's moment of fame was fresher in the mind. She recalled how amazed Ken was by the discovery that she had been Kurlia when Marion first brought him home. He'd 'never met anyone off the telly before' and gave the impression he had previously thought TV stars sprang fully formed from the loins of Zeus and tarried but briefly on this mortal plane. Unfortunately, she had long since gone from seeming something intangibly exotic to merely his mother-in-law, and it stung all the more when that was all you were to someone as unremarkable as Ken.

As a physical specimen he was attractive enough, but in the grander scheme, there was no escaping her disappointment that the first daughter, first *child* of Celia Wilde and Max Temple should end up a schoolteacher married to a plumber.

She glanced over the breakfast bar into the kitchen, where Marion was busying herself. She really ought to have got her hair done, and surely could have shed a few pounds before a holiday when you know you'll be in a bikini. She was looking old beyond her twenty-eight years, frumpy and dumpy. Celia thought of how she looked at the same age, also having had two kids by that point. There was no comparison. She could still turn heads today, whereas Marion never knew how to sell herself.

She'd met Ken at the age of seventeen and married him before she even graduated, like she couldn't wait to get away. She reckoned Marion had settled for Ken, knowing she'd never need to raise her game again if she ended up with someone uninspiring. Shame. Marion could have been so much more. She just never seemed to push herself. Never seemed to believe in herself. Celia had made her peace with it, though. She had read that this was often the case with children of prominent and high-achieving parents. The important thing was that Marion was happy, she supposed.

'What fascinates me is not so much the twisted evidence, but the mental processes that cause people to seize upon it,' Max was now saying, Celia having tuned out for a moment. 'The brain doesn't passively observe the world: it actively constructs from sometimes surprisingly limited material, and to compensate, it has a catalogue of shortcuts that it uses to make sense of the piecemeal input it receives. This leads to all kinds of illusions and misperceptions.'

203

Celia stepped alongside him and put an arm on his shoulder.

'Now, come on, Max, we shouldn't bore everybody with this stuff. They all must have heard it a dozen times.'

'No, not at all,' Calum assured her, Svetlana, Vince and Ken joining in agreement. 'It's been a bit of a whirlwind for Max and this is the first time we've really had him to ourselves since it all kicked off. We want to hear everything about it.'

The whole room seemed in his thrall apart from the kids. Hughie and Lia were playing with toys, separately and quietly: the way they could when they knew it was late and a wrong move could precipitate bedtime.

Then Celia realised there was an exception among the adults: Laurie. Normally she would be too pie-eyed to be paying attention by this stage of the evening, but on this occasion she was still sober. Maybe it was an indication that Celia was a bit pissed if she thought Laurie seemed dry in comparison, but to be fair she appeared to have been cutting down this holiday. Perhaps she was on a programme.

Laurie was standing close to Vince, leaning on the edge of a sofa sipping from a glass of orange juice. Celia began to notice that she never made eye contact with Max, despite him holding the floor. It felt weird, sounding a warning in Celia's head that there was something she ought to be aware of.

Now she came to think of it, Laurie had been like this when they all had lunch the day Sylvie and Calum got here. At the time, Celia had thought Laurie was just hungover, but now she realised she was observing the same weird chemistry. Laurie never made eye contact with him, but she was constantly looking at Max when his gaze was elsewhere, intent in her eyes. She was like a teenager at a school disco furtively checking out the guy she was obsessed with.

Celia cast her mind back to the last holiday, around Easter. She tried to remember if Laurie had seemed like this then but recalled instead that Vince had not come with her. He stayed back in Scotland and Laurie had been out here on her own. A chill ran through her as she put it together. The only question was whether this meant it was still going on. Had something happened at Easter and now it was weird between them? Or was she playing it cool so that Celia didn't cop on to what was still happening now?

Celia drained her drink and walked away from Max, heading to the kitchen in search of another gin. She poured herself a measure appropriate to dealing with what she had just deduced, topping up with tonic and taking a large gulp before she even closed the fridge door.

She almost forgot Marion was nearby, but as it happened she was distracted by a commotion in the living area. Celia looked across the breakfast bar towards the sofa, where Hughie had looped a slipknot over Rory's head from behind and pulled it tight.

Rory dropped his bottle of beer to the floor as he reacted to clutch his neck, and Hughie got a fright at the disproportionate response his prank appeared to have precipitated. He was looking teary, afraid he was in big trouble.

'I was only playing,' he said.

Ken was calmly – maybe too calmly – explaining why this wasn't a fun game for everyone.

'It's okay to do this with dolls, but not with Uncle Rory.'

'Why?'

'It's dangerous. Why do you think they hanged those prisoners in *Robin Hood*? That's how they used to execute people.'

'But they escaped,' Hughie countered, sounding unconvinced.

'I think it's maybe time for bed,' Marion suggested. 'The supper's going to be ready in about half an hour anyway.'

There was an immediate squeal of complaint from Lia, but Hughie seemed resigned, even relieved. He already knew he'd blown it.

'But I don't feel sleepy,' Lia said.

'I'll give you a story then,' Ken told her.

Celia heard opportunity knock.

'I'll come and give you a hand.'

Lia climbed eagerly into her father's toned and muscular arms, while Hughie allowed Celia to lead him with unusually timid gratitude. He got a head rub from Rory on his way out, which cheered him, but he seemed tired.

They crossed the grass to the other villa, which Marion's family were sharing with Rory and Svetlana.

Celia and Ken supervised face-washing and toothbrushing, then tucked the pair of them into the twin beds.

'I want *The Little Mole*,' Lia said.

'I'm okay from here,' Ken told Celia, lifting the book.

'It's fine. I want to hear it too,' she replied.

'Why don't you read, then?' he said, offering her the volume. 'You're the professional.'

It was both true and a flattering suggestion, but she didn't want to risk him leaving her to it.

'How about I do some of the animals' voices,' she suggested, addressing the kids.

'Yay,' Lia replied.

A few minutes later, the story was complete and the children seemed quite settled. Ken turned off the light and withdrew, closing the door.

'Thanks,' he said.

'Quid pro quo. You obliged me with the sun cream earlier.'

Celia stopped at the end of the hall, opposite the open door to Ken and Marion's bedroom. She turned to face him as he approached and took hold of his hand.

She knew she was a little drunk, but who wouldn't need a few, with everybody fawning over Max like that. If they knew what he was really like. She deserved a little compensation, and if her daughter was stuck with some plumber, why shouldn't she get something out of it?

'You know, you could rub more than just my back if you want to. I know you enjoyed it.'

She took his hand and placed it beneath her collarbone, just above her right breast.

'I think Marion might have some thoughts on that,' he replied, calm and measured as always. It was hard to get a read on him. Was he looking for reassurance?

She placed her own hand on his chest and began moving it down. His pectorals were firm.

'She's my daughter, I know. You're good to Marion, and I'm grateful. But you could have a little fringe benefit to being part of the family.'

Ken removed his hand from her chest and used it to stop her fingers travelling any further.

'I don't think Max would like it either, Celia.'

'Max? Hah. Are you kidding? You don't think he hasn't strayed? Right under my nose? Trust me, there are plenty of little indiscretions going on around here.'

She grabbed his hand again and placed it directly onto her breast.

'I deserve a treat, and I think you know you deserve a little something too. I might be twenty-odd years older but let's be honest, I'm still in better shape than Marion.'

Ken's expression darkened. He lifted his hand and gripped her elbow with a firm authority.

'I think you've had one too many, Celia. Maybe you need some food. Marion should have supper ready any minute.'

Something cold immediately settled in Celia, a glimpse of how the past few seconds would look to her in the very near future.

'I'm just . . . it was a test, Ken,' she said, her voice faltering from nerves, booze and humiliation. 'I'm just looking out for my daughter. Testing you, that's what it was. Testing if you would stray. And you passed.'

'Good to know.'

As she re-entered the other villa, Celia felt conspicuously flushed, like her face was a beacon signalling shame and inviting questions as to the source. She hoped to God everyone thought it was just the heat and the alcohol, and prayed Ken wouldn't say anything to Marion later. He wouldn't, surely. It would be too awkward for everybody.

She would deny it happened, or stick with the test story. Problem was, unless Marion said something, she would never know whether he told her or not.

Celia had returned to find that Niamh was awake and crying, held in Sylvie's arms as she sat on the sofa. Typical. They had just got the other two down and the baby had been woken by the voices from the living room.

Svetlana, Vince and Rory were all gathered around, trying to humour the little one. Which was of course the worst thing to do when you were trying to get a child to calm down and go to sleep. Celia tried not to dwell on the fact that even an unwanted illegitimate baby seemed to be capable of drawing more notice than she could this evening.

Marion emerged from the kitchen carrying a tray of lasagne and placed it down on the table.

'That looks amazing,' Laurie said. 'We're really grateful for the invite. In fact, Vince and I were talking, and we thought we should all get together for a barbecue at the end of the holiday.'

'Yes, we'll lay on all the food,' Vince said. 'It's about time we returned the favour. Big blow-out next Friday. That's the last night of our stay.'

'That sounds lovely,' Marion replied. 'That's our last night too. But we'll be up early the next morning for flights, and we'd need to pack, so . . .'

'Of course, of course,' Vince said. 'We're off on the Saturday flight as well. Thursday then. How does that sound, Celia?'

'I'm looking forward to it already,' she told him.

She drew upon all her RADA training to fake her smile, but her words were not entirely insincere. Celia was indeed looking forward to it, because by Thursday night there would be only a day left of an utterly disappointing holiday. And once it was over, she wasn't sure she wanted to put up with this whole Portugal palaver any more.

2002

Rory

Rory was lying in the afterglow, listening to the sound of Svetlana in the shower, when he heard a knock at the door. They had finally enjoyed some furtive and what he had thought was fairly quiet sex, so the presence of someone outside the room was a jolt to remind him they were living at close quarters with Marion and her family, while the fact of knocking at all suggested an awkward awareness on the part of whoever was out there that it may not be a good time to come in.

Svetlana had been clingy and emotional when he came to, sleeping until ten thirty after maybe overdoing things last night. Turned out she had been lying awake for hours, lying there running things over in her head and had worked herself onto the edge of a panic attack. She could get like that, in ways that made him wonder just what the hell she had been through in the years before they met. He had held her close to calm her down, and one thing had led to another, as the tabloids liked to put it.

'Just a sec,' he said, getting up and pulling on some shorts.

He opened the door and found Ken standing there, holding a mobile phone.

'There's a call for you,' he said apologetically. 'It came on Marion's phone. She's outside. I heard it ring and picked it up and it's for you.'

'Cheers, Ken. Sorry you were disturbed.'

'Don't worry about it.'

Ken handed him the phone and walked away.

Rory didn't have a mobile. It was just another expense he couldn't stretch to, trying to pay London rents on a record store salary. You had to make economies and prioritise. These days any funds spent on a phone contract constituted money he could otherwise be spending on, ahem, necessities.

Svetlana had a mobile, though he didn't know how she was paying for it. Maybe when you had lived in so many far-flung places, it was more of a priority to be able to get in touch with people.

He held the phone to his ear, a clamshell device like a *Star Trek* communicator.

'Rory speaking.'

'Rory, it's Danny. Mate, I'm really sorry. I've got to warn you.'

His flatmate sounded out of kilter. Shaken up.

'These guys came to the flat looking for you. No, looking for Svetlana, but they knew you were with her. Like, Russians or something, Eastern Europeans. Fucking gangsters anyway, that's the point. Man. I'm so sorry . . .' His voice was wavering, tremulous. He sounded really scared.

'They pushed their way in when I answered the door. Fuck, man, they had a pair of pliers. I told them where you are. That's why I'm calling, to warn you. Told them I didn't know exactly where you are, but I told them Portugal, the Algarve.'

'Are you okay, Danny? Did they hurt you?'

'They didn't have to. One of them held these pliers to my earlobe. Didn't even have to squeeze, man. It was all I could do not to shit myself. These are scary bastards.'

'You okay now? Did you call the police?'

'Fuck no. They were pretty clear about that.'

'How much did you tell them?'

'Everything. Everything I know.'

'Yeah, but what *do* you know?'

'Just that you're with your family. I don't know where, exactly. I let them go through your stuff. Showed them that the only contact number you had left me was for your sister's phone. That's why I'm calling you now. I'm sorry, mate, I was so scared. What's going on, man? What you mixed up in?'

Svetlana emerged from the shower, a towel wrapped around her middle. She had a quizzical look as she noticed that he was on a

210

mobile. He had to watch his words and get out of this conversation, call Danny back when she wasn't around.

'I'm really sorry you got hit with this, mate. But it's going to get sorted, okay? Thanks for the heads-up. I'll see you in a few days, all right?'

He terminated the call.

'Who was that?' Svetlana asked. She sounded concerned.

'Just a friend.'

'Calling here? On someone else's phone? Must be . . . emergency.'

He didn't want to tell her what was going on. Didn't want her scared.

'Ach, it was just Danny, my flatmate. There's been a burst pipe and he's having hassle with the landlord.'

He wondered if he should tell her the truth. She had a right to know, but knowing wouldn't change their situation, so what was the point? There was only one course of action that could resolve this. It was time to bite the bullet and get it done.

2018

Ivy

Ivy is listening to the sound of the waves and the cry of birds as she lies in her bedroom, awake but not quite ready to open her eyes. It is morning, too early for the speed launches trailing water-skiers and paragliders, a time of tranquillity, but for her one tainted with too many memories of mornings after. She remembers those more clearly than the nights before, a combination of her father's mind games and her own defence mechanisms.

Lying here alone, staring at the ceiling, feeling guilty and confused and ashamed. Lying here with Calum, feeling lost and helpless and so very afraid.

Easter 2002. That was when she understood the depths to which desperation could take her. She had been unable to sleep and had gone for a glass of water, which was when she noticed Max sitting outside on the far side of the pool.

She went out to join him. She was sleep-deprived and crazy angry. She wanted to lash out, wanted to hurt him, and she finally thought she knew how.

'I often sit here at night when everyone's gone to bed,' he had said, his voice soft. 'I look at the sea illuminated by starlight and it's impossible not to feel that everything's right with the world.'

'I know what you mean,' she replied. 'So exciting about the way everything's taking off for you after that TV show. And Mum says there might be a book in the offing. You're going to be a star.'

She let him think about that for a few seconds, then hit him with it.

'Of course, I could take it all away in a heartbeat. Tell everybody what you did to me.'

'What?'

He acted like he had no idea what she could possibly be talking about. He was good at that.

'Having sex with your own daughter. Grooming her for it, building her up to it. That probably wouldn't look good on the jacket. Then all those years you messed with my head, made me not sure what was real, made me think it was my fault. Why shouldn't the world know about it, *Daddy?*'

'Oh, Sylvie. You're just in an angry frame of mind, what with the baby keeping you up nights. You'll calm down, and I strongly suggest you do. I know you're upset, but that's not a time to make decisions. Especially about the kind of things you're suggesting.'

'My life has turned to shit because of what you did to me. I don't feel like I've anything to lose. You got me fucking pregnant.'

That wiped the look of calm self-assurance from his face, as he finally saw what had been before him the whole time.

'Yeah. Poor Calum. I conned him into thinking Niamh is his, but she's not. Do you know what that means? It's no longer my word against yours. A simple DNA test would put you in jail. I've now got hard proof of what you did. *Living* proof.'

She thought this would be the moment he crumbled, begging her forgiveness, begging her not to reveal the truth. She thought this would be when she finally had power over him.

He regained a look of calm, but only on the surface.

'As I always have to remind you, you wouldn't want to do that to yourself, to the family. The fallout, the things you would unleash.' He gripped her wrist hard, twisting. 'The law of unintended consequences.'

As he spoke, it was what was in his eyes that frightened her: a glimpse of how dangerous it was to have threatened him; what her father might be truly capable of.

All these years later, it seems almost alien to be in this room and not be scared, but nor is she entirely at ease. Max is dead, but that doesn't mean there aren't still things here that could hurt her.

Her phone vibrates on the bedside table, prompting her to glance at the clock on the wall. To her surprise she has slept into working hours, and to her greater surprise, the call isn't from the office.

She feels a surge of something she is not quite ready to name when she sees the caller identified: L. Though their discussion yesterday had been civil, and he'd said he would try to help, it is only now he is calling that she realises she didn't really expect him to deliver.

Why would he? she had asked herself, but she knew the answer to that question. He's a far softer touch than his reputation would suggest, if you just know which buttons to press. At least, he's proven a soft touch to her, and maybe only to her. She doesn't like to think what that implies, any more than she likes to dwell upon what that L has come to stand for. If she's prepared to use his feelings for her to further her own aims, then that tells a harsh truth about what she is.

It's always been that way though, by necessity. It's the survivor in her. Priority number one has always been protecting herself, protecting her secret; and sometimes protecting other people *from* her secret.

'Hey,' she says.

'You sound croaky. Did I wake you?'

'No. But I'm not up yet.'

'Really? On a school day? You okay?'

'I'm fine. How are things your end?'

'Fine,' he replies, noncommittal.

'No, I mean, seriously, how are you?'

There is a pause.

'You know, Ivy, we don't need to make this hard. I've got some information like you asked, and you don't need to meet any requirements to get it.'

'I appreciate that. And I'm guessing you're sparing me from hearing how you're really doing, because how you're really doing is all my fault.'

Another pause. Then he speaks.

'That's about the size of it, yeah.'

She knew this would be the case, but it's still painful to hear him confirm it.

214

'And yet, you've gone out of your way to help me.'

'More than that. I've called in favours to help you.'

'Why?'

'Because you asked.'

'I mean why, after what I did to you?'

'Maybe because I'm still hoping you can undo it.'

It's her turn to pause. She feels that little surge again, knowing that he's just told her the door is still open. Part of her wants to rush through it, and it hurts that she can't.

He got close, way too close, before she realised. Maybe that's his superpower, how he does what he does.

'What did you find out?'

When he speaks again, his tone is more businesslike, having parsed her failure to respond to his last statement. They both know where they stand.

'I spoke to my contact, Detective Superintendent Catherine McLeod. You were right. The police are treating the death as suspicious. Me calling and asking about it was suspicious too. That set a few alarm bells ringing, so McLeod is now very curious as to what I know and who I know it from.'

Ivy feels a different kind of surge, something more worrying.

'I trust you didn't give up my name.'

'No, but there may have to be a quid pro quo at some point on this.'

'I can't make any promises.'

'I told her the same, but I also said I'd let her in on anything I found out. She wasn't happy, but experience has told her I'm worth a punt.'

'You mean the Black Widow thing?'

'Among others.'

'What else did she say?'

'In this case, "suspicious" means he was murdered but they don't want to go public with that yet, or to give out any details as to how. He was found in his office. No sign of a break-in. They're reckoning he let the perp in, so it was someone he knew, possibly a client, or a prospective client. They're ruling out robbery because he doesn't keep money or valuables there. Only thing taken was his phone.'

'Can the police trace it?'

'In theory. Unless the battery has been removed, even if it's switched off, the network provider can turn on the phone remotely. But to get them to do that, the police need a warrant, and there's a lot of legal and privacy hoops to be jumped through.'

He leaves it hanging, but only so that she recognises he's left it hanging.

'Is this where you tell me you know a guy?'

'No. I know a girl. Do you have the number?'

Ivy sees the possibility rise and fall again. She doesn't have Vince's number, and she can't ask anyone else for it because why would she possibly need it? Then she remembers the list taped to the wall just inside the kitchen door: the numbers of an emergency doctor, take-aways, restaurants in the village, and their next-door neighbour.

'Give me a minute.'

She gets up and pulls on some clothes. A few moments later she is in the kitchen looking at the list. The number is right there, just beneath Casa Padaria Pizzas. No surname, just 'Vince'.

Ivy reads it out and he quotes it back to her to verify.

'I'll get back to you as soon as I hear. Meantime, you going to tell me your connection to this?'

'Not yet.'

'I noticed it was a weird ringing tone. Where are you?'

'Abroad. I'm with family.'

'I wasn't sure you had any. Never heard you mention them.'

She feels a growing anxiety, a fear that he is probing, a fear about what he may already have found out.

She says nothing until she is back behind her bedroom door, not wanting to talk beyond it where she might be overheard.

'Tell me the truth, Jack,' she says. 'Do you know who I really am?'

It's one of the few times she's called him by his real name. It makes her feel strangely vulnerable, like she's speaking to who he really is rather than the version he only is to her. Or is it that she is calling him what everybody else calls him because she's afraid of what she has invested in the name that only she uses?

L. Middle initial. Jack Lapsley Parlabane.

216

'Is this your way of saying I never quite understood you?' he replies.

'I'm asking literally. Do you know who I am?'

'You're Ivy Roan, PR dark arts mistress. I'm still not sure I understand the question.'

'Come on. You're an investigative journalist. Surely you've looked into my background.'

'I was never investigating you. Apart from in the ways you'd occasionally let me. Is there something I should know?'

Jesus, she thinks. By telling him there is something for him to find, she is inviting him to look for it. But hadn't she been doing that from the beginning?

What a fool. She's a bloody vampire and she's been sleeping with Van Helsing.

2002

Rory

Dad put down his book and stood up, arcing his back and extending his arms. The stretch and accompanying yawn was a familiar enough prelude that his subsequent words were redundant, but he said those every day too.

'I'm going for my mid-morning constitutional.'

His regular walk along the clifftop path that he undertook even in the fiercest heat, usually on his own.

'Hey, I think I'll join you,' Rory said.

'Really? Are you sure?'

Dad was trying to make it sound like he didn't want Rory to feel obliged to keep him company, but really what he meant was that he'd prefer to be alone; alone with his brilliant thoughts. Rory would have preferred to leave him alone too, but he was running out of days.

It wasn't quite now or never but it felt like the time was right. The family had got to know Svetlana; not just got used to her being around, but having her part of things, helping out with Marion's kids. She also seemed to be making a good impression on Dad last night, when Vince and Laurie had come over. Dad had been holding forth to the gathered audience and Rory noticed that Max addressed a lot of his answers specifically to her regardless of who had asked the question. People sometimes depicted academics as bloodless and asexual, monastic intellectuals cloistered in their ivory towers, but Rory knew for sure that at least one of them wasn't immune to the attention of a beautiful face and a flash of braless tit.

They walked at a leisurely pace in the sunshine, their conversation accompanied by the crash of water against the cliff-face beneath. They spoke in neutral generalities, the awkward exchanges of two people wary of the distance between them. Rory feared Max would interpret the small talk as a conspicuous prelude to discussing something else, though offering to join his dad on the walk had probably been signal enough.

'How's London treating you?' Dad asked.

'Much the same. Margins are tight, and my wages don't go far. I'm not planning to work in a record store for ever, if that's what you're wondering. Been treading water for a while, I will admit.'

'You know, you'd have a few more doors open to you in terms of your earning potential if you considered going back and completing your degree.'

That old saw, like a cut scene in a videogame that you kept seeing over and over: the Gatekeeper stating: 'You cannot proceed any further in your quest until you have completed this challenge.'

It wasn't like Dad expected it ever to happen, or genuinely sought to convince him to go back to uni. Max was merely reiterating his disappointment and laying down the consequent terms of their relationship.

But today, at least, it gave Rory the angle he needed.

'I kind of feel I've got renewed impetus about a lot of things since I met Svetlana. She's been really good for me.'

'Yes,' Dad agreed, smiling. 'She is quite the catch. Any man would count himself lucky to have a woman who looks like her.'

'I felt rudderless for a long time because I never had a strong sense of vocation. I lacked the drive to get where I was going because I never knew where that was. But now I'm seeing that what I needed was to find the right person rather than the right purpose.'

'Have you got grand plans now? Is that what you're telling me?'

There was a cheery note to his father's voice, but Rory wasn't sure if the humour signalled that he was pleased at his son finally discovering some gumption or amused in his scornful scepticism that this would actually lead to anything.

'The record store isn't the greatest job, but I am getting a lot of experience in retail management. Neither of us want to stay in

London, so I'd kind of like to go somewhere really new to make a fresh start.'

A paraglider went past, pulled by a motor launch. Rory could hear the shrieks of the woman in the harness a hundred yards out and as many yards up, her laughter carried on the breeze.

'How new and how fresh?'

'Extremely. I've got a friend in Cairns who is looking for some help running his surf shop. We thought we might have a crack at it over in Australia.'

Dad nodded, contemplating.

'That would indeed be something very fresh. When it comes to a change of scene, it would be physically impossible to get much further away from your current one. I can't imagine your mother would be delighted at the prospect of you being on the other side of the world. She'd never see you.'

She'd never see you, he noted. Not we. Rory tried not to dwell on this.

'You guys could come and visit. You've never been to Australia. It would give you the impetus to take the trip. For all you know, you might even be going there on a book tour.'

Rory swallowed.

'This is the new beginning I need, Dad.'

He was surprised by the depth of the sincerity in his words, not having appreciated how much he believed them until he heard them coming out of his own mouth.

Dad slowed his pace but didn't stop walking.

'I'm guessing I wouldn't need to be a professor of psychology to anticipate that we are approaching a request for funds to help realise this great vision.'

Rory felt a pang of disappointment in himself that he had indeed been so transparent.

'Well, yes, but it's actually a little bit more complicated than that.'

'I'm listening.'

Surprisingly, Dad's tone didn't sound like a door closing. He seemed curious, albeit in his dry and dusty way.

Rory seized the moment and outlined the situation. He told him everything Svetlana was mired in, though he skipped the part about her working as a high-end call girl.

'And how much do you two need to extricate yourselves and start again as far away from these people as you can both get?'

Rory sighed, wondering what kind of figure his dad was expecting to hear. He wished he had seeded the idea that it might run to six figures, so that the truth didn't sound so bad.

'She owes them twenty-five thousand.'

'Twenty-five thousand what? Pounds? Euros?'

He had gone for Sterling as it made the number itself sound smaller.

'Pounds. Probably more by now, because of the way they keep jacking up the compound interest.'

They walked on for a while, neither speaking. There was a bench up ahead, looking out over the cliffs upon a horseshoe inlet. He knew it was a spot where Dad often stopped for a rest and a drink of water. He sat down, gazing out to sea, while Rory remained on his feet, on tenterhooks.

Dad tapped the wood alongside him, inviting Rory to join. They sat together quietly for a few moments, then Max spoke.

'She's a truly beautiful woman, Rory. A real prize. I can understand why you see a bright future with her. It's no mystery why you've fallen for her. But I'm rather disappointed that you've fallen for her story.'

Rory turned to him.

'What?'

'Come on, Rory, she's miles out of your league. You're too love-struck and blinded by your apparent good fortune that you haven't stopped to ask yourself what someone who looks like her would be doing with you. And this fantasy woman just happens to walk into your life not long after I start to develop a media career and land a widely reported book deal? She's playing you, son. She's a grifter.'

Rory felt a punch to the gut: a horrible dawning realisation of how naive and stupid he had been. But it wasn't his stupidity in believing Svetlana genuinely cared for him: it was his stupidity in believing his father did; his naivety in thinking his dad might see him as anything other than a washout. He used to think Max had always shown him tough love in the hope that it would encourage him to realise his potential, that his dad still believed he could make more of his life. The very fact that he was incredulous someone like Svetlana wanted to be with him told Rory all he needed to know about how his father truly perceived him.

Nonetheless, Rory had evidence on his side. Max had always prided himself on basing judgements upon empirical data rather than emotion.

'They came to my flat, Dad. I got a phone call yesterday from Danny. They threatened to torture him. They came looking for Svetlana in London and now they know she's here in Portugal.'

Dad rolled his eyes. Not an encouraging sign.

'How well do you know this Danny? How do you know he's not a part of this stratagem to bleed me for a whole load of money I would never see again?'

'It's fucking Danny. He works in Halfords. This isn't some two-bit scam cooked up down the pub. We're talking about international human traffickers. These are ruthless people, Dad.'

'I suspect the most ruthless person in this equation is your supposed girlfriend, and it's what she does once you've told her the bad news that should be most instructive. I do hope the honey in the trap has been sweet and you've had some great sex out of the deal, because that tap's about to be turned off for ever. Whether she gets the money or not, I guarantee you're never going to see her again after this trip, so given that the outcomes would be identical, I'm going to opt for the course of action that is twenty-five thousand pounds cheaper.'

Dad got to his feet.

'Anyway, shall we resume our walk? Or would I be right in assuming you'd prefer to be alone at this point?'

Rory remained on the bench. He felt like a weight was pinning him there, because he knew that once he got up, once he walked back to the villa, he'd have to break this to Svetlana. She had been abused and disappointed by so many people. He wanted to be the one who was different.

Meantime Dad strolled off like he didn't have a care in the world, probably because he hadn't. There was always a side of him that was utterly unfeeling. Sometimes Rory thought the bastard had proven so adept at deconstructing human psychology because he was an external observer: an alien studying a species to which he didn't belong.

2018

Marion

Marion is giving Arron a bottle, the tears drying upon his little face now that he has got what he was crying for. He is warm in her arms, a beautiful feeling that takes her back twenty years, same as it does whenever she holds little Emily. The two babies she once cosseted on this very patio are sitting at the table right now, making chit-chat with Amanda. It gives her a glow to see them being welcoming and supportive.

'Did I hear right that you're a doctor?' Amanda asks Lia.

Marion is pleased to see that she is a little more talkative this morning. The girl seemed understandably shell-shocked and withdrawn yesterday, reeling from the situation in which she had found herself.

'Not quite,' Lia replies. 'I just sat my finals. Waiting for the results.' She holds up crossed fingers.

'Oh, you'll sail through,' Mum tells her. Marion wishes she wouldn't, scared she's jinxing it by tempting fate. It's always easy to be confident like that when you don't have skin in the game.

'If all goes well, I'll be starting as an FY1 in August.'

'What's that?' Amanda asks.

'Oh, Foundation Year One. What used to be known as a Junior House Officer.'

'And do you have a specialty you're aiming for, or is it too early?'

'It's way in the future, but I'd like to go into paediatrics.'

'And what do you do, Hugh?'

'Hugh is following his grandfather's footsteps into academia,' Celia answers for him. 'He's got his PhD and soon we're going to have another psychology professor in the family. A fitting tribute, if you ask me.'

Hugh looks bashful, like he always does when Mum makes a fuss.

'Gran's a few pages ahead,' he tells Amanda. 'I'm a lecturer at the University of Liverpool.'

'But not for much longer,' Mum butts in. 'Hugh's going to be teaching at Yale.'

'Oh, wow. Seriously?'

Hugh makes an anxious face, reflecting Marion's own feelings.

'I've been over for to the US for interviews and it's looking positive, but I'm not counting any chickens. I've got mixed feelings about having to uproot the three of us with Emily so small, but my wife Maggie keeps saying totally go for it. It's one of the reasons she stayed home: she's researching places where we might live and doing groundwork on the immigration process.'

'Maggie's right,' his sister tells him. 'It's an amazing opportunity.'

Marion looks at Hugh and Lia, still able to feel them in her arms, still able to picture them here when they were running around playing with dolls and water guns. She remembers how worried she always was for them back then and realises the catch they never tell you about parenthood. You do everything in your power to make sure they grow up safe and well, but there's no finish line. Your shift never ends. She knows she'll never be able to stop worrying about them. She'll always be trying to protect them.

Every time someone mentions Hugh going to Yale, she feels something close to panic. Part of her gets anxious about how crushed he will be if he doesn't get the post, while another part worries about Trump and mass shootings and all the dangers he'll face if he does go to the States.

Just like when they were little, everything still seems so precarious. Both of her babies are about to take major leaps forward in their careers, and she feels no different to when they were each about to start nursery, start school, start uni.

Ken says she needs to learn to let go, take pleasure in their taking flight. She knows he's right.

She looks across to where he sits on the edge of the pool, dandling his granddaughter on his knee with her feet dipped into the water.

She was kicking off just five minutes ago, but Emily always calms down whenever she is in his arms.

Marion knows the feeling.

She used to worry about what Hugh would be like as a father because he was so tempestuous when he was younger. She was always afraid whatever she was doing as a mother was making it worse. He grew out of it though, became more and more like his dad. Calm and unflappable.

Ken is the best of men, truly. He is a far better man than her father was. It took a long time to admit it to herself, because it felt disloyal, but it's true. He is a better person than either of her parents, and he was the first person to make her feel that she was worth more than them too.

They were always so snooty about him because he was 'a plumber'. He ran his own business, for God's sake. It used to annoy her, until she realised that prior to Dad's book deal, Ken was probably making more money than either of them. She suspected they knew that too, which was what really pissed them off. But the thing they really didn't like about Ken was that he made her happy. They had never done that.

Just as importantly, Ken helped her understand all the ways in which they had made her *un*happy. They acted permanently disappointed because she didn't have some glittering career like they had hoped, but Ken made her see that how they felt about it didn't matter. Marion liked what she did, and that was what counted.

A few years ago, Ken told her that Celia had once made a pass at him. He had never mentioned it before because it was during *that* holiday in 2002, which they didn't like to bring up in any context, but one night he got a little tipsy and spilled the story. It was not merely a revelation, but an epiphany. It made her see that Mum was actually jealous of her, of what she had, and even of who she had.

What Ken told her broke the spell of how Marion had always perceived her mother. It provided the key to understanding her behaviour and thus picturing it from the outside for what it really was. Celia had this aura of importance that Marion had bought into throughout her whole life, but now she could see that Celia was just needy and insecure, permanently hostage to her own narcissism. Everything she did, everything she said was ultimately about drawing attention back to Celia. If Marion ever found herself wondering 'Why is she acting this way, why is she saying that to me?' the answer was always the same. Once she understood that, from then on, she was able to observe rather than absorb.

She thinks of all the subtly disparaging remarks Mum makes about Marion's appearance. She used to feel hurt by them, until she realised that Mum was the one who was hurting. Mum was the one spending every day wishing she could regain what she had when she was an adolescent TV star.

During her failed seduction, Celia had boasted to Ken that she was in better shape than her daughter. Mum thought that meant something, thought that mattered, which was why Marion came to find her ridiculous. Marion doesn't care if anybody thinks she looks glamorous. She only cares about how she looks to Ken, and Ken loves what he sees. They are in their forties now and the pair of them are fucking like teenagers. Getting incorrigibly worse after Lia left home, in fact. No reason to keep the noise down. No reason not to do it in the wet room either.

Mum isn't harmless though, and Marion remains wary of her repertoire of dirty tricks and passive-aggressive mind games. But crucially she now understands that Celia is only ever as powerful as you believe she is.

Marion hears the buzz of a mobile. Amanda gets to her feet.

'It's Kirsten,' she says. 'I gotta take this. Are you okay with . . .'

'Arron is just fine,' Marion tells her. 'On you go.'

'Thanks.'

Marion watches her walk away briskly towards what she still thinks of as Vince's villa.

There's always an unreality about death, initially. You can't accept that someone won't simply reappear, that you'll never see them again. But Marion had an immunising dose of it just a few weeks ago, so it's easier to accept this time.

In fact, it cements the sense of an ending to know that Vince is really dead. She has this strong feeling that she won't be back here again, that this is the end of their relationship with this place and with everything that happened here. That's why the little ceremony at the clifftop yesterday meant more to her than the service back home. To Marion, it wasn't merely about saying goodbye to Dad.

She'll encourage Mum to sell up. All down the years Celia was determined to gather everybody together here again, saying it would help them get over the past, but Mum never truly wanted to confront it. What she wanted was for them to reunite here and act like the past didn't happen, to create a parallel timeline in which her family are harmonious.

It's time to move on. Every death is a chance for a new beginning. She feels sad for Kirsten and little Arron, but if Vince's death spells the end of a chapter, it means another one can begin. A better one.

She notices some movement inside and sees Sylvie walking into the kitchen holding her mobile. Ivy, rather. Marion can't get used to thinking of her as anything but Sylvie, especially in this place. She's looking at the list of phone numbers they keep taped to the wall.

The sight is a reminder of everything she needs to move on from. Marion is still uncomfortable around her sister, wary of some hidden agenda she might have for coming here. She realises that Sylvie's very presence makes her feel guilty. Every time she hears her sister's new name it causes Marion to worry how much she contributed to that transformation. And always, always, she wonders what accusations Sylvie secretly harbours towards her.

Everybody in this family harbours secret accusations though. When there is no definitive evidence, nobody can ever be sure about what's true, which means that among the Temples, everybody is potentially guilty. But the consolation for Marion is that as far as everybody else knows, it's still possible nobody is.

2002

Rory

Rory was sitting on his own outside a little café on the front at Praia Mexilhões. His table was right on the edge of the sand, next to a hut selling inflatable dolphins, Spider-man boogie boards and Luis Figo T-shirts. The beach was busy, full of people whose vibrant good cheer was an ample demonstration of how undetectable human emotion could be: all of them oblivious to the turmoil going on behind another person's eyes mere feet away.

He watched as a toddler upended a bucket of water into the hole her daddy was digging, a small action that seemed to disproportion-ately amuse the toddler and consequently delight her parents. He looked at their expressions and thought how he had seldom if ever witnessed such simple joy on the faces of Sylvie or Calum. The two of them were stuck with this kid they seriously didn't want, and Rory couldn't help but worry what the impact would be on poor Niamh. You only had to look at the three Temple children to see how fucked up you could get even when you were raised by two parents who had planned to have you.

The waiter brought him a coffee and placed it down on the table. Rory didn't like to think how much he would prefer it to be a beer, or five beers, but he needed a clear head. He had needed to get away from the villa, away from everybody: grab himself time and space to think.

Everyone was going home in less than forty-eight hours. Vince and Laurie were throwing some kind of party tonight, which would make it difficult to talk privately to anybody. He was running out of options.

He had been expecting Svetlana to really lose it when he told her

Dad's response. In a way it would have been easier if she had been hysterical, bawling and rending the sheets. Instead it was like she was used to it. Resigned to being let down.

'I'm so sorry,' he told her.

'It is not your fault, Rory. This is something I got myself into.'

'There's still time. I'll talk to my mother.'

He knew Dad would have told Celia already, but Rory thought he might be able to convince her to act independently, get their to see the truth. Maybe she wouldn't be blinded like Max was by his low opinion of his own son.

It didn't sound like Svetlana was listening. She had balled up on the bed, looking numb. Defeated. She didn't emerge from their room for a few hours after that. Rory had told people she wasn't feeling well, though he reckoned they all just assumed the two of them weren't getting on.

When Svetlana did appear, she had to act like nothing was wrong. They both did. Sit by the pool, chat and share meals, behave as though he and Dad hadn't had this shattering conversation. Fortunately, the awkwardness probably wasn't that conspicuous, because at any given time there was always some degree of weird tension around the Temple family.

Rory was planning to choose his moment for speaking to Mum, but she beat him to it. She had appeared alongside him in the other villa's kitchen about an hour ago, while Svetlana was playing with Lia in the pool.

'Your father told me,' was all she needed to say.

'He's got it all wrong, Mum. Svetlana's telling the truth. You don't know what she's had to put up with in her life. Seriously, we're two people who can help each other start again.'

Mum had listened attentively while he told her all about Svetlana's first marriage and what came after. This time he didn't hold back on the details.

'I do want to help, Rory,' she had said. 'If the situation is as you say, then when we get back home, we will all go together to the police.'

Rory had struggled to control his exasperation.

'Mum, this isn't a school bully asking for your dinner money.'

'Yes, and by the same token, if you just give them twenty-five thousand pounds, they're going to be back asking for fifty. I'm prepared to help Svetlana, Rory, but only on my terms. You can think about it.'

He sipped at the coffee, bitter, sharpening.

He hadn't broken this to Svetlana yet. He couldn't face how despondent her reaction would be. And yet, he asked himself, wasn't there some sense in what Mum was saying? Would it make for a more stable and assured resolution if they went through official channels to deal with this? Maybe when they got back to London, Svetlana would see that Celia had a point. The UK wasn't like the Ukraine or Russia. They could trust the police to help.

Or maybe they could just run, like he previously suggested. Liquidate everything they had. Cash in his rental deposit on the flat and spend it all on two tickets to Australia, take their chances on the far side of the globe. Despite Svetlana's fears, he doubted these guys would have that kind of reach.

Rory was pulled back from his thoughts by someone placing a coffee cup down on his table. He was about to say he hadn't ordered this when he looked up and saw that it wasn't the waiter who was standing there. It was a muscular blond guy in a crisp linen shirt and aviator shades, a five o'clock shadow failing to conceal the scar on his jawline.

'Rory, is it not?' he said, sitting down.

His accent was East European.

Rory made to get up. The guy grabbed his forearm with an unnervingly strong hand.

'You are with Svetlana, yes? You are . . . boyfriend?'

He had paused to search for the word, then seemed amused by the term in a way that Rory found menacing.

Rory nodded, feeling his guts turn to liquid.

'Svetlana not free to be girlfriend.'

The man made the universal gesture, rubbing his fingers against his thumb as he sat down. He sipped his coffee, staring at Rory over the rim of the cup. Then he indicated the T-shirts on the rack behind him.

'You like football, yes? Luis Figo. Very great player. Go Madrid from Barcelona. Sixty million euro. What is the word? Transfer. Now you want Svetlana transfer to you, but she still play for us.'

Now he made a cruder gesture, circling his left forefinger and driving the middle finger of his right hand through it.

'Still work for us. Svetlana does not come to you on Bosman, you understand? There is transfer fee. Or she must buy out her contract.'

'We are planning to pay,' Rory said. 'We're working on that. We just need a little time.'

The man shrugged.

'Time is okay. But here you are in Portugal. Maybe you think you can take Svetlana and run.'

Rory understood why Svetlana was so scared of these people. He felt like the guy could read his mind.

'We're on holiday,' he explained. 'With family.'

'Maybe you think you go further. America? Brazil?'

The man took a sip of his coffee then reached into his trouser pocket, from which he produced a pair of pliers. He placed them onto the table between the cups, the weight of it causing them to jingle on their saucers.

'I am here to show, like football, we are international business. We play all over the world. I go to Portugal, I find you, I find her. Is okay. Is holiday. You go somewhere else, but you go without pay transfer, I find you, I find her, and next time, we don't have coffee. You understand?'

Rory's mouth was too dry to speak. He merely nodded.

The man finished his drink, lifting the pliers and dropping a couple of euros on the table before walking away.

Rory sat and stared at the sea, unable to touch the rest of his cappuccino. He knew now why Svetlana hadn't been bawling and rending the sheets. There was too much fear and anguish to process, so he just felt numb instead.

His glazed eyes were called to focus by the approach of a familiar sight: Sylvie pushing Niamh in a buggy, Calum by her side. Niamh was crying, so perhaps some instinct in him had recognised the sound and reacted to keep his head down. He couldn't handle a conversation with anybody right now.

Sylvie was oblivious anyway, lost in her own world of misery, the centre of which was howling in front of her. Rory had heard someone say that the really intelligent infants cry a lot because they're frustrated at their inability to express themselves, insatiably curious but unable to ask questions. If this was true, then Niamh was going to be a fucking genius. He suspected it was just something that had been dreamed up to make suffering parents feel better.

Neither Sylvie nor Calum spoke as they walked along the front, Rory tracking their progress. The best he could say was that his sister looked lost in thought, but really the two of them just seemed utterly crushed. Nonetheless, Rory would gladly trade their problems for his right now.

If only it were that simple.

In attempting to debunk a conspiracy theory, the mistake we make is to think we are arguing against a hypothesis: rather it is a process, a permanently evolving entity. The official version is a fixed account, there to be tested, whereas the conspiracy theory is by nature non-disprovable. It is a tantalising trailer for a movie you will never see: the finished version is forever just beyond your grasp.

Max Temple

2018

Amanda

I get up from the table as soon as I see who the call is from.

'It's Kirsten. I gotta take this. Are you okay with . . .'

'Arron is just fine,' Marion tells me. 'On you go.'

'Thanks.'

I make my way back to the privacy of the other villa, where I swipe to answer as I walk through the sliding doors. I noticed Kirsten never fully closed them, not even at night. Neither do the Temples. I guess security isn't a big issue way out here, at least while the places are occupied. Maybe it's a reaction to being cooped up throughout the rest of the year. I can relate: I start to long for the smells of outdoors and the feel of milder air during the long winter back home. Right now though, my instinct is not to open up the barrier between outside and in, but to shut myself away.

'Kirsten. You doing okay?'

'Been better. Is Arron all right?'

She sounds tired, hoarse. She's been doing lots of crying, not so much sleeping. Like mother like son.

'Peachy. Marion's giving him a bottle right now.'

'I suppose he's the one who doesn't know what's just happened.'

'Ignorance is bliss.'

'How you doing? I'm so sorry to have dumped on you like this.'

'I'm good. I can handle things.'

'I've been looking up flights and I can get you both back to Glasgow tomorrow morning. It's the soonest I can manage.'

'No, sure, that's great. I mean, if you need me to keep Arron out here longer, if it would help you deal . . .'

237

I say this because I feel I ought to, and because it's what Rob and Sadiq would want me to say.

'It's easier to get things done when you ain't got a baby to worry about, but I don't feel like myself when he's not around. I miss him so much. All the more now, you know? He's all I've got. I'll get the flights booked on my phone now and I'll email you the details.'

'Thanks.'

I don't want to intrude, and yet I have to ask. It's just like I felt regarding the fact that Vince hadn't been in touch. Feels like a month ago, yet it was still the situation less than twenty-four hours back.

'You heard anything more about what happened?'

'Yeah. That's partly why I'm calling. The police . . .'

Her voice breaks up. She was trying to hold it together and clearly can't now that she's having to say whatever this is.

'They're treating it as suspicious. At first they thought he'd had a heart attack but then they noticed this bruise on his neck. They reckon he was injected with something. They think somebody killed him.'

'Holy shit.'

I hear Kirsten sniff back tears.

'I know, right? They're asking if I know anything, if I can think of any enemies he might have had, anybody he might have been on the wrong side of. Vince? Who was he ever a threat to? All the bloke did was work. Only thing I could think of was that he'd been talking about this deal, and being very cagey. I'm starting to wonder if it was all on the up and up. They won't tell me what actually happened, just little things like his phone is missing. Anyway, they need to get into his emails and they don't have the password. I need you to do me a favour.'

'Sure, anything.'

'I left my tablet over there at the villa because I wasn't thinking straight, and I bailed in a total blur. Vince sometimes used it for email and stuff.'

I noticed the tablet was still here last night. It's sitting on the arm of the sofa. I go over and pick it up, swiping to wake.

'I need your PIN.'

Kirsten tells me six numbers. I recognise them as Arron's date of birth, which I know because I had been looking after his passport on the flight. It seemed absurd that it would do him until he was five, I had thought. The picture had been taken a few weeks ago, and it barely even looked like him now. It could have been any baby.

'There's a password manager app on there. It's called PassKeeper or PassGuard, something like that. Anything Vince logged into on there, it will have saved the details.'

'PassKeeper. Found it.'

'Christ, when I was his secretary, *I* was his password manager. Vince is useless at this stuff.' She pauses. '*Was* useless. Anyway, you're going to need the master password for it.'

Kirsten dictates something complex that I can't imagine there being a mnemonic for, and the manager app decrypts itself. It provides a long list of accounts for programmes and websites.

'What do you need?'

Kirsten lists three email accounts. One has the name of Vince's business as a domain, the others Microsoft and Google accounts, created by default. I copy the usernames and passwords to an email and send it to Kirsten.

'I just feel like such an idiot who knows nothing about her husband, so I want to be able to give the police something, you know?'

'Absolutely. And if there's anything else, just holler.'

'Thanks, Amanda. You've been a diamond through all this.'

I hang up, wishing this were true. I've done next to nothing and feel pretty useless. I really want to help.

It suddenly hits me that I can.

Kirsten said Vince's phone was missing. She also said he sometimes used this tablet. Chances are whoever took the phone has switched it off to prevent precisely what I have in mind, but it's worth a shot. Even if it's lying in a trashcan someplace, the location might be a clue.

I google 'Android find my phone' and within seconds I am looking at a street on a map: the device is switched on after all. My heart races as I zoom out to see where it is.

Stirling UK.

That's when it dawns on me that I've only found Kirsten's phone, because that's who I'm logged in as. The PassKeeper app is still running, however.

I scroll down the list of programmes and websites until I reach the Google accounts. I find three.

SpecialK92@gmail.com. I figure that for Kirsten, probably her year of birth. Below it is vincible67@gmail.com and witness02@gmail.com. Vincible67 sounds the obvious bet, so I try that first.

I log in and once again google 'Android find my phone'. The screen hangs. I'm expecting the search to time out because the device is switched off, but a few moments later I'm looking at another map. This time I don't need to zoom out.

It's Baia Serena.

I feel like the walls just shook.

There is an explanation here that I'm not quite ready to contemplate. I need more information. My eyes are immediately drawn back to the list of accounts.

witness02.

2002. The year Niamh Temple died.

I quit out of the vincible67 account and log into the new one. I'm not looking for a phone this time, but for Vince's emails.

The inbox is empty apart from automatically generated notifications. I check the sub folders and trash. Still nothing. Then I open Sent Items, where I find two messages. I click on the one at the top and parse it in a blur.

To: XX171174@truemail.com
Subject: Back pay
My condolences re the late professor, but before you divide up his estate, I would like to stake my claim for a share as recompense for sixteen years of silence. I see that there has been quite a spike in his book sales, so I know there's plenty to go around.

I know what you are. I know what you did and what you covered up. I have always known, but now I've got hard proof, and the whole world is going to find out everything unless we can come to a fair and equitable accommodation.

240

Call when you're ready to talk terms. But if I don't hear from you, I'm going to produce the evidence right in the middle of your big family holiday.

Remember: you wouldn't just be doing this to protect yourself, but to protect your family from the truth.

He doesn't leave his name, only a cellular number. There is also an attachment. I click to download it, at which point the connection hangs. I can barely breathe.

A few seconds later, the glitch resolves itself and the download completes: a Word document. I open it but am presented only with a page of gobbledegook: just endless random sequences of letters. The file must have corrupted. I delete it and download the attachment again.

Same deal. Just a meaningless shitload of Gs, Ts, As and Ds.

Dammit.

I've no way of finding out what the doc was supposed to show, but that hardly matters next to what I now know for sure, which is that one of the Temples not only murdered Vince, but killed Niamh too. And I'm stuck here in the middle of them with Vince and Kirsten's baby.

2002

Marion – Rory – Sylvie

Having been told off by Laurie and Vince for trying to help with the food preparations, Marion decided to make herself useful by spelling Sylvie to give Niamh her bath. As was becoming a regular fixture, Lia was helping out, the upside of which was that she understood it to be a precursor to her own bedtime ritual.

Marion was anticipating some resistance tonight because the kids could always sense when the adults were gearing up for something and they got curious as to what they might be missing out on. Lia and Hugh had both watched with interest as Ken helped Vince move their patio table to the side of the pool. She knew there would be reappearances tonight, on various flimsy pretexts.

That said, the greater worry was that they got out of bed at night in a place like this and *didn't* come bother her – at least this way she'd know what danger they might be getting themselves into.

'Can I do it myself?'

Not this again, she thinks.

'Mummy needs to be here in case anything goes wrong.'

She caught Lia running a bath on her own yesterday. She said it was for her dollies, but she volunteered this information a wee bit too swiftly, the way the kids always did when they didn't want you to guess their true agenda.

Kind of like how weird Hughie was about the hanging thing now. She had spotted him on his own down by the cliff path, practising tying slipknots and hanging more of Lia's dolls. At least he seemed to be doing it surreptitiously since he'd become aware that the adults were all creeped out by it. She worried when he took himself off alone though.

She had always said she thought he was too young for some of

242

these movies. He had first seen that *Lord of the Rings* film when he was still only seven, and he had been watching *Robin Hood: Prince of Thieves* since he was five.

Ken just laughed off her concerns.

'They used to tell us daft shows like *Power Rangers* would make kids dangerous and violent,' he said. 'Though to be fair, I do have my concerns that it might make my children think they can solve their problems by morphing into a gigantic mechanoid.'

She should listen to Ken, she knew. He kept saying they'd be fine, that all they needed was love and common sense and you wouldn't go far wrong. He was probably right, but she wished he could tell her at what point she was going to stop being worried for them.

Rory was sitting in silence, looking at Svetlana as she sat before the mirror applying her make-up. He felt kind of sick at the prospect they might actually be going through with this, but he knew that if they were going to do it, it had to be tonight. Everybody was going to be distracted, and probably drunk.

The fact that it was even an option, that she had the connections to make this possible, had Rory asking himself whether this was her plan from the start. He was starting to wonder what kind of person she really was, wonder at the circles she moved in, the associations she might have. Starting to wonder if his dad was right.

'I understand what this is I am asking,' she said. 'To make you choose between me and family. But I want you to know, if you do this for me, we are for life.'

Rory knew this would be an unforgivable violation of family trust, that once you crossed a Rubicon like this, you could never come back. But he was prepared to do it – for her. He wanted to believe she wanted him. He wanted to believe his father was wrong. But more than anything else, he wanted to be with her, and he knew this would make that possible.

This would solve so many problems at a stroke.

There was a steady beat of music coming from Vince's villa, beneath a tinkle of laughter and a hubbub of voices. It carried on the night air but Sylvie doubted it was loud enough to wake the kids across in the other villas, assuming they were all asleep by now.

The gathering was well under way, the food all but gone. Things were panning out as anticipated: everyone gathered between Vince and Laurie's patio and the barbecue; people traipsing in and out to the kitchen where the drinks were. The activity centred where she wanted it.

Sylvie was sitting by the edge of the pool, watching everyone else eat and drink. Calum was hitting the beers hard and early as he sometimes did, like laying down a marker. He was already quite drunk, or pretending to be, as a signal that the baby was going to be her problem tonight.

She would get annoyed when she saw this, until she remembered Niamh wasn't his baby. None of this was his responsibility. It was something she had done to him. It was why she was a soft touch in that respect, always letting him get away with this. It created a vicious circle. Calum knew she would pick up the slack, so he pulled this kind of thing more and more often.

Mum was hitting it quite hard too. It was a reliable sign that she had given up on being the centre of attention: had to be pissed to tolerate people talking about something other than her. Dad by contrast was being typically abstemious. He could nurse a whisky for two solid hours, that man.

Laurie had her own supply, of course. No going in and out to the kitchen for her. She had that steadily depleting vodka bottle close by and she wasn't leaving it unattended. Her vigilance was probably unnecessary, Sylvie reckoned, as nobody would dare pour a measure from it. It was weird how people acknowledged someone's alcoholism to themselves while simultaneously pretending it wasn't happening.

Sylvie could have done with a drink to help her nerves, but she feared it would only make her sick, especially as she hadn't felt like eating anything. She had been on edge since the party was announced, understanding that a countdown had commenced to the moment when she had to commit fully either way: act ruthlessly or live for ever with the hand she'd been dealt. Now the time was almost upon her and every passing minute made her more anxious. No matter how much she thought she had prepared herself, it was all still hypothetical until the moment that it wasn't.

She looked up at the night sky above the sea. The stars were always so vivid here, and there seemed so many of them. It was darker than at home, less light pollution.

She just worried that it would be dark enough. They seemed like a billion little eyes, ready to bear witness.

Stars hide your fires. Let not light see my black and deep desires.

2018

Amanda

I look through the sliding doors towards the villa on the other side of the pool, and the people seated outside. I feel a sudden and profound sense of threat, as though somebody over there knows what I have been looking at. I tell myself this part is nuts, but that doesn't change what I'm feeling. There is no innocent explanation for what I have just seen, or for Vince's phone being here. Someone over there has got it. Someone over there killed Vince, and whether they know it yet or not, I am now a problem for them.

I'm scared, and I know I'm right to be.

I think back to Saturday morning, when Vince bailed on us just before we were due to leave for the airport.

This is worth a lot of money, but I have to tie it up now.

This is what he was talking about toasting with Champagne: he was blackmailing one of the Temples, and he must have believed they were about to deal. He thought he was going to get his payout, but ended up dead in his office. I don't know why he went to the airport in between times, some kind of double-cross maybe, but it's what happened next that really matters.

I realise that's why they took his phone. Those texts to Kirsten: only texts, no calls. Making out he was still alive to buy somebody time, and maybe even buy them an alibi.

I open the second email in the Sent Items folder, noting it was sent more than a couple of weeks before the other one.

There's nothing ambiguous about the addressee this time. It's to maxtemple@st-andrews.ac.uk.

I feel my scalp tingle as the words unspool, like my own hair is suddenly alien.

I know you were the father of Niamh Temple. I know you raped your own daughter.

And I can prove it.

A shudder seizes me like a cold darkness just passed over the building.

Jesus H.

Incest. Rape. Murder. Who the fuck are these people?

The email carries the same demand for recompense for Vince's years of silence. I wonder how he could have known something like this, how he could prove it.

I notice that this email has an attachment also, the file bearing the same name as the other. Maybe this time it will work. I download and open the document, but again it's just swathes and swathes of random jumbled-up letters. Then it hits me. They're not random, they're sequences.

On a hunch I go to Google Images and type in 'DNA sequence'. Several of the results show me something very similar: banks of text comprising Gs, Ts, Cs and As.

The file wasn't corrupt.

I look again at the date on the message, belatedly sussing its significance. The email was sent on the day Max Temple died. That can't be a coincidence. He had a massive heart attack when he was confronted with evidence of crimes he must have long since assumed he'd gotten away with.

I feel a surge of anger and revulsion, mixed with self-disgust at the way I'd previously felt about him. I'm glad he's dead. The fucker got what was coming to him, but Vince's plan hadn't died with him. Knowing there was still money to be had, especially with Max's book sales soaring in the wake of his death, he moved on to blackmailing someone else.

XX171174

witness02

Vince knew who killed Niamh, and he had been silenced for ever to keep that secret. But if I was to find out who murdered Vince, I would have the answer to a mystery nobody has been able to solve in sixteen years.

A hell of a scoop for an aspiring journalist.

I can rule out Celia and Marion because I saw them at the airport Saturday morning. They were both airside, as airtight as an alibi gets. The two of them had seen Vince in the departure area, and though Kirsten and I hadn't, the woman at the departure desk confirmed he had cleared security. When he bailed to go back to his office, Celia and Marion were getting on an airplane to Faro along with me, Kirsten and Arron.

I'm kind of relieved. I like Marion, and although I felt we got off to a bumpy start, I'm warming to Celia too.

Rory arrived several hours later, which puts him in the frame. He had flown here after connecting in London, but that's only what he told everyone. It's not like anybody would ask to see his flight itinerary. I think of the forums and blogs I browsed, the speculation over his girlfriend travelling under a fake name and passport. She was connected to Eastern European people traffickers, so who knows what she might have coerced him into back then.

I reckon I can safely rule out Hugh and Lia, as they were just kids in 2002, but then I remember the theory that one of them had killed the baby by accident or misadventure. Hugh was up for a post at Yale and Lia was about to start her medical career. It would be a disastrous time for this story to come out, even if they weren't legally culpable. And they were both still in the UK at the right time.

It sounds a stretch, though. When people talk about motive, means and opportunity, they often misunderstand the second one. It's not merely the gun, the knife, the rope or candlestick: it's about whether you have it in you to take a life, to make that decision outside the heat of the moment and follow it through. It takes someone coldly resolute, calculating and ruthless.

Wow, who might that be?

However, according to Marion, Sylvie got here before any of us. She had flown from Edinburgh on a flight that landed an hour ahead of the Glasgow one. But why from Edinburgh when she lived in London?

Someone coldly resolute, calculating and ruthless might bring in a third party, making sure she was out of the country at the time and therefore giving herself a solid alibi. It might even have been cheaper to pay a professional than to pay off Vince, who not only knew what happened to her baby, but what her father had done to her too. She wouldn't have wanted that to become public knowledge either.

But if I allowed the possibility of the killer paying a third party, then Marion and Celia were no longer in the clear either. If Marion had covered up her child's role and Vince knew about it, she might still be protecting that child now. Same went for Celia. Maybe she had played a part in covering up what happened in 2002. The email did say its recipient would be doing this 'to protect your family from the truth'.

It's still an impossible riddle, and I realise there's a damn good reason this person's previous crime has gone undetected for sixteen years. And yet the truth is tantalisingly close: hidden behind a single email address. If I could gain access to each of their phones, I would soon find out who the address belongs to, but with that thought I remember what my priority ought to be right now. I need to call Kirsten, get her to relay all this to the cops.

I pull my cell from my pocket, but as I hold the device in my hand and unlock the screen, I suddenly envisage how I can unlock the truth.

Occam's Razor simplified states that the simplest explanation is usually the right one, but to the conspiracy theorist, the obvious explanation is never correct. There must always be dark forces and occult motives hidden beneath the façade.

Max Temple

2002

Celia – Vince

Celia wasn't sure she wanted to do this any more. She used to look forward so much to getting the whole family together here at the villas, but it just felt like hard work these days. It used to mean something that Marion and her family still came here, and she had been pleased that Rory was making the trip for the first time in ages, but instead of feeling like they were all coming together, it just seemed more obvious how they were drifting apart. They were all so caught up in their own lives. Only ever interested in themselves.

It had been brewing in her mind a while, but it hit her extra hard on Sunday, when once again she had found herself the only one at mass. She used to love taking her children to the little church down in Praia Mexilhões. She had done it many a Sunday long before they bought the villas, when they used to come here and rent a townhouse down in the village.

Marion and Rory had each stopped going to church when they went to uni, falling in with trendy student group-think, but she had been sure they would come back around. She remembers glowing with pride (and not a little vindication) when Marion had each of her kids baptised. Her eldest was full of promises and noble intentions when they were little, but she didn't follow up. She hadn't even sent Hughie to a Catholic school.

Celia gazed across the patio to where Marion stood, her arm around her husband's waist, his resting on her ample thigh. The two of them were always pawing at each other. It made her sick. Her schoolteacher daughter and Plumber Ken.

She couldn't watch them any more. She looked towards Rory instead, but that didn't help. She had been briefly impressed that her son had snared someone remarkable for a change, instead of the usual tattooed tramps and body-pierced slackers, but the tarnish came off right quick when Max sussed her out. She was just some scheming gold-digger who had cooked up a tale, and Rory had fallen for it. He had always been a soft touch for a sob story. So disappointingly wet.

She had to give the gold-digging whore her due, though. Svetlana had to know they weren't biting, and yet she was remaining in character, pretending she didn't know certain conversations had happened. She was being not merely polite but soft-hearted and solicitous, hoping if her performance was convincing enough, Max and Celia would start to have doubts and ultimately relent.

And then there was her youngest, the unmarried teenage mother. Didn't that make her heart swell. Maybe it was true that talent skipped a generation, and it would be her grandchildren who did her proud. Or would they find some way to lay her low too?

Frankly, she couldn't wait for this holiday to be over.

She glanced across at Marion and Ken once more, like probing a hurting tooth. The sight of him made her cringe inside as she kept replaying the incident of a few nights ago.

It was because she had been drunk: both the impetus for trying to seduce him, and more significantly the reason it didn't succeed. Ken was so much younger, and always a little intimidated that she had been a TV star. He hadn't wanted to take advantage of her in case she wasn't sincere, probably not believing she would want him if she wasn't half-cut. And he was right. But more significantly, the booze meant she had been off her game. If she had been straight, she wouldn't have failed. She still had what it took. She could have any man she wanted.

With that thought, Celia drained her gin and tonic and headed for the kitchen.

Vince knocked back another mouthful of Sagres and wished his dad had been alive to see this: iconic seventies' actress Celia Wilde and her husband, academic, author and lately TV talking head Professor Max Temple, partying with their extended family here at Vince's private villa in the Algarve.

254

Not that he would have wanted to share any of it with the old man. Just wanted to show him he was wrong.

Look at the state of this. Can't trust you to do anything properly. You're a no-user, son, that's what you are. You'll never amount to anything if you don't buck up your ideas.

Vince took in the villas, the swimming pool, the starlit sea and the people.

I've amounted to this much, you miserable prick.

On reflection, he was glad his father had never come here. He'd have found some reason this place wasn't good enough either. Nothing Vince did was ever good enough.

Christ, he thought, why was the bastard still in his head all these years later? A grown adult with his own life, his own business, all this.

Maybe because he knew the old man was right. What he had *wasn't* good enough. He only had to look at his wife to see that.

He watched her pour another straight shot from the vodka bottle she was jealously guarding. He had thought she was doing better this holiday, but though Laurie had never exactly been on the wagon, she was falling off it hard tonight.

He kept catching her looking at Max again, too. He had noticed it any time they were together at close quarters, a weird, obsessive vibe coming off her. He wondered again about Easter, when she came out here alone at a time when he was too busy to join her. Was it only so that she could get pissed, drink in peace without his disapproval, or was she having an affair with the esteemed professor? It certainly fucking looked like it.

It would be kind of hypocritical for him to get outraged, given the blind eye Laurie had turned to his many indiscretions. But those indiscretions – and that blind eye – were a mutually unspoken response to the fact that they had all but stopped having sex, so Vince had a right to be royally pissed off if she was giving it out to someone else.

He saw Celia come through the sliding doors carrying an empty glass, headed for the kitchen. Their eyes met, and she gave him a warm smile.

'Excellent soirée, Vince. Truly, one of the highlights of the holiday.'

As usual, he could not be sure whether she was sincere or simply very accomplished at faking that sincerity. Also as usual, he didn't really care. He was happy enough to bask in it either way.

'You ready for a refill of something?' he asked as she joined him in the kitchen.

'Oh, why ever not?' she replied, putting her glass down on the worktop. 'Another Bombay Sapph, please.'

Vince reached for the bottle of gin at the same time she did, her hand briefly gripping his arm.

'Hmm,' she murmured curiously.

'What?'

Celia placed the same hand on his bicep and squeezed.

'I didn't think a busy lawyer would have much time to work out. The evidence appears to be to the contrary.'

'I don't get to the gym nearly as often as I'd like, but I force myself to make time because I spend so much of my day sat behind a desk. I find it's crucial for mind and body.'

'I hope Laurie appreciates the effort,' Celia said as he poured her a generous measure. 'It's a long time since Max's arm felt like that, if it ever did. Comes to us all though. The toll of the years.'

'Some more than others,' Vince suggested.

'That's very kind and much appreciated,' she replied, smiling. 'To be honest, there's a double-edged sword to my showbiz past. Other women my age, people only see what's there: they don't have an image of what she looked like twenty-five years before. Whereas when people look at me, they can still see Kurlia. Sometimes I suffer by comparison, but sometimes I think they merge the two in their minds. I'll get the benefit of that for a little bit longer, I hope.'

Vince felt a spark of something, like an electrical signal, uncertain if its source was chemistry or wishful thinking. He thought of words he wasn't sure he ought to say, but what the hell, it was only a compliment, wasn't it? Her husband was just outside, not ten yards away, so it wasn't like Vince could be accused of seriously chancing his arm. Even though he totally was.

'I think the only thing that matters is that you look great right now. What you looked like twenty-five years ago doesn't come into it.'

'Oh, you're so sweet,' she said, letting out a chuckle.

He felt a weird mix of relief and disappointment. Relief that he'd got away with it being taken as a polite compliment. Disappointment that she hadn't read more of an edge into it.

Celia crouched down in front of the fridge and opened the door. She was leaning forward. The way her dress was falling open, he could see right down it. Vince couldn't stop himself, couldn't not look. He saw the curve of her right breast and just the tantalising upper edge of her aureole before it met the material of her bra.

'Is the freezer part the bottom or the top half of this thing?' she asked, glancing up. Catching him looking.

Celia stood straight again, closer to him now.

'You weren't just being sweet, Vince, were you?'

'Not entirely,' he said.

He felt her fingers wrap around his.

'I don't know how to put this delicately, so I'm going to come right out with it.'

Her voice was low and quiet, intimate. He could feel the warmth of her breath on his cheek.

'I am increasingly of the belief that your wife is fucking my husband.'

She looked him deep in the eye, perhaps waiting to see if he was shocked by the revelation.

'The thought had crossed my mind too,' he replied.

She placed a delicate hand on his crotch.

'How would you like to even up the score?'

Vince had to swallow before he could answer.

'I'd like to even the score and take a commanding lead.'

She told him to give it a couple of minutes, so they weren't seen going into her villa together. It was a bloody long two minutes. Vince's heart was thumping throughout, afraid that the moment had passed and she might have changed her mind by the time he got there. It seemed a wonder his heart had anything to pump, as it felt like all the blood had already gone to his cock.

He took the long way, around the back of the villas, and glanced across before entering, to check if he was being observed. Everyone seemed consumed by their own conversations, and most of them were too pissed to be paying attention. The law student kid Calum was already flaked out on a lounger.

Celia was waiting for him at the near end of the hall, next to an open doorway. It didn't look like she had changed her mind. She was unbuttoning her dress.

'We'll have to be quiet and we'll have to be quick,' she said in a whisper.

Vince reckoned he would try his best with the first but feared the second would be a given.

He was surprised by the ferocity with which they went at each other, Celia dragging him through the doorway and onto the bed. They stripped each other with desperate impatience, his jockeys barely off before Celia had pulled him inside her.

Part of him wished he could turn the light on. It seemed a hell of a waste to have Celia Wilde's body writhing naked beneath him yet be unable to see it properly. What light there was spilled from the half-open door to the hall. In their tangled rush they hadn't closed it, but it wasn't like he was going to interrupt proceedings to pull it to.

Besides, if they got caught, it wasn't going to be because they hadn't closed the door. Celia had said to keep things quiet, but she was not as good as her own intentions. She was pushing upwards against him, arching her back, eyes closed, oblivious to the sounds of her own passion.

Vince did not allow himself to get similarly lost in the moment for fear doing so would hasten the moment being over. He wanted it to last, and he wanted to remember it. That was why he noticed the sound of soft footsteps, why he looked up and saw her as she passed the doorway, carrying the baby wrapped in a purple blanket.

2018

Amanda

I've got everything set after only a couple of minutes, but I can't act until everyone is present. I might need to wait until lunchtime for Sylvie to physically join us around the table, but she only needs to be in earshot, and if she's guilty, she'll be listening.

The rest of them haven't moved. They're waiting for me to return. Waiting for news.

I see Sylvie emerge on to the patio. She doesn't head for a sun lounger though. She's hovering.

That's my cue.

I walk back around the pool, lifting Arron from Marion's arms. His weight and warmth are a comfort after all I have been forced to confront.

'How is everything?' Marion asks, her tone solicitous but not optimistic.

'Not great. Kirsten sounds pretty messed up. The cops think Vince was murdered.'

I take in all their responses, trying to gauge who looks less surprised than they ought to be, who is maybe faking it to compensate. I see nothing that makes it any clearer.

Lots of 'My God's and 'How awful's.

'She's in bits but she's booking flights to get the two of us back home in the morning. She's really missing having Arron around. He was her life before, but he's *all* her life now.'

'Of course,' Celia says.

'She says she just thinks about him all the time. He's everything. Turns out even the PIN for her iPad is his date of birth. At least if I forget it I can look at his passport.'

I let this apparently incidental information rest for a while, before going on.

'I just can't believe it. He was meant to be right here, right now. Murdered.'

'Who would want to kill Vince?' asks Marion.

'I know, right? That's why Kirsten had me looking at her tablet. A whole bunch of Vince's emails are on there, stuff that wasn't on his laptop. The police need to see them.'

With the bait in place, I wait a few minutes before priming the trap.

'I think I'll take Arron for a walk along the cliff path. Doesn't look like we're gonna be here much longer, so I figure I better make the most of it.'

'Yes. You do that,' Marion says. 'Use it to clear your head.'

I rub a little sunblock onto Arron's arms, legs and face. He doesn't resist. He's starting to get sleepy after his bottle.

I push the buggy out onto the path, past the fated spot where Niamh supposedly fell. I keep walking for ten minutes or so until Arron is asleep, by which time I can no longer see the villas, and crucially their inhabitants can no longer see me.

There is a bench up ahead, looking out over the cliff beneath the shade of some trees. I engage the brake on Arron's buggy, check he's definitely nodded off and pull out my cell. Even in the shade I need to angle it against the brightness of the day, but the image is coming through clear and steady. I'm streaming live from my laptop, which I've set up in the living room of the villa. Its screen is black and apparently off, but the webcam is pointed directly at the sofa, upon which Kirsten's tablet is sitting.

I sit down on the bench as I stare at the phone, willing something to happen. Wondering how long I've got. Glancing up now and again to see if anyone's coming. Glancing at Arron in case he wakes up. If he starts bawling, I'll have to intervene.

I am alerted by a flicker of shadow on the screen, a change in the light. Something moves past, mostly out of shot. I only catch a glimpse of bare feet. Shit.

I contain my frustration when I remember that whoever it is will first be looking for the passport, which I have helpfully left in plain sight on the sideboard next to Vince's hi-fi.

A few seconds pass. The light changes again. More movement. Then I learn that my spidey sense is pretty good after all, as I watch my prime suspect literally move into the frame.

I can barely breathe at seeing the truth finally revealed, and yet there seems a tragic inevitability to it.

Occam's Razor simplified states that the simplest explanation is usually the right one.

The damaged and emotionally cut-off teenager dropped her own baby over the cliff-edge and left the blanket for someone else to find. She got rid of the daughter who was a product of incest, so that she could be free of the man who raped her. That was why she was so cold and defiant in the photographs.

The conspiracy theorists had been right in this case, but Occam's Razor still applied, and so did Temple's Law.

A conspiracy theory collapses at the point where it requires greater complexity than the official explanation.

There was never a conspiracy, because it was one person acting alone. Sometimes one is all it takes. Especially if it's one as smart and ruthless as Sylvie Temple.

2002

Rory

Rory was worried that things were winding down, concerned that they might have left it too late. He had spotted Mum go into her villa a while ago, and the plan was screwed if she didn't emerge again. He forgot how early some folk could head for their beds. Parenthood seemed to turn people into sleep addicts, and there didn't appear to be a recovery programme.

Marion had wandered off before that, saying she was just going to check on the kids. Rory would have expected her to be back by now. She had been gone long enough for him to wonder if there was a problem, or if she had just decided she'd had enough and hit the sack.

He hovered by the table where the last scraps of barbecue sat, pretending he was still after a bite. Rather, he was waiting for the time to be right.

He watched Svetlana standing on the patio with Ken and, more significantly, with Dad.

Rory didn't feel so conflicted now that it came to it, looking at his father being a hypocritical prick as usual. Acting all nicey-nicey to Svetlana's face when he had made it clear he thought she was essentially a whore: sleeping with Rory as part of a scam. In fact, it had struck him that there was a worse possibility: that Max might believe Svetlana's story was true, and believe she really did love his son, but he didn't give a fuck.

Yeah, choosing family loyalty or choosing Svetlana. It wasn't a tough one.

He glanced at his watch, wishing he had taken note of what time Mum went in there. Then finally he saw her emerge through the patio doors.

That was his cue. Now or never.

It was Svetlana's job to make sure Max was occupied out here while Rory snuck into his parents' bedroom. His role was to note all his dad's credit card and bank details, sort codes, passport number: everything they needed so that Svetlana could facilitate a wire transfer to an anonymous account. Dad was funding their new beginning whether he liked it or not.

He waited until Mum had joined the others on the patio then slipped away, heading towards his parents' villa. That was when he encountered Sylvie coming in the opposite direction.

He could tell something was up right away. She had this frantic, hunted look on her face.

'Is everything okay?' he asked, though clearly it wasn't.

Her voice was faint, frightened, disbelieving.

'I can't find Niamh.'

2018

Ivy

Ivy sees the tablet lying on the sofa as soon as she enters Vince's villa through the sliding doors. She is about to go straight to it when she remembers she needs the passport first.

L's contact had worked worryingly fast in remotely switching on Vince's phone, and when she saw its location plotted on-screen, the implications hit her hard. She was desperate to find out what else might be known by whom, which was why she came out to the patio when she saw Amanda join the gathering.

There had been nothing reassuring about what the girl said. It was exactly as L intimated, but far worse in light of what she had learned subsequently. Ivy needed to know more. If the police were about to read Vince's emails, then she wanted to see them first. She always worried that Vince knew something, and feared he knew everything.

Amanda heading out for a walk provided the perfect opportunity, though Ivy had to wait a while to be sure she was well gone, and not about to come back because she'd forgotten the baby's dummy or whatever. She had to choose her moment, waiting for the others to disperse or occupy themselves with their phones and books so that she wasn't observed trespassing on their neighbour's property.

Ivy keys in Arron's date of birth. The tablet tells her the pin is incorrect.

She tries it again, this time in eight-digit format, giving the full year. The lock screen vanishes, and she is presented with a Gmail page, the account named as witness02. She goes to the Sent folder, where there are two messages: one to maxtemple@st-andrews.ac.uk and one to XX171174@truemail.com.

She reads them both. It is everything she feared.

264

Now I've got hard proof.

'Oh, Vince, you stupid bastard.'

She looks at the document attached to both emails, recognising the content immediately. It is Niamh's DNA, the sample she got analysed and documented back in 2002 after that Easter holiday, when she became afraid Max might harm the baby because she constituted living proof of his crimes. This was her way of warning him off, her dead man's pedal: hard evidence that he was Niamh's father.

Max had been appalled and offended when she confronted him with it, and not just because she had changed the rules. He seemed genuinely hurt by the idea that she could believe he would 'pose a danger to his own flesh and blood'. She was aghast at the sincerity of his response. Yeah, why would she think a man who raped one of his daughters might possibly be a threat to another? Aware of the twisted distinction in his mind, she immediately began to worry about him starting on Niamh.

But what's confusing her is that she had ordered the sample itself destroyed. She no longer needed it after Niamh was gone. Only the data remained.

Max wasn't to know that though, so maybe Vince was bluffing. He had to be, because he had no way of proving the DNA result belonged to who he claimed it did.

Unless . . .

Ivy feels dizzy for a moment, like the whole room is spinning. She snaps back, a truly ancient instinct taking over.

She looks again at the second address: XX171174@truemail.com. It is Marion's date of birth. She had recognised it right away, but now it makes her think of the PIN she just entered, and the passport that had been conveniently sitting there in the same room. Amanda telling them all she was going for a walk, leaving everything unattended.

Ivy looks up from the tablet and notices a laptop sitting a few feet away. Its screen is black, but there is a tiny lens in the centre of the bezel above.

Clever girl. She set a trap. But Amanda doesn't have the full picture, and now she's the one the jaws are closing on.

265

2002

Vince

He glanced at his wife. She noticed and looked back, holding his gaze. They had been sitting there for close on an hour, neither of them uttering a single word, but they both knew that had to change, and soon.

Vince finished his coffee and put the mug firmly down on the table like he was calling a meeting to order.

'So, before the police come knocking,' he said, 'do you want to talk about what we saw?'

Laurie reached for the vodka bottle and began to pour.

'You're going to need a drink,' she told him.

'I really don't think that's a good idea.'

'Trust me, it'll help. I insist.'

She poured out half a glass, a ludicrously large measure for any time of the day, and placed it in front of him.

'Drink.'

Laurie's expression told him not to refuse.

He smelled it as he raised the glass to his lips; or rather, he smelled nothing. There was no odour. Vince took a sip.

It was water. This was what she'd been drinking last night.

'I guess this is the part where we both say: "it wasn't what it looked like",' she suggested.

'No,' Vince confessed. 'What you saw was exactly what it looked like. I was screwing Celia. So why don't you tell me what the hell you were doing with the baby everybody's looking for, and why you were pretending to be pissed while you were doing it?'

Laurie picked up the bottle and contemplated it. She let out a joyless laugh.

'Do you know why I started drinking, Vince?'

She pinned him with her gaze, making him understand that it wasn't a rhetorical question.

'We never talked about it,' he said. It sounded feeble and he knew it.

'But you must have speculated.'

Vince said nothing. He nodded, though.

'I never felt it was my place to ask.'

'Sometimes I wish you would. Mostly I'm glad you haven't. But we're here now, so I'll tell you, and then we won't talk about it again. I was raped. It happened when I was a student. I was eighteen and it damaged me for keeps. It was someone I trusted, and someone whose word everybody would have believed over mine, which was why I was never able to tell anybody. I should have told you. I realise that. I thought being with you would help me get over it, that I could have a normal relationship, but the marks it left were indelible.'

Laurie swallowed, stiffening in her posture. She looked him in the eye.

'So now you know,' she said.

Vince nodded. He didn't know what to say, but figured his role was to listen. What he couldn't figure was where this was going.

Laurie gazed across towards the other villas.

'When I came here at Easter, it was to drink: I think you guessed that much. I was out there on the patio one night, sitting on that sunbed, drinking until I passed out. I must have fallen off the lounger and been too comatose to feel anything, because when I came to I was lying on the tiles. I heard voices nearby: Sylvie and Max having what they thought was a private conversation. They hadn't seen me because I was spark out on the floor.

'They were talking about how well everything was going for Max with the book deal and everything. Then Sylvie told him she could take it all away in a heartbeat.'

'How?'

'By telling the world he had raped her, and that Niamh was living proof.'

Vince felt frozen for a moment, caught in Laurie's stare, which conveyed that there was nothing nuanced or ambiguous about what she was telling him. He had to look away, so he gazed down into the glass. He was wishing it really was vodka now. He drank it anyway.

'I realised I should have seen it myself. The signs were right there, but for years I'd been too shitfaced to put it together. I remembered seeing that little girl so full of potential. She looked like she could do anything. Then I watched her diminished by teenage pregnancy and early motherhood. Utterly defeated, the light gone out of her eyes. And once I learned why, I couldn't stand by and do nothing.'

Vince felt as though the room had shuddered, but it was just him.

'What did you do, Laurie?'

'I let her know she could talk to me. I told her I knew the truth. And I told her how I could help.'

It was an answer and not an answer.

He asked the question again.

'What did you do, Laurie?'

2018

Amanda

I watch Sylvie look up from the tablet and stare directly at the webcam. She then puts down the device and exits from view.

I've been made.

I feel suddenly vulnerable out here on the path, the plunge to the water and rocks below no longer a postcard view, but a stark warning. I need to get to where there are other people. I need witnesses. I already told Kirsten to relay all this to the cops back home, but it wasn't like they were going to come screaming around the corner over here. Less than an hour ago I fancied myself the investigative reporter, but now I'm in way over my head.

As I stand up from the bench and take the footbrake off the buggy, I hear footsteps approaching from around the bend. I stop dead, temporarily paralysed by fear.

To my relief it is only Celia, out for a stroll.

She must have read the alarm in my face.

'Is everything all right, dear? I mean, apart from . . .'

I feel my lip tremble. I shake my head.

'What's wrong?'

'I've got some very bad news. Terrible, in fact.'

'From Kirsten?'

'No, but it is about Vince. We're going to need to get the police.'

'What on earth's the matter?'

Jeez, how could I tell her something like this? And yet I had to. I was in danger and I needed allies.

'This is going to be very difficult for you to hear, Mrs Temple, and I really hate having to be the one who tells you.'

'Celia, please. And you can tell me anything.'

'I've reason to believe it was Sylvie who killed Vince.'

Celia looks confused, almost like she didn't hear right.

'Sylvie? No.'

'I'm serious.'

She gives me a patient little semi-smile.

'Look, I appreciate the two of you didn't hit it off, but with respect, Amanda, I think you're being irrational. And not in possession of the facts, either. Sylvie was already over here when Vince died.'

'I think she may have paid someone to do it.'

Celia's starting to look pissed.

'This is horrible. Why would you say this?'

I need her onside, and fast.

'When I said the police wanted to see Vince's emails, it was bait. I set up a camera to monitor who would go get Kirsten's tablet. I *watched* Sylvie do it. I've got the recording backed up to the cloud.'

Celia still sounds calm, though it's like she's keeping a lid on her anger at me.

'I'm sure there's some other explanation. She was maybe just curious about what happened. She's had her own tragedy to deal with, after all. Why should she wish Vince any harm?'

'He was blackmailing her. His email said he's got proof that . . .'

I need to take a breath, steel myself to actually voice this.

'He said he had proof that Sylvie killed Niamh.'

Celia's irritation is growing.

'Oh, that's preposterous. Honestly, if you knew what this family has had to endure, and the work my husband did to combat these peddlers of fantasy and innuendo. I'm disappointed you would even begin to entertain—'

I wonder why the woman's not more curious. I figure I'm not getting through. Celia's rejected the notion from the get-go, so she's not hearing what I'm telling her.

'Vince was blackmailing your husband too,' I interrupt. 'He said he had proof that Max was Niamh's father.'

Celia is hearing me now.

'He said he knew that Max raped his own daughter. Vince sent an email threatening to expose this on the day Max died.'

270

Celia looks frozen, like a video that's buffering. She seems vacant, suspended, as though she's completely absent from the moment.

As I look at her, I'm reminded of the first time I saw Celia, only a few days ago. It was while we sat in the departure area at Glasgow Airport, waiting for our flight, waiting for Vince. If only it had been me and Kirsten who caught sight of him, rather than Celia and Marion, everything might have played out differently. Kirsten would have railed at him to just get his ass on the goddamn plane.

But that's when I realise. Vince was never in the departure area. He didn't make it to the airport. His boarding pass was on his phone, which meant that whoever took it simply needed to scan it at Security to create an electronic alibi, putting Vince in the departure lounge when in fact he was already dead. And then to seal the deal, she had claimed to see him in Starbucks.

The revelation shows on my face, just as Celia snaps back into the here and now.

She's looking at me differently. We hold each other in a frozen gaze. I feel like the air has just electrified around me. I know I'm in danger.

2018

Ivy – Amanda

Ivy puts down the tablet and bolts from the villa. She has no care to be discreet about her exit for fear of being seen. There is nothing left to hide.

She knew her mother had killed Vince the moment she saw her email address on his blackmail demand: her first child's gender and date of birth. The last time she saw it had been on the message she was sent about Mum's secret Catholic funeral for Max. That was another instance of her mother inhabiting a version of the world as she envisaged it ought to be, caring nothing for other people's wishes or feelings if they got in the way.

That was why Vince hadn't merely given her a reason to kill him. He had inadvertently triggered the means too. She had an extreme defence mechanism when reality threatened to broach her fantasy vision of herself.

Killing Vince had not wiped away the evidence, however. That was why Amanda, in laying her trap, had identified herself as a new threat.

Ivy sees Marion coming out of her villa clasping a magazine and a bottle of sun cream, and sprints towards her.

'Where's Mum?'

'She went for a walk. Said she was going up to Dad's bench. Is everything all right?'

'No. Call the police. Right now.'

Ivy leaves Marion's subsequent questions unanswered as she takes off running between the villas, through the gap in the hedge and onto the clifftop path.

Vince had known all along. He'd known everything. Laurie must have had to tell him, for whatever reason. Maybe the burden was too heavy to bear alone. For all their difficulties, she and Vince had been close back then, and she trusted him. But Laurie never shared with Sylvie the fact that Vince was in on their secret. She must have figured there was nothing to fear, and she didn't want Sylvie worrying needlessly. Vince couldn't tell anybody what he knew without incriminating his wife and indeed incriminating himself for his silence and thus complicity.

But Laurie had died last year, when Vince had a new wife and a baby on the way.

Ivy catches a glimpse of them as the path emerges from between bushes. They are up by Dad's bench, stood facing each other in conversation. Something about it feels wrong. It suddenly strikes her what it is: they're not speaking, only staring. They're not in conversation. They're in a stand-off. At the cliff-edge.

I want to get away but I feel paralysed, pinned to the spot. I dare not take my eyes off Celia because I'm scared of dropping my guard. There is nothing but cold fury and hatred in her expression, and she looks suddenly so much older. It's like she's put on a mask, or that the mask she was wearing has been lifted.

I feel so very alone. I want my dads.

I sense movement in my peripheral vision and I can't stop myself reacting to it. I glance to my right, over Celia's left shoulder, where I am relieved to see Ivy running towards us. But as I break our mutual stare, Celia seizes on it, pushing me hard in the chest with both hands, driving forward with surprising strength and determination.

I feel my balance lost, my centre of gravity thrust backwards. My feet scrabble on gravel and dust. The sky fills my vision and I am falling, then rolling on the ground.

I reach out a hand to dig my nails in the dirt, the crudest of brakes. It's not enough. My momentum is taking me over the edge.

My arm hooks around a rock as my body slides over the precipice. I swing outwards for one horrific second, but my right arm is locked and I'm left dangling. I reach over the side with my left hand, fumbling for something to grip. Then I feel an explosion of pain in my fingers and pull my hand away.

A second pain shoots through my right arm. Celia is stamping on me, trying to force me to let go. Raw survival instinct battles with reflex and I manage to keep my hold, but my grip is loosening. I feel another blow. My arm is weakening and my fingers beginning to slip.

Ivy hares into the next bend, an outcrop temporarily masking Celia and Amanda from view. Racing around the corner, a cry catches in her throat as she watches her mother viciously push the girl backwards. Amanda tumbles towards the edge of the cliff but manages to wrap her arm around a rock. Celia notices and begins stamping on it.

Ivy is running flat out but there is too much ground to cover. She isn't going to get there on time.

But that doesn't mean she can't intervene.

Ivy screams out as she runs.

'Get away from her!'

Mum turns, startled. There is an instant transformation, the snarling fury in her face erased, replaced with an expression of concern. It is what Ivy was relying upon. With Celia, all you have to do is give her an audience and she becomes instantly a different person.

'Help, she's fallen,' Celia says, overflowing with concern and sincerity. 'I bumped against her by accident and she lost her footing.'

Ivy covers the last few yards at full pelt and dives to the ground, locking both hands around Amanda's wrist. Then with a strength she did not know she possessed, she hauls the girl back over the cliff-edge to safety.

2018

Amanda

I wince from the sting as Sylvie dabs gently at the scratches on my arms and legs, cleaning the wounds with a cotton pad moistened with antiseptic. It seems stupid to care about a little pain after what could have happened, but it's pure reflex.

My heartbeat has just about returned to normal, though it has taken a while. I know I'm going to be reliving those moments for the rest of my life. Fortunately, there will be a rest of my life because of the woman in front of me.

Is it ungrateful to wish my dads were here instead? They were who I thought of as I tumbled and skidded over the edge. Who I wished would come rescue me. They hadn't been there though, and Sylvie had.

Not Sylvie. Ivy. It's polite to start thinking of her by her preferred name. I understand fully now why she changed it, and I want to respect that. There is still plenty I don't understand, however. I have so many questions but I'm not sure it's my place to ask.

I'm still kind of reeling from the weirdness of what happened after. Once I'd been pulled to safety, I wondered what we were going to do with Celia. Were we supposed to restrain her in some way, out there on the path, until the cops showed? If I'd had rope, I'd have happily tied the psycho bitch to the bench. Instead, Ivy calmly suggested Celia make her way back to the villa, and she had complied, walking a few paces ahead of us, like nothing had happened, nothing was wrong.

Celia is now sitting in her own villa with Marion and Rory, who are effectively guarding her until the police get here.

I feel I have to mention all this.

275

'Your mom came in quietly. I can't believe she just gave up without a fight.'

'You don't know her,' Ivy replies. 'Inside her head, she'll already have erased what she tried to do to you. What she did to Vince, too. She'll deny all of it, and she'll believe herself. In part of her mind, what's about to happen to her will be some Kafkaesque inexplicable injustice. But there's also a part that knows the truth, and that's the part that murders lawyers and pushes people over cliffs. It's called narcissistic rage. It's what happens when something threatens to shatter the grandiose illusion a narcissist has of being perfect, always in the right, always in control.'

She looks me in the eye. 'You read those emails, I assume.'

I bite my lip, just about managing a nod. It's hard to admit you know something like that about a person. There's no option but to admit it though. Ivy saw the tablet. She knows I read them.

'My mother built this fantasy of herself as the matriarch of an exceptional family. Her need to preserve that fantasy caused her to ignore what her husband was doing to me. Vince threatened to tear down the walls and let everybody see what Max really was, and therefore who she really was. She thought if she killed him, the truth would stay hidden. Add to that, she was bound to have worked out that it was Vince's initial threat that caused Max to have his heart attack, so there was a revenge motive too.'

I picture the cliff again, replay that look in Celia's eyes. The moment she realised I was a threat, she hadn't hesitated.

'Vince's emails also said he knew what happened to Niamh. Does that mean that Celia . . . ?'

I let it hang, unwilling to say it out loud.

Ivy puts down the cotton wool and stands up straight. She seems far away for a moment. Then she walks over to the windows. It's like she's checking we're not being watched. Everybody's indoors though, not just Rory, Marion and Celia. Hugh and Lia have been told too, and it's not like anyone would feel like swimming or lying on a lounger after what just went down.

'We haven't exactly hit it off, have we?' Ivy says. 'I understand. I'm not the most warm and fuzzy person.'

'Hey, look, with everything you've been through—'

'It's okay. It's who I am. I've read that children of narcissists sometimes can't handle being liked by others. I got comfortable being disliked instead. But I like you, Amanda, despite what you might think, and I don't want you to hate me.'

'I don't hate you,' I insist.

'You will in a minute.'

Ivy crouches down in front of me again, but this time she isn't dabbing my wounds.

'Because we kept coming here when I was younger, I decided to learn some Portuguese. I've lost a lot of it in the years since, but there is one word I'll never forget, because it has no equivalent in another language. The word is *saudade*. It is a feeling, a melancholic yearning. It is described as the love that remains after what you love is gone, or the simultaneously painful and beautiful feeling of missing something that will never return. I've also heard it called the presence of absence. Because it's not translatable, it's hard to define, so I never knew what it truly meant until I felt it for myself. I've felt it every day since the summer of 2002, when I gave up my daughter.'

I feel an adrenaline surge, a combination of shock and elation. I keep my voice low, though there is nobody nearby to hear.

'You're telling me Niamh didn't die?'

2002

He could hear the crashing of the waves against the rocks just yards away, only a few bushes between the edge of the road and the drop. He had come here earlier, in the daylight, so that he would have his bearings. The wait was going to be nerve-wracking enough without the fear that he was sitting in the wrong place.

He saw twin beams weaving across the dusty track, a vehicle coming around the bend and fully into view. He felt the same surge he had with the last two false alarms, but this time the headlights flashed off and on again to confirm it was Laurie's car approaching in the dark.

There was no going back now. This was really happening.

He glanced into the back once again, where the baby seat was locked in place. He had formula, bottles, snacks, blankets, nappies, wipes, fresh clothes and toys. He had been on a ready footing for the best part of a fortnight.

The waiting and hoping had been a purgatory, feeling like his life was in a state of suspension. But a few days ago, he got the call to say it was on.

He had borrowed – albeit without the permission or knowledge of his sister – his niece's passport. She was around the same age, give or take a few months. It was issued when Keira was only three months old, so the fact that the picture looked nothing like Niamh wouldn't matter. It looked nothing like Keira now either. It was just about getting her out of the country.

All the other documentation was being worked out with Laurie's help. Some of it legitimately, some of it not so. Through her job, she knew people on both sides of the law.

The car stopped alongside his and he quickly stepped out onto the road, scanning the darkness for potential witnesses. Laurie emerged from her vehicle then opened the rear passenger door before leaning inside. When she stood up straight again, she had the baby in her arms.

She was sleeping. That would help. When she woke, she would be far from here, opening her eyes to a new life.

2018

Amanda

I look down at Ivy, kneeling before me. She seems smaller, a vulnerability to her I have not sensed before. My heart is pounding as I wait for her to speak.

'In the spring of that year, I was approached by Laurie, Vince's late wife. She had overheard a sensitive conversation I had with Max. She knew everything, and she offered me a way out of my situation. She had friends who wanted a baby but couldn't have one.

'I deliberated for a long time. But when I came here again that summer, I realised I couldn't go on. I wanted my future back. I did it so that Niamh and I would both have the lives we deserved. Laurie made the arrangements. That was why it was her idea to have a party that night, so that we could stage the disappearance. She drove Niamh a few minutes down the road to where someone was waiting to take her to a new family. So there really was a conspiracy, ironically enough.'

There's a rushing in my ears, as though more blood is pumping to my brain to help it process this. I feel worried someone can hear us and yet simultaneously like this room and the two of us are utterly isolated from the rest of the world.

I am relieved to learn that Niamh didn't die, though I'm still confused by one thing.

'But why—'

'Didn't I just have her adopted legitimately? A number of reasons. Mainly because I didn't want my parents involved. I didn't want them obstructing it, trying to talk me out of it. I didn't want them taking over the process either, choosing some couple they knew so that they still had their claws in Niamh.

'Then there was Calum. He didn't want to be a father at that stage, but equally, he was a good person who would always try to do the right thing. He wouldn't have liked the idea of giving up his own baby, so if he resisted, I would have had to prove that he wasn't the father. If it came to that, then everything would have to come out. I just wasn't ready for that.'

I get the impression there's more to it, a further reason she's not telling me, but I have a more pressing question right now.

'Do you know who Niamh was given to?'

Ivy looks towards the windows again, but it's not like she's checking this time. More like she's hiding from me. When she turns again, there are tears in her eyes.

'I didn't *want* to know. I got Laurie to promise never to tell me, and she was as good as her word. But I found out. Today.'

I think about what I read in Vince's emails, and about the DNA sequence in the attachment, but there's something I'm not seeing.

'I don't follow.'

'Vince threatened Celia that he would produce his evidence in the middle of her big family holiday: DNA evidence that Max was Niamh's father.'

I think I get it.

'Vince obtained a DNA sample,' I suggest, 'which means he must still have been in contact with Niamh's new parents. And you've worked out who they are.'

Ivy places her hands upon my arms, shaking her head.

'He obtained more than a sample,' she says, her voice breaking.

It is like a leviathan rising from the depths, so vast that its approach can't be observed because it is all around. I have no sooner finally seen it than it swallows me.

2002

Rob

He held out his arms, impatient for the feeling of her weight and warmth. Laurie stalled for a moment, the sleeping form cradled against her shoulder.

'Are you sure you're ready for this?' she asked.

'As much as anyone is ever ready for this.'

He and Sadiq had been on tenterhooks for several months, since Laurie got in touch and told them Sylvie was seriously considering her offer. They'd had a lot of time to plan. A lot of time to think about everything that might go wrong. A lot of time to think about what happens if it goes right too.

That had been the hardest part. Once they'd allowed themselves to truly contemplate the possibility, the notion of it not happening became almost unbearable. It was like they'd already been loving this little girl in advance, waiting for fatherhood to begin. Waiting for her to be theirs.

They desperately wanted to have a child, but they couldn't adopt in the UK at the time as a gay couple. They had started looking into surrogacy, because if the baby was biologically his or Sadiq's child, that solved a lot of issues. Then their friend Laurie stepped in and offered the possibility of a shortcut.

They were going to move to Sadiq's native Canada. Start a life there. Start a family there.

Laurie nodded sagely at his answer, gazing in the direction she had come from. All the subterfuge and illegality had been less of a worry than the notion that the vulnerable young mother back there might change her mind, but Laurie had explained in disturbing detail why that wasn't going to happen.

Laurie delivered the child into Rob's arms. He felt his heart race. He was afraid in a hundred different ways.

Rob wanted to just stand there and hold her, but there wasn't the time. He placed the child into the car seat, carefully fastening the clips and adjusting the straps so that she was snug and safe.

When he closed the door gently, Laurie was already back inside her vehicle. She rolled down her window.

'Don't read the papers. Don't watch the TV. Don't feel guilty. You're giving Sylvie and Niamh the lives they both deserve.'

Rob looked along the track.

'What about the rest of them?'

'I won't sugar-coat it. There will be collateral damage, but for the most part, they'll be getting what they deserve too.'

2018

Ivy

They are standing next to Dad's bench, just the three of them: Max and Celia's children. The venue had been Rory's suggestion: they needed somewhere to talk away from everyone else, and it seemed appropriate. The afternoon sun is blazing but there is a breeze coming off the sea that makes it tolerable, and for Marion and Rory at least, the heat is far from their greatest source of discomfort.

Nobody is speaking. It is a great Temple family tradition.

Ivy has just told them how she knows Mum killed Vince, and why she tried to kill Amanda. Unavoidably, that has meant telling them what Dad did too. That is all she has told them, however. What she confided in Amanda would stay between the two of them. With Vince gone, there are only four people in the world who know the truth, and none of them has a motive to disclose it.

Ivy changed her name legally when she moved to London in the autumn of 2006, shortly after graduation. She fully appreciated the prescience of this move when the Madeleine McCann story broke six months later.

Rory and Marion might one day work out why she calls herself Ivy, but they will never know why she chose Roan. It is an anagram of Nora, the heroine of Henrik Ibsen's play, *A Doll's House*, which she studied at university. Nora refused the role of wife and mother, and did what at the time was considered unthinkable, leaving her husband and her children. Consequently, her departure at the end of the play was known as 'the door-slam heard around the world'. It said fuck you to everyone who wanted to put a woman in a box. That had spoken to her.

Amanda asked her why she didn't go through normal adoption

channels. The answer she offered was honest, but it was not the whole truth. Giving her daughter away had merely been her deliverance from Max and Celia.

Faking Niamh's death had been her revenge upon them.

She hadn't just wanted to break out of the dungeon they kept her in: she wanted to pull down the whole castle and burn their banners. Celia always blamed her for driving the family apart, and in that much, she was right. It was Ivy's intention, and they had it coming.

Not everyone did, though. She had always justified the fall-out for Rory and Marion because the tragedy loosened their parents' merciless grip on everybody, but in truth she never lost much sleep over it. Neither of them had suffered like she did. Mostly it was Calum she felt guilty about. She wonders whether she should tell him, wonders how air-tight the restrictions will be when Mum goes to trial. Perhaps it's best to leave it to fate. It won't change much for him now. Calum put it behind him way back. He's married with three daughters. He's a good father, as she always knew he would be, given the right chance.

Rory looks shell-shocked at what he's just heard, more so even than after watching his mother being taken away by Portuguese police. He keeps staring at the bench, as though looking at the man who isn't there.

Rory always cared the most, always felt other people's pain.

'You okay?' Ivy asks him.

'I'm just so sorry, sis. I had no idea. It must have been going on right under my nose the whole time, but I didn't see it. I mean, I knew Dad could be a cold and callous prick, but I just didn't know . . .'

Rory puts his hand on the metal frame of the bench.

'I only saw what I wanted,' he says. 'That's always been my problem. You know, back in 2002, I asked for Dad's help here at this very spot. I needed money. Svetlana had told me about these people traffickers she was in hock to. Once they were off her back, we were going to start a new life together. Dad refused. He said she was playing an angle. Said it was the only reason a woman like that would be interested in a loser like me.'

Rory looks at the ground and shakes his head.

285

'Turned out the bastard was right. She was a grifter, working with a couple of Eastern European heavies. She ended up in jail for travelling under a false passport. Svetlana wasn't even her real name. Maybe it takes a manipulative, calculating sociopath to spot another one. Dad clocked her for what she was right away. I only saw what I wanted.'

That is when Marion sits down on the bench and starts to weep.

Her voice is quiet, as though coming from a place deep inside, a place of darkness and fear.

'I did know,' she states.

'You what?' Rory replies, anger rising. 'You knew? How?'

Ivy puts a hand on his arm, calming him, reminding him that it is not his place to be the angry one here.

Marion looks up at her.

'He came to me when I was twelve,' she says. 'It only happened once. He stopped because I was crying. He told me I must have dreamed it. Said he had been walking past my room and came in because I was having a nightmare. He said I was confusing the dream with him holding me when I woke up. I knew what had really happened, but I needed to believe his version, because otherwise . . . I don't know. It was just easier. The alternative was too frightening.

'That day when you blew up at him, deep down I knew what you were saying might be true, but I couldn't let myself accept it. If I did, it meant this thing I had suppressed would come to the surface, and it would also mean I hadn't protected you. It was easier to tell myself this was just more of your acting out, when in fact all your attention-seeking was your way of crying out to tell someone what was wrong. I'm so sorry. I'm just so sorry.'

Ivy puts a hand on Marion's shoulder. She has always harboured a suspicion that this was the case, and she thought she would feel angrier and more bitter when her sister finally admitted it. Instead it is as though all the rage she feels has been dissipated by being released into the open air, beneath a wide blue sky.

It hits her that she has been weighed down for years with a burden she doesn't need to carry. All her life she has been putting up walls because she thought they would protect her, but in the last few hours she has learned that hiding a truth only makes you its prisoner. Telling the truth makes you powerful. And among those powers is absolution.

'I forgive you,' Ivy says.

Marion squeezes her hand.

Another silence follows, the three of them gazing at the view: cloudless blue sky and the twinkling sea below.

It is Rory who finally speaks.

'So, same time next year?'

Ivy is hot and damp with sweat by the time they reach the villas.

'Do you want something to drink?' Marion asks, heading inside.

'Sure. The usual would be most welcome.'

Ivy walks around the pool and takes her ease on a sun lounger beneath the shade of a parasol. A couple of minutes later, it is not Marion who appears at her side and hands her a cold beer, but Amanda. The gesture is a small one, but it means a lot. It tells her she can heal. It tells her they're both going to be okay: Ivy who used to be Sylvie; Amanda who used to be Niamh.

She says thanks. Amanda nods and walks away again.

Ivy takes a few gulps then reaches for her mobile. It's time.

Jamie answers after a single ring.

'Jamie, I need you to set me up a call with DKG tomorrow morning.'

'Consider it done. Does this mean you've finalised your strategy proposal for dealing with the depot fire?'

He sounds calm and neutral, but she can tell he's bracing himself for the worst.

'It's a slight update. I'm recommending full disclosure, total transparency and a policy of setting a new gold standard in worker safety.'

'That's . . . I mean . . .'

Jamie almost splutters he sounds so pleased, but it only lasts a moment before caution colours his tone.

'Our consultations for DKG are covered by a confidentiality agreement. If they don't like this, they can take their business elsewhere, to someone prepared to manage things differently. I can only imagine how Sir Jock will respond if we lose the account and the cover-up happens anyway.'

'Neither of those things is going to happen. You remember those pictures of the melted toys? I own those personally, remember. I'll let DKG know that they're free to go elsewhere, but either way I'll be releasing those images to an investigative journalist of my acquaintance, so good luck if their strategy is to go low.'

'Understood,' he says, sounding delighted. 'And remind me never to get on the wrong side of you, boss. You are *bad*.'

Ivy smiles, because what he really means is that she's not.

2018

Amanda

The movies had lied to me. As far as I understand, it is supposed to rain in London, but it is hotter here than it was in Portugal. Maybe it's just that they're not geared for it like in Toronto. The closest I've come to air-conditioning today has been the breeze preceding the arrival of a Tube train, and that provided only the briefest sensation of cool before the warm air became clammy and still around me again.

Even Glasgow had been warm and sunny when I flew back with Arron, though the weather felt utterly at odds with the prevailing mood. Kirsten had been gushingly appreciative of all I had done, but it was clear that nothing was going to be the way I planned when I left YYZ. Kirsten's sister had come up from Chelmsford to help out, so I wasn't even needed in the short term. I was sad to leave because I had come to like Kirsten and grown surprisingly fond of Arron, but I was relieved too.

A lot of the details are being kept quiet ahead of the trial, but Kirsten had found out a little about what happened. The cops think Celia went to the office pretending she was there to agree a schedule of payments. She must have chosen her moment when he was sitting at his desk, maybe looking at something on his screen. She stuck him in the shoulder with a hypodermic, delivering a massive intra-muscular dose of insulin. He was wearing a light T-shirt for going abroad, so she didn't even need to find bare skin. It would have barely left a mark when she did it, but by the time the pathologists were examining the body, there was a very large tell-tale bruise around the injection point.

Since flying back from Portugal, I have spent a lot of time on the phone to my parents, though I'm not ready to tell them what I know. A big part of me is glad I don't have to see them right now, because I was really angry with them at first. I'm dealing with it, though. I've a lot of conflicting emotions but the bottom line is that I've experienced enough of the Temple family to know that Rob and Sadiq and Sylvie and Laurie all did the right thing.

When Ivy told me the truth, it was as though the Earth had disappeared from beneath my feet. I was falling, and when I landed, I thought the whole world had changed. Since then, the weirdest thing has been coming to terms with the reality that almost nothing has. Rob, Sadiq and I all still mean the same to each other. The only difference is that I'm not all messed up about Kara any more. She's simply a friend of my dads who did them a big favour; just not as big as the one they made out she had, which is why pretty soon she won't have to lie any more.

I wonder how long it will be before they suss how much I know. They're aware Vince was murdered, but many of the details have been suppressed due to reporting restrictions, specifically because it was a blackmail case. I can plausibly plead ignorance, but I suspect they're going to put it together when I tell them how I'm now going to be spending the rest of my summer, and in particular who is putting me up.

I'm on my way to meet her right now. She called a couple of hours ago to say she'd organised some work experience for me. She didn't give details, only the name of a bar. I assumed it would turn out to be some upscale cocktail joint, but as my phone tells me I'm approaching my destination, it doesn't strike me as somewhere that would be Ivy's speed. It looks kinda rough and ready, more your traditional British pub. I wonder if it's actually a bartending job.

I walk inside. It's dark and low-ceilinged, the temperature only marginally cooler than on the street. I can't see Ivy and worry momentarily that I might have the wrong place: a lot of London bars have the same name. Then I spot her at a booth near the back, sitting next to some sandy-haired dude in shorts and a Savage Earth Heart tee. Cool band, I think, though he looks kind of old to be into them.

Ivy beckons me across and the guy gets up to greet me, extending a hand.

'Amanda, this is Jack, to whom we both owe a great many favours. He's organised a work-experience placement for you at *Broadwave*.'

I'm glad I don't have a drink, because I'd have done a spit-take. 'Are you kidding me?'

Broadwave is one of the fastest-growing news websites in the biz, a multi-media platform with international reach. Clearly Ivy has some major-league connections. Pays to be on the dark side, I guess.

'Do as you're told, try not to get in anybody's way, and learn as much as you can,' she says. 'Though try not to learn too much from Jack and you'll probably stay out of jail.'

Jack brings over a fresh round of drinks and they toast. He asks a few questions about what I'm going to be studying, what I've written, my YouTube channel.

I answer as best I can, trying not to sound like a dweeb, still totally reeling.

'It's a hell of a solid you're doing me. I really appreciate this.'

'*I* really appreciate this,' Ivy tells him. 'How many favours am I into you for now?'

'Friends don't keep score,' he replies, though he says it in a way that sounds like he is totally keeping score.

'So, how do you guys know each other?' I ask.

There's an awkward micro-pause, just long enough to read some complicated vibe between them that makes me think I might have missed something.

'Oh, sorry. Are you two, like, an item?'

They answer at the same time.

He says no. She says yes.

Further reading

If you are interested to know more about the complex psychology that makes us naturally susceptible to conspiracy thinking, I can wholeheartedly recommend *Suspicious Minds: Why We Believe Conspiracy Theories* by Rob Brotherton.

For a historical contextualisation and vigorous debunking of some of the biggest conspiracy theories still stalking modern culture, look no further than David Aaronovitch's excellent *Voodoo Histories: How Conspiracy Theory Has Shaped Modern History*.

And on the tender subject of narcissistic parents and the impact they have on their children, there are many impassioned first-hand accounts out there, but for a well-researched and evidence-based look at how child abuse can take many varied forms, I would recommend *Toxic Parents* by Susan Forward.